AMY
OLIVEIRA

*INTERNATIONAL BESTSELLING* AUTHOR

# Keepsake

First e-book edition January 2023.

*Cover Book design by The Pretty Little Design Co.*

*Edited by Karen Washo at Utterly Unashamed*

*PAPERBACK:* 978-1-7397895-6-5

*www.amyoliveira.com*

# Content Warning

Death of a family member, infertility, suicide, depression, anxiety, panic attacks, graphic violence, domestic abuse (off screen).

*For you*
*Who felt too anxious to be yourself*
*Too unlikable to open up*
*Too depressed to see a way out*
*I love you, I am you.*

# Prologue

I LOOKED DOWN AT the dirt covered grave with a whimper lodged in my throat.

I wasn't the first person to stand in front of a grave and blame the world for its injustice, but today I felt like the only one. I swallowed something reminiscent of gravel. My eyes stung with unshed tears. I read her name over and over again, waiting for the new reality to sink in.

*Sofia* is *dead*, I told myself.

The rest of us could go ahead and wander aimlessly through life. She wasn't coming back.

This time the tears fell, the whimper was freed, and I was left there alone, staring at the grave where they buried my best friend.

# 1. Logan

I FELT THE URGE to say I hated funerals, but everyone hated them.

I grabbed a cup of soda, desperately trying to find something to do with my hands as I strolled around the house.

No one stopped me. I didn't know many people, and the ones I knew probably didn't remember me after all these years. It felt weird to be at a funeral when I didn't know anyone but the deceased. Funerals were for the living, after all.

Tired, I slumped on the couch and held the soda with both hands. With my eyes fixed on the wall, I almost missed the small body landing beside mine on the couch.

I spotted the dangling feet first. Pink sequin sneakers with vibrant yellow laces. My gaze went up to her face, watching me with curiosity. She had long brown hair and a pink hairband with a tiny bow on top. Whatever she was wearing wasn't funeral appropriate. It was awfully colorful. But I was glad she wasn't wearing black. She was just a little girl.

"I know you," she told me.

My eyebrows rose. "Do you?"

She nodded. "You're the one with mommy in that picture." I followed her finger and sure enough, right on top of the mantel, I spotted a picture of me and Sofia about sixteen years ago. We were grinning at the camera, my arm over her shoulders while she munched on gummy bears.

It was the day we found out she was pregnant. It was a revelation scary enough to shake us to our very core, but I didn't want her panicking. Well, not until it was time to panic, so I bought a shitload of candy, and we got drunk on sugar.

I forgot about that day, Sofia didn't. As my gaze left the picture, it found Dashiell walking around with a deep frown on his forehead. Lanky and taller than any fifteen-year-old ought to be, I wondered if he knew he was—in a way—in the mantel picture too.

My eyes were still glued to him when he caught me sitting next to his sister. His frown was now clearly directed at me. I held my breath as he turned to Vienna. "What are you doing?" he barked, flashing me a look and then turning back at her.

"I'm sitting with mommy's friend," Vienna replied. "She's the one in the picture, see?"

Dashiell didn't turn to look at the picture, even though his sister pointed to it behind him. But he looked right at me, his eyes narrowing.

I shrugged apologetically. "I was about your age when we took that picture. I have no idea how she recognized me."

It felt like a victory when Dashiell turned to check out the photo. Deciding neither I nor Vienna were lying, I got a stiff nod from him. My heart skipped a beat. He was too serious for a fifteen-year-old. Too protective, too suspicious. Those weren't qualities people were born with, but rather earned through suffering.

The last time I saw Dashiell, he was still a small child with bright eyes like his mother.

"You went to school with mommy." Vienna's voice brought me back again.

I smiled at her. "My whole life."

"That's super best friends," Vienna said.

"I think that's true," I agreed.

"If they were such great friends, how come you don't even know her, Vi?" Dashiell scoffed.

My smile fell into a hard line. He wasn't wrong, but I also knew he was not lashing out because of the true reality of my friendship. It was because his mother was dead. It sliced through me every time I thought about it.

Sofia was dead.

She left children behind. There was an eight-year-old girl with pink sneakers grieving just by my side, and my brain couldn't even understand that kind of pain.

Dashiell was right. I never deserved the title of Sofia's super best friend, but I would have liked to have it anyway for the years of gummy bear consumption and rom-com watching. I wished someone would have told me it was going be my last moments with my best friend. I wish I treasured those moments at the time.

I opened my mouth to reply to Dashiell, who was still glaring at me, but someone else cut me off.

"Oh, Logan, you're here." There was surprise in her tone, and it was laughable. It was Sofia's funeral. Where else would I be?

I nodded, standing up and smoothing the black dress I had on. Caridad, Sofia's mother, looked me up and down like I wore something wrong. The dress was an appropriate knee length, no cleavage and nicely shaped. My heels weren't excessively high, and my brown hair was secured in a tight ponytail at the nape of my neck.

Caridad wasn't impressed. It was clear by the way she studied me. A chubby hand patted her on her cheek, breaking our stare off. I blinked, only then really noticing she had Lachlan in her arms. His eyes were green like mine, but his were light with yellow in the corners and mine were deep emerald green. I wasn't done watching the boy, but Caridad shuffled him in her arms, giving him to Dashiell. "Hold him for me."

The teenager took his brother and offered his hand to Vienna. Again, I was struck by how much older he looked doing that. *That's wrong*, my heart told me. He was a child still. He was supposed to rebel when people asked him to do things. Instead, his eyes were somber when he took the toddler in his arms and led Vienna away from Caridad and me.

I sighed, and the woman stiffed again. "Come."

I couldn't do anything but follow, even though I knew what was to come. I knew the Castillo home by heart. Nothing had changed besides my picture on the mantel that I had to believe was an addition from when Sofia moved back to her parents. Caridad led me out of the living room, across the hall, heading to the bedrooms. My heart lunged to my throat as we passed Sofia's old bedroom but thank goodness she didn't open that door. Instead, she led me to Sofia's brother's old room.

It was a mix of old and new. A room untouched by time, and the family's storage closet at the moment. I was studying the old posters sellotaped to the walls when Caridad started, "I know we have to talk."

I turned; my hands laced in front of my body. "I didn't expect a conversation in the middle of her funeral."

"No?" Caridad questioned. "It'll be a quick one."

Filled with dread, I opened my mouth, but Caridad was already speaking over me.

"This won't work, Logan. I'm not trying to be cold." It was hard to believe, but I said nothing. "You need to see why this won't work, right?"

"It's what Sofia wanted," I argued.

"You haven't seen Sofia in years."

Yes, once more that was thrown in my face with no ceremony. We recently reconnected online, but I couldn't pretend a few messages on social media were enough to repair the severed bond.

"You know I didn't want to stop being her friend," I tried instead.

Caridad nodded. "It doesn't change the outcome."

"Sofia wanted the kids with me, Mrs. Castillo. It's in her will. It's your right to feel however you want about it, but we'll have to tell them. They deserve to know"

"You don't know them!" She got right into the argument. "You're a stranger to those children and their mother just died."

I understood what she was saying, and maybe she was right, but there was a reason for Sofia's decision, and I'd be damned if it wasn't honored. "I have the means to provide for them and give them all they need—"

"This isn't about money, Logan," Caridad bellowed, and I recoiled.

We watched each other, and not a word was spoken for a full minute. I licked my lips, fighting the urge to curse, but before I could speak, the door swung open breaking our staring contest.

I held my breath as Sofia's older brother, Alvaro, barged in. His expression murderous as he narrowed his eyes between his mother and me. He was tall and barrel chested, filling the whole doorway before stepping in and closing it behind his back.

"In the middle of the funeral?" he growled.

I had the decency to tuck my head down even though I didn't choose to have this conversation right now.

"She was talking to the kids," Caridad said, and I gaped at her.

"What do you think I am going to do? Tell them? Run away with them?" I prodded more, offended.

Caridad closed her mouth in a thin line, and it was all the answer I needed. She wasn't going to give them up. She wasn't going to let me fulfill Sofia's wishes. I decided to try a different angle.

"I'm not taking the kids and disappearing with them. I want to have a chance to talk to them and let them get to know me."

"They are kids," she replied. "Fragile kids who just lost their mother. They can't make decisions right now."

"I want a chance to fulfill my best friend's wishes." I was nearly begging.

Silence followed my request.

"Mamá?" Alvaro sighed, making me glance his way. My memories of Alvaro Castillo were fragments of a tiny TV screen, rather than a complete person. He was long gone from the house when we were teenagers having sleepovers, but Sofia adored him. He was her hero. Her mother hated what he had done with his life, but we used to watch his MMA fights on the VCR in secret.

"She's not a mother," Caridad declared.

"Sofia wasn't a mother at first."

"Sofia was an excellent mother." Caridad reeled back, and Alvaro sighed again.

"She was, Mamá. But Sofia needed to learn. Why can't Logan learn too?"

I bit on my cheek to keep from smiling. Big brother was helping. He was the first person who didn't sound disgusted with the idea of me raising those kids.

"I can learn," I said quietly, trying to put as much humility as I could into my words. Caridad needed to see I wasn't above groveling.

The woman broke eye contact with her son and turned to me, hatred steaming off her. She always disliked me, even when I used to sleep at her house and was her daughter's best friend. She always refused when Sofia asked to come over to my house. Now, it wasn't just a birthday or a trip Sofia was asking of her mother. It was to give her grandchildren to me.

"You chose career over family, Logan," the woman said. "You have a life in the city and a demanding job. You can't take three kids and think they'll fit in with your life. They need to stay where they feel comfortable. They need to..."

"I told you I don't want to uproot the children." I tried. "I want to get to know them first and..."

"First and then what?"

I frowned. "Try to be there for them—"

"You're never going to be their mother." And without any more words, Caridad left the bedroom.

I heard the door click behind me and then, only then, I let a tear fall. It wasn’t her harsh words that affected me. I knew I’d never be a replacement for their mother, but it was the raw quality of her voice.

I sniffled, and the rustling of fabric reminded me Alvaro was still in the room. “My mother is grieving,” he explained, but I couldn’t look at his face.

I nodded, eyes cast down. “I know.”

“I’ll talk to her,” he promised.

I nodded again, words failing me.

We were stuck in place, my hands shaking and his breathing coming through in big gulps of air. Finally, he moved. I heard the door clicking close behind me once again. Only when he was gone did I stop to think it was his bedroom that I made him leave.

I DIDN’T SAY GOODBYE to the kids.

They didn’t know me, and I couldn’t anger Caridad again. My shoulders were heavy as I went to my car and drove to the hotel.

My hands gripped the wheel in front of me and I blew out an exasperated breath. This feeling? I had never felt like this before. It was eating me alive, distorting my beliefs. I blinked like it would make me see things better, but if I was confused before, now after talking to Caridad, I was even worse.

At the hotel, I took my time with a long shower until my skin couldn't take the scalding water anymore. My tears ran freely down my cheeks, my hands balled into fists, pounding the tiles in front of me.

Sofia was a better person than me. She deserved to live. She had *something* to live for.

My funeral clothes were tossed to the side. All I wanted was to burn them. I squeezed myself into jeans and a top, my hair up in a bun and my face devoid of makeup. I went downstairs pretending to look for the restaurant, it had been a week since I had a proper meal.

I parked my ass in a booth in the most secluded space of the hotel bar and bistro. When the waitress arrived to take my order, I didn't order food. No, it was whiskey I needed, and it was whiskey she brought me.

I sipped it and let it burn on its way down. I never liked the drink, but it worked like a charm.

My fingertips touched the glass in front of me. Caridad was right. I was unfit to raise those kids. But so were all of us.

My head whipped up when a loud scratching on the floor brought my attention away from my pity party. The dismissal died on my tongue when I saw it wasn't just a random person sitting in front of me, but Alvaro.

He was clutching a whiskey tumbler, still dressed in the suit he was wearing this afternoon. I wanted to ask him what he was doing here, but I couldn't find it in me to care. It was a hotel bar, and he buried his baby sister today. He was miserable, and misery loved company.

"She has that power," he said when I remained silent, only my throat working on a knot. "Of making us feel unfit."

I looked down at my glass, chuckling. "She's right. I'm not a mother."

"But you want the kids."

"I want the kids."

"Why?"

I raised my head up to look at him. Alvaro carried the Castillo's whiskey-colored eyes adorned with dark long lashes. His jaw was strong with a five o'clock shadow so precise I knew it was a look he sported, no matter the circumstances. Dark caramel colored hair, just one shade darker than his tan skin, looked golden under the lights. Small patches of gray hair by his temples were a constant reminder he was sixteen years older than me. That made him forty-six. There was something familiar about him, and it hit me. *Sofia*. The man was not someone I knew very well, but he carried Sofia's softness somewhere inside.

My stomach churned.

"Sofia asked," I simply said.

Alvaro studied me. I lifted a shoulder, not sure what else to say.

"She left you three kids after not talking for years," he started. "And you're willing to try?"

"I didn't stop being friends with Sofia because I wanted to," I explained to a Castillo again.

Alvaro nodded.

"I always cared for her. We were like sisters. She asked me one last thing. One thing that is nothing in comparison to all she gave me."

"Nothing?" He lifted an eyebrow. "Raising her children? Lachlan is only three."

I didn't want to get into details, so I just shook my head. "I love her. I have the money. I have the space. I can do this."

My skin burned under Alvaro's gaze. "That won't work with my mom. That's why she thinks you're unfit."

I nodded. "Yes, because I'm the girl who chose career over family. Did she even wonder if the option for a family was ever given to me?"

Alvaro licked his lips. "Explain to me why you don't have a lawyer starting to push my parents back out yet."

My eyebrows lifted, surprised by his suggestion. "Because I agree with her. They are kids and they just lost their mother. I never wanted to take them from here or destroy all that they ever knew. I thought I was going to have a chance to get to know them and at least offer the possibility of taking me as their guardian. I thought..."

"Dashiell is fifteen, Vienna is eight, and Lachlan is three," Alvaro said. "You thought of talking to them?"

I nodded. "I thought they'd have a choice. I don't know. But then your mom said I couldn't trust what they say because they are traumatized." I rubbed my temple.

A moment passed and I reached for the whiskey, taking a big swig of it. It burned on the way down, but it didn't feel as bad as I already did.

"I can talk to my mother," Alvaro offered again.

"Will she listen?"

Instead of replying, he pinned me with a look. "Do you really think you can do it?"

"Yes, I really do."

He tsked. "If anything, you have money to pay for a nanny."

# 2.

# Alvaro

Bloody knuckles over the wheel, it was a bad idea to work my frustrations out like I used to. It was an even worse one to go see my mother in this state. But the clock was ticking, I couldn't stay away much longer.

As I drove through the familiar streets, the same words chanted over and over in my thoughts.

*Sofia is dead.*

*Sofia is dead.*

*Sofia is fucking dead.*

It was when I stepped on the brake, the red light blaring in front of me and the asshole behind blaring his horn without mercy, that the curses flew off my lips in the most amazing symphony.

*Sofia is dead, my fucking baby sister is dead.*

I strangled the wheel. I couldn't think about what life would be like now. I had a business to run and apparently a life to live. How the hell was I supposed to live my life when she was dead and buried underground?

I couldn't think of what to do to soothe the ache, so I simply made a to-do list. They said to focus on one day after the other, one step at a time. I occupied my mind with busy-work and overlapping tasks because when I closed my eyes...

I saw my sister.

She had brown eyes and a bold attitude. I taught her how to curse when she was just a small child and Mamá chased me around the house when she caught her baby girl saying puta. I changed Sofia's diapers and made her laugh with raspberries on her soft belly.

And now every time I thought of her, I didn't see that smiling kid anymore. I saw the dead woman in a casket.

I squeezed my eyes shut for a moment, held on to the wheel, and kept driving. I couldn't think of how things would be from now on. I already couldn't deal with staying in Mamá's house, so I booked a hotel telling her it was best if she gave a bed to one of her sisters.

But the truth was I couldn't sleep there beside Sofia's bedroom. I could barely breathe when I was in our childhood home.

I parked the truck in front of the house and inhaled through my nose. I was crumbling, and I wasn't allowed to.

After a moment too long standing by the front door, I barged in the house determined to accomplish my mission.

You could barely tell we had fifty people over for a funeral just yesterday. The house was spotless, mostly because I made my mother hire cleaners. She protested, but I tried my best to make her understand that after a funeral you want to fall apart, not clean.

The kids were in front of the TV. Dash at the left-hand side on his phone and knees apart while Vienna had baby Lachlan between her legs. Pointing at the screen, she tried to explain the plot to the baby.

"Good morning, everyone." I tried to inject any kind of cheeriness in my tone.

Dash looked over his phone. "Tío." He dipped his chin, but a second later, I lost his attention. Vienna smiled, holding Lach's hand as she made the toddler wave at me.

My smile was constricted. I wanted to scream every time I looked at these children. I knew it was unfair. They needed love more than anything right now, but I simply couldn't. I looked at them and I wanted to fight. I wanted to make the world as bloody as my goddamn knuckles.

Mamá and Papá were sitting at the table in the kitchen. Papá read a newspaper and commented on the news while Mamá bobbed her head mindlessly.

The rage ran freely through my blood and squeezed my throat. I wanted to shout my sister's name. Why weren't they overwhelmed with grief?

The second the thought came to my mind, I felt guilty. My parents were suffering, the kids were suffering. My feelings were raw and foreign and I just wanted the world to cry with me.

"Alvaro." Mamá smiled my way.

I swallowed all that down and sat on the chair across from them. Not sure how to start with this, I decided on being direct. "You have to listen to Logan."

"Don't you dare," came out so quickly I reeled back. Mamá had that locked and loaded on the tip of her tongue.

"Mamá..." I started shaking my head.

"No, Alvaro," she spat. "Those children don't need to stay with someone who doesn't even know them. They need their family."

I kept my voice down not to be overheard. "Logan said she wanted to take her time with them. Let them get to know her."

"She's a stranger."

I nodded, that was true. It had been more than a decade since Logan was in Sofia's life. And yet, Sofia wanted the kids to stay with Logan.

Sofia was sixteen years younger than me, a miracle baby Mamá called her. They didn't have the agility to raise children anymore, not when Lachlan just turned three. This kind of dysfunction wasn't good for children, but you try telling that to a Latino mother.

Familia comes above anything.

"We should give her a chance."

"Whose side are you on?" Mamá challenged.

I sighed, pinching the bridge of my nose. "There are no sides. We just have to—"

"You don't understand. You don't know these children."

I flinched, her words cutting right to the cruel reality. I was no better than Logan. Probably worse, since the children were part of my family and I knew nothing about them.

"Mi príncipe..." Mamá started as she realized the wound she just poked.

I shook my head, cutting her off and facing my father. "Papá, you know Logan isn't a bad person."

"She's not a bad person," he agreed.

"Geraldo!" Mamá huffed like he betrayed her.

"She did nothing wrong."

"She did nothing wrong." I went with that lukewarm sentiment. "Can we give her a chance? She wants this."

"Why?" Mamá fired up. "She's a big shot in the city. Why would she want the kids?"

I shrugged, if she wanted to talk about Logan, she'd have to talk to Logan. "We'll honor what Sofia asked. At the very least, we tell the children."

She bit her lip, her face twisted like she ate a sour lemon. I had to put the hammer down. We couldn't hide this from the children.

"It's the right thing to do." Papá decided to cooperate. "They need to know."

I wasn't going to pressure them by saying Logan could go about this in the legal way. She had money to throw toward legal fees that we didn't. That was going to push Mamá further away. It was clear she had a problem with how much money Logan had. There was nothing to hate about the girl, so I had to assume it was the last name attached to her.

Hart.

The Harts owned half of this town, we saw it in the complex buildings and their faces spread over gossip magazines. Maybe Mamá had a good reason for trying to keep the kids away from that life. Besides being insanely rich, I knew next to nothing about the Harts. How could we trust them?

Sofia knew enough. She knew about Logan, and she was their mother. I understood where my mother was coming from, but I was relentless. Even if it was the last thing I did, I had to honor Sofia's wishes.

"Tita, can we have pizza rolls?" Vienna put her head on the door, her expectant smile bright.

Mamá switched to a motherly gaze. "Of course."

We all smiled at the girl until she disappeared once again. Mamá stood up and opened the freezer.

"I don't think I was ever allowed to have pizza rolls." My eyebrows rose.

Mamá never let me have junk food, or food that looked like what the other kids were having. She would tell us, "*They do not know what they are eating.*" It was Mamá's version of, *"Father, forgive them, for they do not know what they are doing."*

"Their mother died," Mamá whispered and turned to the freezer again, sniffling when she turned her back to me.

My forehead met the tips of my fingers and I massaged for a second as Mamá disappeared through the door. My father looked over his shoulder, watching her leave. "She needs time."

I breathed in and out. "We all do. I just want to do what is right for the kids. What Sofia wanted."

Papá was a strong man, righteous, someone I always wanted approval from. I knew I fucked up many years ago when I left and broke their hearts in a million pieces. Even now, as they grieved for their baby, Papá's eyes scanned my bloody knuckles and shame overwhelmed me.

The hands holding the newspaper shook, and he put it down, his eyes closing in a disappointing sigh.

Forty-six years old and that sigh still cut me like a knife.

"A month," I said, trying to avoid a confrontation.

Papá's eyes left my knuckles and met my eyes, his eyebrows raising from the sudden change of subject.

"I'll give Mamá a month to settle down and then we'll bring Logan in and tell the kids. That's enough time."

He nodded. I knew he was holding himself back from saying anything.

Mamá came back a second later, breaking our silence. "You think we should send them to school on Monday?"

"Lachlan goes to school?" I asked.

She nodded. "A fancy preschool Sofia put him in because of work..." She trailed off, the silence speaking for itself.

Sofia was a receptionist in a big corporation after years of being a cashier in a supermarket. It was a better job and came with a couple of perks. But she was a receptionist. The preschool wasn't going to be an option when she wasn't—

"If there's a problem, I'll pay for it." I swallowed down any other thoughts.

"You don't need to."

Refusing to listen, I raised my hand, stopping her in her tracks.

"I talked to Papá. We'll leave things as they are for now. For a month."

Mamá was back on the defensive once again, her back straight, eyes trained on me. "And after a month?"

"Then we'll talk to the kids and tell them." She opened her mouth to argue but I was faster. "That's it, Mamá. One month. It's the right thing to do. I'll tell Logan she needs to wait."

"A month and then you take them away from their home?"

Yes, the kids lived with them now, but it wasn't always like that. They used to live with Sofia and her good for nothing partner until Sofia left him and he disappeared from the kids' lives. Still, she moved to another house and tried to make it on her own. Only recently she asked if she could stay with my parents. The room Dash slept in still looked exactly like I left it with the addition of the boxes they brought with them.

Sofia, Vienna, and Lachlan shared her small room. This house wasn't something Sofia wanted; I knew that much. I wasn't going to tell my mother that, but Sofia only came home out of necessity.

Maybe that was why she chose Logan. The kids would want for nothing. If it was only to make them comfortable, Logan was a good choice.

"A month."

# 3.

# Logan

THERE WERE FOUR RULES I lived by when analyzing an investment risk.

First, diversifying. Everyone knew that one. You can't put all your eggs into one basket. I never did, and I advised my clients of the same.

So, I didn't put all my hopes on Alvaro Castillo. He told me to wait a month for things to settle down with his parents. He promised I'd meet the kids, but diversifying was key. I contacted my lawyer, aka my favorite cousin Willa, and she assured me we had this even if Caridad refused to let me in the house.

Second, establish a probable maximum loss plan. I've been called a pessimist before, but things change. It was that easy. The market could flip, and you didn't want to be caught off guard. I always assume I'll lose a little.

So, I assumed I might lose Alvaro's support. I might never win Caridad over. But I couldn't lose the kids. That was the only thing on my mind as I drove over for our first meeting. My margin of loss was on the adults. I didn't care about what they thought. Well, I cared a little, but it wasn't a deal breaker. The kids, though? I couldn't lose them.

Third, require a margin of safety. A margin of safety left room for judgment errors, mistakes, or unforeseen adverse conditions. It might sound like rule number two, but not quite. This one was about the mistakes I would make. Some things were out of my control, but I had to prepare for the things under my control just as much. I couldn't bet on my perfection.

That was why I ordered about fifty parenting books. Dash was fifteen, Vienna eight, and Lachlan only three. The age range was too great. No one could be a perfect parent, but I could minimize my gap knowledge. I was prepared for mistakes, but I'd try my best to avoid them.

Fourth, think long term. Investing was a marathon, not a sprint. Just like parenting.

I inhaled and let out a calming breath. The kids needed time. Even though I had waited a month already, they needed time to adjust.

My hands shook when I thought of them refusing to live with me. But quickly I dismissed that thought. *Rule number two*. I refused to lose the kids. I wasn't going to do it.

I checked myself in the mirror. My long brown hair was in a ponytail, my eyebrows sharp, and my mouth closed in a thin line. Sofia was all heart. She had always been that way. Kind, full of laughter and softness. I wasn't likable. That was the problem.

That might be the reason I was good at my job. As a portfolio manager, I had to tell my clients what they should invest in. No sugar coating. Just the harsh truth. I was supposed to predict the risk, be the pessimist they accused me of. My severity made them trust my judgment. Not something you'd expect from a caretaker.

The Bluetooth rang with a call from my phone, and I pressed the connecting button.

"I'm ok, Willa."

My cousin laughed from the other side. "Are you sure? You sound tense. Forget it. You always sound tense."

"Are you calling just to freak me out?"

"I'm calling to remind you that you're meeting kids today, Lo."

I let out a slow breath, and she giggled on the other side. "Now tell me the truth. How are you?"

I frowned at the road ahead. "I'm scared. They all hate me there."

"Alvaro doesn't hate you."

"Alvaro doesn't know me," I corrected. "A month ago he was on my side, but that was a month ago. I don't know what Caridad has been saying about me."

"Ugh," Willa groaned. "That woman. There's nothing wrong with you. What's her problem?"

*She knows I'm going to be an unfit parent*, I said to myself. Instead of voicing that terrifying thought, I went with facts.

"She was never a fan of my friendship with Sofia. And she knows I never liked David."

Willa never knew about the sack of shit David was. I was never close to my cousins like Sofia was close to hers, but when I was accepted to Harvard, Sofia wasn't talking to me. I got into college feeling like shit. It was my dream since I was a little girl, but I had no one to celebrate with. Dad went to Harvard as well. To him, getting in wasn't an accomplishment, it was a given.

Then, my mom called and said my cousin Willa was attending, too. But Willa was... nothing like the rest of our family. She was bright, fun, and had no table manners. My parents were appalled by her. So we became fast friends.

I felt secure with Willa. She knew the pressure of being a Hart, she understood the need to set myself apart. And she knew we couldn't be stupid...ever. We had privilege.

Money was important. Money brought comforts. I hated many things about my parents and the way they raised me, but I wasn't stupid enough to turn my back on the comforts. I used that privilege and studied my ass off to get where I was. To the point, my last name didn't even matter anymore. I could support myself.

That was the privilege I had to sell to Caridad Castillo. I knew she wouldn't like it, but there were three kids who I could set up for life.

I could pay for Dash's college—anywhere he wanted to go. I could do so much for them. Caridad just needed to accept my presence. Or at least my money.

"It doesn't matter what Sofia's mom thinks," Willa said. "You're not doing anything wrong. Sofia wanted you to have the kids. You're playing nice to her because you're a nice person, not because you don't have a leg to stand on."

I smirked as I turned onto the right street. Willa was unconventional, but she was still an attorney.

"Thanks, Will. I'm arriving at their house. Talk later?"

"Please call me. And relax, ok? They are going to love you."

I didn't believe that, but still I hummed and hung up the call. After I parked at the curb, my hands still on the wheel, I turned to my right to see the Castillo's house.

At the edge of the fanciest public school district you would ever see was the Castillo house. Right there. They almost didn't make it.

My life changed because I met Sofia Castillo.

She was the first person I connected with, the only one who truly saw me. She was my best friend. And sure, if times were different, Dad would have sent me to the same private school where Willa went. Just like, if this house was three streets down, Sofia wouldn't be in my school.

It didn't matter though, because she was there, and she saved me so many times.

But I couldn't save her.

My thoughts were interrupted when the front door flew open and Alvaro stood there, his arms crossed over his chest.

I sighed, grabbed my keys, and exited the car.

The man was bigger than the door. At least he looked bigger. His eyes narrowed like I was doing something wrong by staying in my car a second longer than he desired.

As I made my way to the porch, I glanced at the white pickup truck in front, a blue logo stamped on the driver's door. The image of a castle with written CASTILLO CONSTRUCTION underneath. I turned to the man at the front, my eyebrows raised. "Clever."

"I'm a genius."

I wished someday I could look at Alvaro without the back flashbacks of his MMA days. I urged my brain to not notice the way his thighs were muscly under his jeans, or how his arms bulged stretching the well-worn T-shirt. It was weird seeing him like that, in person. He was just as intimidating as he looked in the MMA cage, maybe even more so.

"What were you doing?"

I reached Alvaro, just his enormous self between me and the Castillo's home. For some reason, I didn't want to lie. "Breathing in."

His eyebrows relaxed when he took me in. A beat passed, and he dipped his chin, passing his palm over his buzzed hair.

At the first step, I felt overwhelmed. I had no idea how they did it. How they looked at those walls and didn't miss her so much, it drove them insane.

Alvaro guided me to the living room. His parents were already waiting. I couldn't help but notice the picture of Sofia with me was removed. So Caridad didn't think I was mantel worthy. Shaking myself off, I stopped, a stiff smile on my lips.

It was Geraldo who moved first. He stood up and offered his hand. "Thank you for coming, Logan."

My feet made the move and brought me to Sofia's dad. He always let us do whatever we wanted when he was home—cookies, pizza. Whatever we weren't normally allowed, we were if Geraldo was in charge.

My smile fell a little when I turned to grab Caridad's hand. That nagging feeling of wanting to jump through hoops to make this woman like me barrelled through my chest. I needed to move on.

I sat down on the armchair opposite of their three-piece couch, facing Caridad and Geraldo. Alvaro waited awkwardly at the door, then with a sigh, he moved and took the other armchair.

With my hands resting on my lap, I let the silence stretch. I didn't care. I dealt with people with worse tempers than the Castillo family. If they wanted to sit in horrible silence? That was fine. I could do that.

Someone couldn't, though.

"So, let's talk," Alvaro started.

"Where are the kids?"

"Neighbors," he replied. "They got an indoor pool."

I nodded and asked nothing about if Lachlan was allowed to swim by himself or if he had a floaty.

Clearing my throat, I started, "It's been a month. I hope things are better—"

"Things will never be better again," Caridad interrupted me.

I squeezed my eyes shut but kept going as I opened them. "What I mean is, things are more settled now, and I'd like to talk about the kids' future."

Caridad took a breath, her eyes darting to the two men in her family, and when they didn't say anything, she took it as an incentive to say her piece.

"There's nothing to talk about. The kids belong to their family. We are their family. We'll raise them."

I sighed, exhausted even though I'd only been there three minutes. "I'm trying to be reasonable."

"So leave the kids be," she said sharply. "Leave them well enough alone."

"What makes you think I'm so bad for them?" I couldn't resist asking. "What makes me so unfit to..."

"You aren't their mother!"

"Neither are you."

I knew it was a mistake the second the words flew out of my mouth. My skin buzzed, my brain scrambled, trying to understand how quickly I lost my temper.

"Let's calm down..." Alvaro started, but I stopped him by raising my palm.

Opening my eyes slowly, I focused on Caridad. "I waited a month as you requested. I said I could adapt in any way. I never wanted to take them from here. I only asked for a chance, but you insist on treating me as a villain. Tell me what is so horrible about me that you can't allow your grandchildren to even meet me?"

"There's nothing wrong with you—" Alvaro shook his head.

"We might not have money," Caridad interrupted. "But we have values. We have hard work."

"I never made this about finances. But if that's the route you want to go? Yes, I am comfortable. What is the big deal?"

Caridad shook her head. "Familia is everything. We are the kids' family. They should stay with us."

"Sofia wanted—"

"You haven't been her friend for years."

My laugh was so sarcastic, I snorted. "And that was my fault?"

"You left and cut contact."

"I didn't do it. It was Da—"

But I never got to finish his name. Something dislodged from Alvaro's throat and the next word that came out of his mouth was so final, it laid over us like a heavy blanket.

*"Enough."*

My breathing was erratic. I've done everything I promised myself not to do. I came over to negotiate, to make them trust me, but instead I did nothing but argue with Caridad since I arrived.

This wasn't how I fixed my problems. It wasn't how I liked to deal with anything in life. However, Caridad was never going to like me. She wasn't going to be charmed by anything I said, and it was clear the kids weren't here, so it didn't matter. I came here to talk to them, but once again I wasn't allowed.

Only five minutes in and I could understand this was a losing battle. Thank god I always diversified my investments.

Smoothing the pants over my legs, I took a breath. "I came here to talk. To try to make this happen amicably." She huffed, refusing to look at me. I nodded to myself. "Of course you've now proven that's impossible."

"The kids are not going anywhere," she made a point of saying.

"I see." I breathed in.

It was only Alvaro who picked up on my tone. He was alert, his body turned to me, "Logan..."

I shook my head, standing up. He did, too. "Logan, sit down. We can talk."

"No." I faced him. "I waited a month like you requested. I came here to talk to the children. I've done nothing wrong, yet I'm continuously being treated like a criminal. I'm done here."

With a last nod to Sofia's parents, I let myself out. I heard Alvaro coming after me, but the steps ended when Caridad said, "Let her go."

And I ran to my car.

# 4.

# Alvaro

"Let her go," Mamá said.

I shouldn't let Logan go, but the simmering anger in my blood just boiled over. I swirled around, facing my parents with a tick in my jaw.

"Do you understand what just happened here?"

"She's gone," Mamá said, nodding to herself after a good day's work. "The subject is dropped."

"It is not dropped. She's getting lawyers involved. Do you understand what that means?"

"I won't fight her." She stood up, heading to the kitchen. "She can fight alone at court."

I laughed. I never used such a cruel laugh with my own mother, but then again, I remembered her being reasonable.

"She'll take the kids."

Mamá shook her head. "No one is going to take kids from their family."

I breathed through my nose, trying to calm myself. "Sofia made Logan their guardian. Logan has money to bury this family in legal fees. It is nothing for her and might be everything for us."

"I am their grandmother," she started again.

I couldn't let her say it one more time. "You are in your late sixties. Logan is young, rich, and their legal guardian. And even if it wasn't for all the obvious reasons, how selfish could you be?"

She almost tripped on her feet, shrieking unintelligent words for the way I dared to talk to her.

"If this is dragged out in court, do you understand how bad it's going to be for the kids? How horrible is it going to be for them to have to go through this? And they will read the letter."

Mamá moved so fast I barely saw it coming. One second she had her hand on her waist, a disapproving face, the next she was close to me, her face scrunched in a murderous glare.

"No one is reading that letter."

There again. Mamá had rules which we all had to obey. She decided our fates and made sure to always double down on the guilt trip if we ever dared go against her.

"They will if you bring this to court. You're hurting them."

Low? A little. That was her argument, wasn't it? Family was everything. People were expected to make sacrifices for their family. Right now, our concept of family was broken. Sofia broke us. She left this world and left us behind, not knowing what to do without her.

Saying the words I might regret, I looked into my mother's eyes, knowing I was about to hurt her. "Sofia knew she wanted to leave this world. And she knew who she wanted to raise her kids. It's about time you respect her wishes."

Without dealing with the consequences of my words, I left, got into my truck, and drove away.

"PICK UP, PICK UP," I chanted in the car on my way back to the city, blowing up Logan's phone.

She finally picked up.

"Don't call your lawyers." It was the first thing out of my mouth.

As much as Mamá's stubbornness infuriated me, I knew bringing this to court could destroy my family.

That was the last thing I wanted.

"Your plan isn't working."

"Logan, listen..."

"No," she replied sharply. "I can't keep tiptoeing around your mother. Those kids deserve the best."

"This is hard for her."

"It's hard for everyone. I lost Sofia, too. You lost a sister. And more than anything, those kids lost their mother."

I nodded to myself. "So you see how making them go through a court dispute is the worst way to handle this?"

I held my breath as she released hers, her voice sounding tired on the phone. "I'm not going to drag your family through that. But I did talk to a lawyer already."

"Logan..." I palmed my head.

She chuckled softly. "It's just my cousin. I needed to go there with someone on my side."

"I was on your side."

She didn't respond to that. Instead, she said. "I want to talk to the kids. I want to tell them about the situation and at least have a chance to be part of their lives. I'm not going to lie here, if they hate me," her voice lost its firm quality, "if they hate me, I won't change anything or uproot them. I just want a chance. At least to be Aunty Logan, you know?"

"Tía Logan?" I chanced.

"If they call me tía, that angry vein in your mother's forehead might explode."

I chuckled at the image. "Don't worry. If it didn't explode when I was doing MMA, I can't believe it would with just a word."

She took a breath, and then she broke my heart with the next thing she said. "We used to watch you fight, Sofia and I. She would tape them, and we watched them together over and over again."

My mouth felt uncomfortably dry. "Yeah?"

"Yeah." I hear a smile in her voice. "The good ones we watched many times. I think I know all your moves. She thought you were the coolest guy on earth. Her big brother hung the moon."

My hands strangled the steering wheel like I could crush it between my fingers. Grief like nothing else took residence on my chest and for a second there, I couldn't breathe. Eyes on the road, but I couldn't see anything else.

"I'll text later with a date to meet the kids," I rushed to say.

Before Logan could say anything, I hung up the call and breathed through my nose. My heart ticked like a time bomb, my mind frail, unprotected. I couldn't keep myself together.

My vision doubled up, it only focused back when my phone chimed with a message.

**Logan:** I'm sorry.

My discontent ripped through my chest, coming out in a horrific scream.

Trying to get back to myself, I headed for the only place that could numb the guilt enough to make me forget I let Sofia feel so alone. She left this world, leaving us all behind…in shambles.

"You're supposed let me know before you come around, huh? I have to work the bets." He tapped my shoulder.

"Hands off," I growled.

Paddy raised his hands quickly like I was an unhinged animal. It was a fair assessment. I disliked the man, but he ran the illegal betting ring, and he let me in whenever I wanted.

And I wanted in now.

I needed it.

As I wrapped my knuckles, my deadly stare ahead, my body buzzing with adrenaline, Paddy moved around. His twitchy body observing me, his yellow teeth showing with a smirk.

"Ya know Castillo, some would say you should look for a shrink. Fixing your life in a ring isn't the answer."

I finished with one hand and moved to the other. "Yet, how would you make money?"

"I'm trying to be your friend."

"Don't."

"Come on." He dared to approach. "We've known each other for—"

I worked fast, closing my hand around his neck, shoving his slimy body against the rusty lockers of his shitty gym. No one would come to this hellhole if it wasn't for illegal betting. This shit wouldn't survive a day.

"Stay out of my business, Paddy," I growled into his face.

"If you want to make money, you gotta tell me when you're coming for a fight."

"I came to break someone's face. I bet half of town would be glad if it was yours."

His nostrils flared, his Adam's apple bobbing under my hand. "Save the rage for the ring."

I chuckled, releasing him to a hop on my feet. Shaking my head, I went back to getting ready. "You have twenty minutes, Paddy. Make it count."

Never saw the man move so fast, his greasy fingers on his phone as he alerted all his regulars. The rules in Paddy's house were simple. Anyone could fight. But at first, they fight for free. You showed up and no one bet on you, so you were just there, punching suckers for nothing.

As bets came in, the cut was still shit because Paddy was a greedy fucker, but I never came in for money anyway. I preferred those days when no one knew about me, when no one was betting, and I could just fight.

Nowadays, Paddy got a stiffy when I walked through those doors. And if that wasn't disturbing enough, he acted like we were some sort of partners. He wanted to schedule my fights, let it brew with his clients. Put me against the other big fighters.

I cracked my neck, rolling my shoulders back as I watched myself in the foggy mirror ahead. The shorts I wore dropped low, my tattoos covered one side of my body.

Another disappointment to my mother. She said I was a good man, that she raised me right and fighting wasn't a good man's path and neither were tattoos.

It didn't matter when I explained MMA was a sport. Even when I proved I was good over and over again, and I started getting sponsors. To her, it was mindless fighting with no technique.

When I left home, I thought they would see my success and change their minds. Proving them wrong was my mission and I wouldn't stop until my picture was everywhere.

Instead, I played the sport with mild success for a long time. My face was nowhere, my name wasn't known, so they never changed their minds. They called for Christmas, but no one called saying they regretted their words about my career.

In my stupid quest to prove myself, I missed what was going on with Sofia.

My hands closed in a fist as I thought about what Logan said. Sofia watched my fights. I was barely part of her life and she thought of me as her hero?

A growl escaped from my throat, and I shot a look at Paddy. "Now."

He glanced at his watch, nodding quickly. Leaving behind Paddy, the lockers, and that gross smell of mold that always lingered, I opened the door. It was the middle of the week, but the word definitely spread in the time I allowed Paddy to work his bets.

The pristine MMA cage I got used to was left behind when I retired. Now, I crossed Paddy's shitty gym, heading to an even shittier ring, as I refused to look anyone in the eye.

I cut through the crowd and headed straight in, only stopping to lift the rope. I waited in a corner, my hands full of tension, cracking my neck to the side.

Their cheers were deafening, and I did my best to ignore them. I waited as Paddy found someone worthy of fighting me. I eyed my opponent, some big guy I saw around. Bushy beard, trying too hard to intimidate me with a sneer.

"Gentleman, are you ready for El Toro?" Paddy shouted, egging on the crowd.

Roars came from each corner, my opponent's eyes narrowing as he realized how out of his depth he was.

*El Toro.* A stupid nickname from my MMA days, but even I couldn't deny it.

Once I was in the ring, I only saw red.

I wiped a finger over my lips, testing my feet on the ring to avoid sliding. Big man watched me, wary for the first time. The crowd screamed El Toro at the top of their lungs, and I knew I had it.

Not because I had a reputation. Not because I had professional training. Not because I was better.

I had this fight because I had nothing else.

I had a shitty relationship with my parents. My little sister killed herself. My failures were overwhelming.

The only person who saw grandeur in me was the little sister I left behind. The one who I let my parents pressure into being with the kids' father even though I hated him from the second I met him.

Big man met me in the middle. Paddy signaled, and the fight started. Blow after blow, I barely felt it.

He got me in my stomach, but I didn't feel a thing. I blocked him after, and he retreated. He came back again, he wore that damn snarl I didn't care about. I hit him in the face, happy when it was so strong I saw the skin on his cheek move. Taking my moment, I tried once again and hit him in the stomach.

Big man recuperated, taking me with a right hook. I tasted blood in my mouth, but I smiled at him.

*More.*

*Just hit me enough so I forget what I've done.*

*I let Sofia die.*

He swung so strongly this time the crowd winced, my eye burning, letting me know it would be completely swollen shut tomorrow.

"Come on, big man," I called for him.

He came mercilessly, one strike after the other. He was getting predictable. Like a rehearsed dance, he did it again and again until my body memorized his tells.

I blocked once, even as sweat and blood covered my eyes. He was big, but he wasn't trained. He wasn't good.

So I punched him like he ended my sister himself, like I blamed him as well.

I released it all on him because I couldn't do anything else. I couldn't protect my sister.

I punched him because I couldn't punch myself.

When my opponent dropped, my ears rang. Somewhere out there, Paddy worked the crowd, their chanting loud, calling EL TORO at the top of their lungs.

I looked down at him, and I felt nothing.

He wasn't me.

And Sofia was still dead.

# 5.

# Alvaro

¿Que es eso en tu cara?

I waited a full week until I dared to visit my parents' home, but I couldn't leave Logan waiting any longer.

Mamá looked sharply at the bruise covering my left eye, and I was quickly transported in time. Thirty years ago? Fuck. I remember sitting in this kitchen trying to tell them my trainer said I had a future.

"Where are the kids? We are doing this now."

The woman who raised me walked toward me, unfolded the arms she had crossed over her chest and reached for my chin, moving it to the light.

"Mi príncipe, eres tan guapo. ¿Por qué?"

"Leave the boy, Caridad." Papá arrived just in time.

Mamá let my chin go with a sigh, and I rolled my shoulders back, trying to not get affected by her. I didn't have a reason. She asked me why, but I had nothing. Why did I still go to Paddy's? It fixed nothing. It never brought me any peace.

Deciding not to think about it for a second longer, I fixed my gaze on my father. "Logan is coming again. Soon. But I think we should tell them before. Prepare them."

Papá nodded, and we both avoided my mother's eyes. She was against it, but I couldn't make myself more clear. Logan was the person Sofia choose to take care of the kids. My mother couldn't hold Lachlan for long. She had a bad back, and I bet anything Dash was taking care of his siblings while they were here. More than he should.

I didn't point out to Mamá about her back and Dash's responsibility with the younger ones. I didn't want her to think she was failing. But I wanted to end this situation.

"I will call them to the living room," Papá said.

"No," Mamá started, and I swear Papá and I held our breath. "In the kitchen. That's where family talks."

I lifted a shoulder, not carrying much, but Papá nodded, mumbling, "Of course, mi amor."

We waited in silence, thankfully, but when she sat at the table, hands wiggling all over her lap, I went to her.

Grasping her hands on mine, I promised, "Nothing bad will happen to the kids. Logan is a good girl."

Mamá looked at our hands, her cold fingers gripping mine. I continued, "She loved Sofia. She's a good person."

"She's not from our world," Mamá said again. "I don't want the kids to lose who they are."

"They aren't going to be less Cuban if they move in with Logan."

Mamá shook her head. "Cuba is not just blood, Alvaro. It's a culture. It's who we are. I don't want them missing out."

"Mamá..." I shook my head, bringing my arm around her. "That's something you can say to Logan."

"If they forget where they come from? They won't understand—"

"I know. But that's not what is happening here. You're not giving away your grandchildren. Logan will take the toll, but we are going to be right there with her."

"Will we?" She unglued from my chest, watching me with an expression that made me uncertain.

I opened my mouth to ask, but steps interrupted me. Soon Papá and the kids were back. Lachlan on Dash's hip. Lachlan could walk. Of course, they just came from upstairs, but still. What toddler didn't want to run around the house and make the adults wince at every corner?

I filed that under one more thing I needed to investigate.

"Hi, tío." Vienna smiled, jumping on me before I even got a chance to respond.

I kissed her soft brown hair, and she smiled at me so brightly it almost made things better.

"Why were you being a dumbass?" she surprisingly asked.

"Vienna!" Mamá scolded.

"Excuse me?"

She lifted a shoulder, taking a seat just beside my chair. "That's the only reason Dash ever gets a black eye."

My eyes darted to my nephew straight away, panic flaring through my veins.

"Don't listen to her," Dash mumbled, taking a seat opposite Mamá with Lachlan on his knees.

Pinching the bridge of my nose, I started. "How are you doing?"

"I'm best friends with Cierra again," Vienna informed me.

"Great."

Dash snorted. "Believe me, it is not."

Vienna gasped. "Shut up, Dash!"

"Language, Vienna," Mamá warned.

"Cierra is a bully, you know it. No one will care if you come home crying again, Vienna," Dash insisted.

"Stop, Dash!" Vienna's voice was so loud, dogs responded to it.

"I'm telling the truth. You have the worst friends."

"You're telling lies! I'm gonna tell mo—"

The whole table held its collective breath. Dash flinched like an invisible hand just slapped him right across his face. Vienna never finished her sentence. Instead, her lip quivered, her eyes so huge they took over her face.

Mamá hiccupped. Papá looked away.

I tried again. "I have something to tell you."

Dash's eyes left his sister and focused on me. "Tell us."

There was a defiance there. Something like he dared me to bring more bad news.

"Do you remember Logan?" I asked them.

I planned a hundred different starts for this conversation. I knew nothing would make this easier. When they all three shook their heads, I kept going. "She was your mom's best friend when they were growing up."

"She's the mantel lady," Vienna said with the smallest of voices.

I frowned, but Mamá was nodding. "Sofia kept a picture of them on the mantel."

It wasn't there anymore.

"Yes, the mantel lady. She was Sofia's good friend and when your mother..." I cleared my throat. "Your mother left a document saying she'd like Logan to take care of you."

"We are leaving Tita's house?" Vienna asked.

"No!" Mamá thought it was good to scream.

"Not if you don't want to. Sofia thought it was a good fit. Logan just wants to meet you. She wants a chance." And as I said it, it was my mother who I faced.

"So mom died," Dash drawled. "And now some lady is coming over trying to take us away?"

"She's a virtual stranger." Mamá's hands went up.

God. This again. I pinned my mother with a look. "You saw her grow up. She's not a stranger. She's not taking anyone, alright? She just wants a chance to get to know you."

I barely finished saying it, and I heard the car parking outside. I looked through the window, finding Logan's Beemer out of place in front of the house. Vienna stretched her neck, trying to see too, and it was Papá who stood up mumbling he was going to get the door.

"No one needs to worry. She's just here to introduce herself." I thought it was best to say.

None of them were paying attention to me. Even Lachlan, who I thought only understood half of what I was saying, was holding his breath as we heard Papá opening the front door.

I heard Logan's voice. She had a gentle tone, feminine and controlled. She was wearing heels. I could hear them as they tapped on the wood floors.

They turned for the kitchen, appearing at the door, where we all waited in silence.

She was so small, but I noticed she always squared her shoulders, her little nose up. Her hair was parted in the middle and secured together in a businesslike low pony.

Logan was wearing her office clothes, a pencil skirt and blouse. Her eyes scanned the table, landing on each one of us as she breathed in, like she was trying to muster some courage.

"Hey there, Logan," I offered.

"Hi," she tried.

Her eyes were back on the kids. She wanted this. She really wanted this.

"Why don't you sit down, Logan? I'll get everyone coffee," my mother surprisingly offered.

"I'll take coffee too, Tita," Vienna said.

"No, you won't." Mamá shook her head and left the table to boil water.

"Thank you, Mrs. Castillo."

She looked painfully misplaced. Awkward to the bone, so I nodded to the chair vacant just beside Vienna. "Sit, Logan. We were just talking to the kids about you."

"Oh." Logan hurried to the chair, talking a place and smiling to Vienna, who was watching her too closely.

"I like your nails," Vienna offered.

I looked down at Logan's nails. They were long, but not too long, and painted in bright orange. I frowned. That was very different from the rest of the business attire she was wearing.

"My work clothes are kind of boring, so I have fun with my nails," Logan told her.

Vienna reached for Logan's hands over the table. Her little pinky touched Logan's nail tip. "Pretty," she whispered.

"So, we are going to live with you? Where do you even live?" That was Dash, of course, not in the mood to be beating around the bush, I guessed.

I sighed, but Logan replied. "You don't need to move in with me."

"How can you take care of us if we don't live with you?" Vienna asked an excellent question.

Logan bit her cheek, shaking her head. "You can if you want. What I am saying is it is up to you."

"If we agree to go with you." Dash waved off like Logan being kind was something he hadn't any time for.

Mamá cleared her throat, her back turned to us as she poured the hot water over the cotton filter.

"I live in the city," Logan said. "I have a..." She looked at Mamá's back and then practically whispered, "I live in a penthouse. And I have four bedrooms, so."

Papá whistled, and I felt the rage energy coming off my mother. I paid attention to the kids, though. Dash's eyebrows rose and Vienna looked excited.

"That's so cool," the little girl exclaimed. "And you live there all by yourself?"

"I do." Logan nodded. "But it will be a full house if you come to live with me."

"You can't raise kids in Chicago," Mom said at once, placing her faithful big thermos on the table.

"Why not?" Vienna asked, genuinely interested.

"People raise their kids everywhere," I argued.

"You don't need to come with me. I can get a house here," Logan rushed to say. "I can... rent first, but if you all liked it, we can buy something."

"So you're rich," Dash bluntly said.

"I'm comfortable."

*Things that rich people say.*

"If we're going to live with you, we can have all kinds of stuff, then?"

"Dash..." I asked under my breath.

"What, tío? I want to know what she's offering."

"You'll have anything you want, regardless."

Mamá made a face as she slammed a cup in front of Logan.

"Not everything." Logan tried to change things. "I mean, I'll pay for your college, Dashiell. If you live with me or not. For all of you." She cleared her throat. "Regardless."

"What's in it for you?" Dash asked.

"Excuse me?"

I poured coffee into Logan's cup. Something told me she needed it.

"You're going to bring us to a penthouse and pay for my college for what?"

I opened my mouth, but Logan shook her head. She faced Dash carefully. A beat passed before she said, "Because your mom asked me to."

# 6
# Logan

It was always like this between us. Sofia was soft and easy to love. I was rigid, a Hart through and through. I didn't know how to say the right things. Terrible at dating, I was too direct. Too much to the point.

I came to this house once again with one goal in mind. I was here to wow the kids and make them want to see me again. My mentor always said you only needed to make it to the next interview. To the next project. One step at the time.

I came to make them agree to see me again. Instead, I talked about paying for their education. The hands resting on top of my thighs clutched the fabric, and I hoped to dear god my smile wasn't too wobbly.

"We can talk about this later." I swallowed, avoiding Caridad's murderous gaze.

I knew she was going to accuse me of buying their affection. I wasn't. At least I didn't think I was. My head turned to Alvaro, unconsciously asking for help, but before he could intervene, Dash spoke up.

"We want to talk alone."

Alvaro blinked at his nephew. I looked from one Castillo to the next, not sure what he meant. Since everyone kept silent, I decided to ask.

"By yourselves?"

Dash shook his head. "With you."

"Dashiell..." Caridad started, but Alvaro stood up.

"We'll be in the other room."

I heard protests from Caridad, but my focus wouldn't waver from Dashiell. He was looking straight at me, Lachlan still on his knee and watching me as much as his big brother. Even Vienna, who was the most talkative of the siblings, was in complete silence now.

I squirmed under his eyes, and we waited in complete silence until one-by-one Alvaro left with his parents and the door closed softly behind them.

"How come mom wants us to live with you?" he fired off the second that door closed.

I sucked in a breath, ready for that question. "We grew up together. We were best friends since we were little. We used to share everything."

"And how come we don't know you?" He narrowed his eyes.

I swallowed, not sure how much I could share. "I'm actually your godmother," I told him. "I organized your baby shower." That did not change the look on his face, so I pressed on. "Things changed when we graduated from school..." I cleared my throat. "But we reconnected later. And she knew she could trust me."

The words felt weird in my mouth, but I had no time to think about it.

"And we would go live in the city with you?" Dashiell pushed.

I shook my head. "I can rent some place here. You don't need to move schools."

Dash and Vienna shared a look. Since I laid my eyes on him during the funeral, I knew he was too grown up. Between how serious he was for a fifteen-year-old, and how Vienna seemed almost jumpy at times while Lachlan wouldn't talk at all… I had my hands full with them.

It wasn't time to think about that. I'd leave it to future Logan and that pile of parenting books waiting for me. Right now, I had one step further to go. And I could only think about that one. *One thing at the time.*

"The thing is," he started again. "We don't want to stay here."

"With your grandparents?" I tilted my head.

"At our school," Vienna whispered.

She lowered her head, her mouth closed in a line as she pressed against the table. I frowned and directed my question to Dashiell. "What's wrong with school?"

"Everyone knows about mom," he said. "They just keep asking questions. Teachers, too."

"Some teachers are nice and ask if I want to talk," Vienna chimed in.

"But we don't want to talk," Dash finished quickly. "We tried to bring it up with Tita that we wanted to move schools."

I nodded, knowing already what she replied. "It's a good school. That's where me and your mom went."

Dash nodded. It wasn't news to him. "But we don't want to stay there anymore."

I looked from one to the other. Lachlan did not offer much, but a blink from his brother's knees. I didn't let excitement run through my veins. This was better than I thought. They were open to coming with me. But...

"We can talk to Caridad," I offered.

"You have custody, right?" Dash asked.

I nodded. "Yeah, your mom's attorney made sure everything was how she wanted. I'm your legal guardian."

"So, it's decided." He nodded and turned to Vienna. "Call Tita."

The girl sprang into action. I barely understood what was decided as Caridad and the others arrived.

"We are going with Logan."

That was how Dash delivered the news. It was blunt and somehow the perfect sentence for the sharp answer it received.

"No," Caridad said.

I massaged my temple. "Dashiell thinks..." but I never got to finish that thought.

Caridad turned to me with a rage I never faced. "You're not taking my grandchildren from me. Their place is with their family."

"I'm not trying to take anything from you—"

But she was now screaming in Spanish at me. I held my breath, keeping my head low as she called me irresponsible for taking the children from their family. I was accused of poisoning their mind, of throwing money at them because that was all a Hart could do.

I didn't flinch. I let her talk. Maybe she thought I couldn't speak Spanish. That was fine. She was upset, and this was her way of showing it.

So, I feigned ignorance because Dashiell was right. As their legal guardian, I had the right to bring them with me.

I won.

"Mamá, calm down, please. Let's talk."

As Caridad sucked in a breath, I could hear her heart shattering.

"I don't want to do this."

"You said you wanted us to live with you," Dash accused.

I breathed in. "Of course I do."

"They will not," Caridad yelled.

God, it was endless. I opened my mouth to try one last time, but Alvaro roared.

He stood up at all his height, his face like thunder. Frowning, making that new shiner he had on his eye even more scary. Why the hell did he have bruises, anyway? But it all worked for him. The snug T-shirt with his business logo stretched over his chest, the menace in his eyes proving he had enough of all of us.

"Dash, is that what you want?" He addressed his nephew, ignoring his mother's sharp look.

Dashiell confirmed. "We don't want to go to that school anymore."

Alvaro nodded and turned to me. "Maybe you can have a look at schools—"

"I have a list of public and private schools close to my house."

"Of course you do," Alvaro said, and I could swear I saw a twitch on his lip.

"This is insane. They don't know..."

"Maybe the kids need a fresh start." My voice was low, but once they all paid attention to me, I continued a little stronger. "This is new for everyone, but maybe they need... time."

Caridad's eyes flew to Dash, and he nodded. "It would be nice not to be in that school anymore." He moved uncomfortably in his seat. "Everyone knows us there."

"It doesn't need to be permanent. It doesn't need to be full time," I added.

My face was hot from them all watching me, but I couldn't do anything but hope. I wanted them with me, and they wanted to go. Why couldn't we just try?

Sofia wanted them with me.

I was sure fighting her family was the wrong move here, but how long could I bend backwards to satisfy Caridad? I'd do it gladly if there was any indication she wanted to be reasonable. But I knew, right in my core, she would never be on my side.

"I think the kids should go visit a couple of schools," Alvaro started.

"It's in the middle of the school year." Caridad was already shaking her head.

"Logan is our legal guardian, and we want to go." Dash stood up, Lachlan in his arms. "Let's go, Vi."

Vienna stood up right away and followed her big brother out of the kitchen.

None of the adults said a word as the kids left. I glanced at Caridad, expecting to see a murderous expression, but instead what I found was a grandmother with a broken heart.

I blew out a breath. Shaking myself I leaned over the table, looking directly in her eyes. "I don't want to fight. Please."

She didn't look at me, instead her eyes were trained on the place her grandchildren had disappeared to. She then turned to me, something wild going through her face.

"They can go with you." She nodded, her eyes on mine. "But Alvaro goes, too."

Silence stretched. Under furrowed eyebrows I stared at her, trying to understand what she just said.

"Sorry?" I spoke up when it was obvious she wasn't going to give me anything.

Dipping her chin, she avoided our glances and focused on her husband. "Alvaro lives in Chicago, too. It's not unreasonable to expect he's invited to the kids' life."

I breathed out slowly, relieved, "Of course. Alvaro can visit them—"

"No." And she pinned me with a look. "Alvaro goes where the kids go. He stays with you or none of them do."

I blinked, trying my best not to point out she wasn't in the position to demand anything. Before I could open my mouth to protest, though, the other person involved decided to speak up.

"Mamá." He shook his head. "I have a business. I—"

"No one said you need to stay with them the whole time. The kids have school. And Logan surely will be back at her job as soon as she can."

I hated that comment. I hated that she used it to make me feel less about having a career. She barely knew me after all. The teenage girl she met was full of dreams, the woman in front of her was full of accomplishments. I wasn't going to say sorry for having achieved my goals.

"I'm actually taking a leave of absence. I asked my boss. She knows the situation here. I want to be flexible and have time until they adapt."

It was maternity leave. I didn't even think about it, but rather Willa, who told me as a new guardian I could argue to my boss I needed to step away from the office for a couple of months. I wouldn't call it maternity leave in front of Caridad, though.

And I was worried. I wanted to have time with the kids so I could plan my next step. I needed to understand them. I wanted to hear Lachlan talking. I knew he could talk, and I couldn't understand why he didn't. I wanted Dash's trust and... well, maybe Vienna was the easiest of the three.

Maybe she was my lifeline in this mess.

"Anyway, I need time and space for them. Space I wouldn't have if—"

"You're suggesting that I move in with Logan?"

"I'm suggesting that you take responsibility for your sister's children," Caridad stated. "I'll gladly keep them here..."

"But Sofia wanted Logan to raise them. Sofia trusted Logan."

"Family is everything. I raised Sofia and I can raise her kids too. If you're so inclined to give them away, then you take on that responsibility. You go with her."

"And keep an eye on what I am doing?" I chuckled a humorless laugh. "Is that the plan? Alvaro spies to see if I am doing something wrong? You clearly don't know me if you—"

"That's true." Caridad's voice softened for the first time. "I don't know you. These are my grandchildren who you are planning to take with you."

I hated the honest quality of her voice. It made me nod and take a big breath. "I can stay here. I can rent a house."

"What did Dash say to you?" Alvaro asked suddenly.

I licked my lips, unsure what to share. But in the end, if I was going to do this in peace, I had to understand Caridad and the others deserved to be involved too. They were the kids' family, after all.

"He said what he said in front of you all. He wants to go someplace else. People know about Sofia and they are constantly reminded. He wants to start new, and I guess that was a big selling point for them."

I didn't expect Dash to be jumping up and down in happiness about living with me. He didn't know me, as it seemed to be the theme for the entire Castillo family.

I watched each person in front of me as they reacted to my words. Geraldo swallowed down a lump in his throat. Caridad's eyes filled with tears. Finally, I faced Alvaro, who breathed through his nose, tipping his head back and looking up at the ceiling before facing me.

"I'll go with you."

"Sorry?" I arched an eyebrow.

"They deserve a second chance. You don't need to stay here. We can go back together."

"You keep saying *we*."

"This is a weird situation. I can help."

I crossed my arms. "And you want to stay with us?"

"I can. Just until things settle down."

"Alvaro will help." Caridad nodded like it was decided.

She was putting a spy inside my house. I knew that much. Alvaro was there to call her every night telling how inept I was. However, he was the kids' uncle, he knew them better than me. That was a fact.

"Lachlan can sleep in Vienna's or Dash's room," I said. "You get a room, then."

"Thank you." And I could swear I saw the smallest twitch on his lip.

"So, that's settled. We can see if that's going to work."

I closed my eyes for just a second to hold myself back from saying something I'd regret. Caridad kept mistaking my soft approach for weakness. I knew my rights. I was ready for a fight, but I didn't want to cause them more trauma.

Shaking my head, I understood in our relationship there would be many times when I had to keep my mouth shut in order to avoid a confrontation.

So I did just that. I avoided another confrontation and said, "Yes, it is settled."

# 7.

# Alvaro

"Lach? You ok there?"

His eyes, that were once focused on the passing views, faced me through the mirror. He had a pacifier, something Dash said he was only allowed on car rides since his third birthday.

Putting the car seat in my truck was an experience. The number of snacks Mamá prepared for our short ride to the city was alarming.

I was out of my depth, plain and simple. Kids had rules I didn't understand. They had to snack all the time, and were allowed to suck on a pacifier sometimes, but not always.

My mother was suffering. As irrational as she was for not seeing they couldn't raise children in their seventies, I knew it came from a place of hurt. She was scared of losing them.

She didn't trust Logan as far as she could throw her. And as tiny as Logan was, Mamá was even smaller.

I understood how weird it was to give Sofia's kids to someone else, to have them live in Chicago full time and visit on the weekends. I understood her pain, so I agreed to something... I couldn't deliver.

I never agreed to a fight I didn't think I could win. Even when I lost, it was by a small margin. I never entered with my fists first, head later. When I started my business, Castillo Construction, I knew I could do it.

But this time, I was getting myself involved in something I couldn't win.

I knew nothing about kids.

And they came in different ages.

I had a toddler frowning, I had Vienna talking non-stop about something or another, and I had a sulking teenager by my side.

Funny to think I was old enough to be their parent. In my forties, I shouldn't feel so out of place with them.

I drove on, letting them eat everything Mamá packed and fill my truck with crumbs.

That was my life now. I was supposed to drive them up and down and they were going to snack and talk and pick the music.

I glanced at my phone to check the address Logan gave us. She lived on the Gold Coast. *Of course she did*. She had a penthouse in one of the most expensive places in this damn country.

Even Dash knew what it meant. As soon as he noticed I added her address to the GPS, he turned the phone in his direction to check it out and whistled when he saw her zip code.

Those houses went for millions. Rubbing my face, I tried not to think about how I ended up in this mess. All I wanted was to help my parents see they couldn't raise the kids. They didn't have what it took anymore, health wise or financially. I could try to send them money, but Papá was never really easy to help. They would end up putting themselves into debt, trying to do the right thing.

There was also the problem with Lachlan. He was too young. He needed a lot. He was only three. A silent, kind of scary, three-year-old.

They were traumatized kids. My mom was trying to hold on to them, but Logan was their best chance.

Not me.

I was no one's best chance.

I was fists. I was rage. I wasn't suited for soft love.

The opposite of what I made Logan believe, I had no relationship with them. I knew I wasn't going to be any help. I was a construction worker who wasn't meant to live in a penthouse on the Gold Coast. And yet, that's where I was headed.

I had a duffle with a couple of old T-shirts and stained jeans I packed before picking up the kids this morning. I wouldn't be surprised if they refused to allow my truck to be parked on the street.

Turning the car off, I glanced at the passenger seat. Dash only pocketed his phone when he noticed we had stopped. Lowering his head so he could see the tall building through the window, he chuckled. "So, here we are."

We both found Logan at the same time. She was standing in front of the building, the doorman just beside her. She stood eerily straight with a severe ponytail pulling her hair out of her face.

"She's intense," Dash commented.

I didn't want to agree and start this off on the wrong foot with Logan, but if she wanted to hide her real self, she wasn't doing a good job. I thought at first it was just her work clothes that made her look tense.

Maybe my mother was antagonizing her so much, the girl was always defensive. But no. I could tell by the way her jaw worked, even the way she blinked too fast, that it was just Logan. Dash was right, she was intense.

Turning in my seat, I looked at Vienna and Lachlan.

"This is it. Logan is waiting."

Vienna nodded but said nothing. Lachlan blinked.

"You have to tell me if you're uncomfortable. So we can... you know. Do something."

"Very inspirational, tío." Dash patted my back. Then his eyes fixed on his sister. "Don't break shit, don't steal shit." She opened her mouth to protest, but he kept going. "Tell me if something is going on before you go off the rails. Lach?"

The three-year-old blinked again. "Yeah, you're cool."

With that, he opened the door and left the car. Vienna tried to follow him but thank god I remembered to enable the child locks today.

"We need to get out, too!" she told me, and then tried to open the door more than one hundred times to see if anything changed in the last second.

I frowned at her. "Vienna, I'll..."

But she kept trying to open the door, aggressively so. Like a cork popping, without notice, no rhyme or reason, Lachlan started to cry. He opened his mouth as big as I'd ever seen, and from it came a wounded cry. Like it was from the bottom of his heart, as if Vienna's distress over the child locks was the last straw for him.

Tears spilled from his eyes, the pacifier falling on his lap. My mouth opened and closed, confused by what I should think or do.

Why was he crying?

I didn't understand.

Why was Vienna suddenly in the middle of a rage trying to open the door?

It knocked the air out of my lungs when I realized these children didn't come with manuals. And it wasn't even a little bit amusing.

No.

In a horrifying, real way. They were suffering, crying in front of me, and I had no clue why.

Vienna kept trying to open the door, all her strength on the handle forcing it again and again as she grew distressed. I barely could hear it now over Lachlan wailing, his cries so loud I felt the glass windows shake.

Paralyzed in shock, I couldn't move until the passenger door opened again, but instead of Dash, Logan's face came to view.

"Oh my god," she whispered over the wailing.

I turned to her, incapable of explaining what was happening. I just shook my head, hoping she could understand I was lost for words.

What did I do wrong? How did we go from driving happily to this?

"I—I'm going to take him," she told me and closed the door again.

The banging door took me out of my stupor. I moved quickly, removing my seatbelt and swinging the door open at the same time Logan moved.

Outside, the world was normal again. I could hear the street, the people, the cars, and my own thoughts. I looked at Logan and we said nothing to each other until she took a deep breath and opened Lachlan's door.

The wailing slapped us right in the face. At least we could all be glad he was a very healthy boy with the strong lungs he had on him.

"Hey, Lachlan. What's up, buddy?" Logan tried her softest voice, but I didn't think he could hear her over his own screams.

I rounded the car to stand behind Logan, my hands in my pockets like an idiot. Vienna's eyes widened when she saw a door was opened. Without thinking twice, she threw herself on her brother, not intimidated by the yelling.

Her body on top of him made Lachlan even more upset. He kicked and waved his arms as she jumped over him unceremoniously. Logan stepped back, smart enough to get out of the way, her back bumping to my front as I held her shoulders with my hands.

Warm under my palm, her head reached right under my chin. We watched dumbfounded Vienna jumping over Lachlan's seat and land on the sidewalk. But at her first step to freedom, a hand stopped her.

Dashiell's arm laced around her waist. "What is your problem?" he asked, tsking.

"My door was locked," she complained, sending me a dirty look.

I opened my mouth, but no sound came out.

"Stay where you are. Don't cross the road by yourself," he told her.

Then he came to Lachlan, grabbing his pacifier from his lap, he stuffed it in the child's mouth.

"Lach, stop."

At first Lachlan did not stop. He had to hold the pacifier or he would spit it out all over again. But after half a minute, Lachlan latched on to it and Dash removed his hand and opened the seat belt.

Taking his brother in his arms, the wailing completely stopped.

Vienna was still angry, but she held Dash's hand when he offered it to her. The teenager eyed Logan and I up and down, shook his head in disappointment and brought the kids across the road and to Logan's building.

It was only when we watched them cross securely that Logan turned in my hands. Her big green eyes were full of tears when she looked up at me.

"I think we fucked up."

No shit.

AFTER DASH TOOK THE kids, I finally removed my hands from Logan's shoulders, and we crossed the street to meet them. I was so busy watching her, I only noticed how ridiculous her building was once I stood at the front of it.

In solid exposed stone, reeking of old money, it stood proudly with a doorman at the front. He smiled and introduced himself as Andrew, nodding when Logan told him I was staying as well as the kids.

"Just let me know if you need anything." He bowed his head slightly.

The scene belonged in a movie, and it took me a second to return the gesture with a dip of my chin, clearing my throat and thanking the man.

Then Logan took a keycard from her back pocket, a card to access her floor. After swiping, she pressed the eleven.

"I gave a keycard to Dash." She explained the kids' absence. "And you can park your truck down in the parking lot. I have three spaces."

I nodded but looked forward, my eyes glued to the reflective metal of the elevator's door. Even if it was clearly renovated and modern, the floors were in light marble, with gold accents in the corner proving this building was old and once belonged to practically royalty.

As we ascended to the eleventh floor, I relaxed a little, and I chanced a look at Logan. She was standing in that way of hers, back straight and tense shoulders. Her jaw was clenched, and she was frowning at her own reflection.

I didn't need to be a shrink to know Logan was freaking out.

The elevator doors opened right in the middle of her living room, and I knew that her penthouse wasn't meant for us.

The first thing I noticed were the windows. Floor-length windows with a curve at the top framing the outside garden with a view of the city. Shelves and shelves of books, artwork on the walls, and a luscious cream sofa where the three kids sat, looking as misplaced as I felt. She also had flowers everywhere. Pink and white flowers in crystal vases on the tables and counters.

My boots hit the dark wooden floors in a zigzag pattern, and I almost missed as Logan took her heels off and rushed to the kids.

"Everything ok?" she asked.

Dash narrowed his eyes at her. "Yes."

That was all he offered. Logan laced her hands in front of her torso, and I really felt bad for her. Those kids were going to chew her up.

I scratched my palm over my buzzed hair as Logan made an attempt to perk up, slapping her hands over her legs. "Do you want to see the rest of the place?"

Lachlan slid off Dash's knees. Vienna took her little brother's hand, following close to Logan. I let Dash go and followed behind.

"This is the media room," she told us, showing the next room with a more comfortable set of sofas and a big screen. "My office is over there." She pointed to the opposite door. We all peeked at it, but it wasn't very exciting. Just a nice table with her laptop, paperwork on top, and a vase of flowers. I stopped counting them at this point.

Logan pivoted to the right. We were all following close by. "The kitchen." My tongue doubled its size when I took in the space. With an island right in the middle, copper pots hanging from the top and a cupboard in glass showing off expensive china covering all the walls opposite from the stove.

"You cook?" Dash asked.

"Sometimes," she mumbled, but judging by the way she pinked from her cheeks up to her ears, I'd say she was lying.

"The dining room is over there." She pointed to the right, where a big ten chair table stood. It was hard to miss.

I scratched my stubble as we progressed in the tour. I wasn't in the business to agree with my own mother, but she was right in her own way.

Logan's world wasn't ours. Every single thing in her house looked and smelled undoubtedly expensive. My work boots scratched her wooden floor. I felt like an elephant in a china shop. I was blue collar and rough, she was fragile and small. The stuff in her house looked like it was ready to break if any Castillo even looked too hard at it.

This wasn't a place for a toddler. I couldn't stop Lachlan from touching things. Even right now, he was leaving sticky marks all over her furniture. Those damn crystal vases with the white and pink flowers were at the perfect height to fall over on his head.

I said nothing, and I wasn't going to say a word. Logan wanted this. She was ready to fight for this. If reality and dreams were going to collide, that was her problem.

"And the bedrooms," she said as we went up the stairs.

They all looked similar, big with king-size beds and beige decorations. The only different one was the one beside her bedroom that had a view of Lake Michigan. I stepped in.

"Tío, will you grab this one?" Dash asked.

I nodded, accepting. This was temporary, I reminded myself. My life was in my crappy apartment on top of my office. An office that was mostly for show and meeting new clients since most days I was at a construction site.

I looked around the room with the view anyway, my eyes on the lake. I breathed in and out.

"I'll get them settled," she said.

I turned from the window. The kids weren't there anymore, and she was standing awkwardly at the door like she wouldn't dare step closer to a room with me in it.

"You do that." I nodded and my eyes turned to the view once again.

# 8. Logan

"Buy a bed for Lachlan." I wrote down on my notepad. What do toddlers even need? I didn't know.

Squeezing my eyes shut, I thought about how little I knew about everything. This had never happened. I always made a point of being prepared.

I scribbled down, "BE PREPARED" even though that one needed a dropdown list on its own. Breathing slowly out, I reached for my ponytail and pulled out the hairband throwing it onto my useless list.

My roots hurt as I raked both hands over the strands, relaxing it after a long day being pushed back. Shoulders slumped, I pinched the bridge of my nose, trying to calm down.

"Don't be so hard on yourself."

Glancing up, there he was. My lips parted as my brain tried to understand his presence. Alvaro was a figment of my imagination. He was that man on the TV with muscular arms who was able to knock out a man double his size.

He was a character, a bedtime story Sofia liked to tell me about. And now? He was in my home watching me with those piercing warm brown eyes exactly like his sister's.

"This is the first time I've seen your hair down."

My hand flew to my hair once again as he said it. It must have looked wild after hours up. I tried to smooth it down, but I doubted it was going to make any difference.

"Today was a mess." I decided to change the subject.

"It was a tantrum."

"That neither of us knew how to react to." I pushed, circling around the desk.

Alvaro shook his head, "It will work it—"

"No." I cut him off. "That's unacceptable."

"Tantrums?" His lip curved. "That's what children do."

My mouth closed in a line, and I stepped closer to him looking over his side to make sure there wasn't any sign of the kids. When it was obvious they were already in bed, I talked, lowering my voice anyway.

"It wasn't just the tantrum. We froze. Dashiell can't be the one doing the heavy lifting."

"He just knows how to calm them better. You're overthinking this."

I stepped even closer. "He's too grown up. Too hands on. He's a teenage boy, Alvaro. Tell me how you were at that age."

He hated that I said it. Hated. I could tell when his jaw ticked and an angry vein pulsed in his neck. Alvaro looked over his shoulders before turning back to me. "He's just good."

But when he stepped away to leave the office, I followed.

"Yeah, he might be good and kind. But..." I searched for the words. "I want him to relax, I want him to know I got this."

"So prove it to him that you do."

"I will." I looked away from him. "But so do you."

He just raised an eyebrow, but it was enough to make me talk again. "You're here now. You're involved in this. And you're going to find a way to do better by them." To avoid bumping into him, I circled to the right and left the office, but not before I said, "I'll send you literature."

I didn't wait for him to complain. Making my way upstairs, I took care going on my tiptoes, holding my breath as I reached the second floor. To my right was Alvaro's new bedroom, and in front the two bedrooms belonging to the children.

The penthouse originally had six bedrooms, but years ago I changed one of the bedrooms to a gym, and another to a living room upstairs. The biggest room was mine, and I thought keeping three empty rooms was enough.

My eyes traced the firmly closed door. Was it safe for them to sleep with the doors closed?

On an impulse, I reached for the knob and twisted before I could think better of it. Vienna was fast asleep, star fishing in the middle of the bed.

I didn't check if she brushed her teeth or ask if she wanted a story. I didn't even tuck her in.

Feeling like shit, I opened the other bedroom just a crack. I could tell Dashiell chose the right side of the bed, his bigger form taking that space. Lachlan was sleeping by his side, sucking on his pacifier. I frowned, looking at the mattress. Pillows were trapped between the mattress and bed frame, creating a slope on Lachlan's side, preventing him from falling.

Smart.

That was another something I didn't do.

I closed the door again, and Vienna's too with something heavy lodged in my throat. With no signs of Alvaro coming up, I let myself inside my room. Pushing the zipper of my black dress down, it pooled over my toes and I stepped out of it, grabbing it and stuffing it into the laundry basket.

Next went my underwear as I grabbed a soft T-shirt and pulled it over my head, jumping into the bed with the sea of parenting books I left from the night before.

They were here now. I wanted them here. I felt like I needed them here, and yet I didn't know what to do.

The books could only help with so much. I read about development. I understood what happened in each phase of their lives and I knew what to feed them.

But this was much more. There were so many moving parts to raising children and the parts I lacked the most, no one wrote a book about.

My list was forgotten downstairs, but I made a new one and added a few points. We needed a bedtime routine. We need a routine for everything.

I grabbed my phone and texted Alvaro link after link of things I wanted him to read. Then I ordered more books, some on how children dealt with grief. That seemed like an important piece of the puzzle I was forgetting.

They weren't just children. They were sad.

I was highlighting passages of a book on emotional development when my phone chimed with a message.

**Alvaro:** ??

**Logan:** Read

**Alvaro:** That's your plan?

**Logan:** Yes

**Alvaro:** Logan, listen. Let's just give them time to adapt... It was just a tantrum.

**Logan:** I'm in charge here and we are doing this my way. And my way is being prepared. Read.

And when he didn't reply, I sent one last text.

**Logan:** Tomorrow morning, we are going to find a bed for Lachlan and visit a couple of schools. Be ready at eight. Goodnight.

My eyes flew open, the light fixture glistening under the ray of sun. I had blackout curtains, but I refused to use them. I couldn't be in total darkness. That was too relaxed.

No, I liked the sun in my face and on the eleventh floor, I often woke up with it burning my eyelids.

I threw the blanket away and headed for a quick shower. In my walk-in closet, I tried to select something that was more casual than my work clothes.

I found a skirt that was still mid, but not as restricted, and paired with high boots and a soft sweater. Instead of pulling my hair in a ponytail, I braided to the side.

There.

Accessible.

Breathing with some sense of trust in myself, I opened my door just to find the two rooms opposite from mine were empty. I glanced down at my watch.

Seven thirty in the morning and the children were already up.

Quickly, I raced downstairs and was shocked to find my house full of life. I could clearly hear the TV, so I went in that direction, stopping by the door to take in the situation.

Dash was lying on the sofa, his head bobbing back, and he was fast asleep. Vienna was sitting on my fluffy rug with Lachlan, both watching TV and eating buttery toast, not caring that they both seemed to be covered in crumbs.

"Good morning," I croaked.

"Hey there, Logan." Vienna waved and then her attention was back to the TV.

"Everything ok?" I asked.

"Yeah. Dash made us breakfast."

I tried not to wince. Instead, I smiled at the girl in return and left the TV room quickly before I embarrassed myself further.

That wouldn't do.

No, no, that was wrong. Beyond wrong.

I gnawed on my bottom lip when I made my way to the kitchen, blinking once and then again as I took in the destruction. Dash might have made them breakfast, but he definitely wasn't adept at the cleaning as you go.

Bringing my sleeves up my arms I started cleaning up the impossible mess. I thought they were just having toast, for god's sake.

I turned on the coffeemaker the exact moment Alvaro came downstairs.

"Morning."

Voice rough from the sleep, his greeting felt like a caress. My saliva thick, I mumbled an answer and looked away, afraid he would notice the blush creeping up from my neck to my ears.

He looked good in the morning. His scruff was even rougher in the early morning, his T-shirt a little crumpled around his barrel chest.

Alvaro stretched his pectorals, looking around and yawning. "Where are the kids?"

"The media room. They were awake already."

He checked his watch. Raising an eyebrow as he looked at me, I nodded. "I know."

"Is that what got your panties in a twist?" he asked.

"I promised myself today was going to be different. Today was going to go right, but before I was even out of bed, I was doing it wrong."

Alvaro groaned like I pained him. "It's too early for this. I need coffee."

I placed the coffee I made for myself in front of him on the island. "Now can we talk about the fact it was Dashiell who woke up and made them breakfast?"

Alvaro sipped from the coffee as I pressed the button and started a new one for me.

"So kids wake up early. Earlier than you."

I brushed a stray hair off my face. "What am I going to do? Dashiell should have woken me up."

"So you want Lachlan to wake him up and he goes to you?"

"Until Lachlan can come to me himself." I shook my head. "I just need to wake up earlier than all of them."

Alvaro breathed out as he took a seat. "I'm going to go back to the site soon. I'll be leaving pretty early. This is the first day and you're already too stressed."

I nodded, his ability to read through me doubling my anxiety. "They are so independent. It's like it doesn't matter if I'm here or not, you know? How were they with your parents?"

Alvaro took a big sip before replying. "It doesn't matter. Listen, maybe ask them what their routine is before going completely off the rails. We can add to the list if we need to."

He was openly smirking when I flashed him a look, narrowing my eyes as he explained. "Saw the list you left in the office last night. Very thorough."

I rubbed my temple, feeling my cheeks tint. "Sometimes I need to write things down, even when it is stupid like this. I never felt..."

Biting my lip, the coffee maker beeped, saving me from making a fool of myself. I turned around, grabbing the steamy mug and proceeded to drink even though it burned my tongue.

"You never felt what, Logan?"

Sipping again, I shook my head.

"Come on, aren't we co-parenting here?"

I had to snort. "No. I'm screwing up, you're a spy, and Dashiell is parenting."

That made him smile. I never noticed he was always frowning until that moment, when his forehead relaxed and he gave me a quick smile. "Tell me what's the problem."

Rolling my eyes, I confessed. "I'm usually on top of my game. I hate being so out of my depth."

He hummed, tapping the marble in thought. "What is it that you do, Logan?"

"I'm a portfolio risk manager."

He cleared his throat. "And that would be?"

"I analyze the risk for my clients on investments."

"So you're a professional overthinker? Go figure."

That made me stand higher on my feet. "I'm a market specialist. I know when something might look good, but it will crash. I know how to diversify a portfolio in a smart way. I know how to minimize risks and make my clients..."

"Richer. Impressive. I'm sure you're great at your job and it's not because of where we are right now," he said, moving his finger to show our surroundings, "but because I can see how much you think before you act. And I'm sure that works fine for you, but maybe you might want my expertise right now."

I looked around my house, trying to see a crack. He was in construction, right? What could—

"Not that," he cut off my thoughts. "What I learned a long time ago when I was fighting was that it didn't matter how much I knew of my opponent or how prepared for the fight I was, there was always something that could go wrong. Just like in construction. Something always goes awry at the last minute."

"I know how to prepare for losses." I tipped my nose high. "That's part of my job, too."

"But you rely on other certainties. On numbers. But like in a fight, kids do whatever they want. No rhyme or reason. You've got to retire making lists and just let things happen naturally."

"I can be prepared. It's wise to—"

"Do you want me to read all those things you sent me?" he asked, pushing the mug away and standing up. "I can. And we can make as many lists as you like, but in the end, you need to learn how to move with the music."

"I can do that and be informed at the same time. One doesn't exclude the other."

Alvaro chuckled in a way I didn't like, dipping his chin, he pierced me with a look, "Alright then, Jefa."

I opened my mouth to say something, but he was already leaving the kitchen.

"Seat belt," I said when we closed the doors and I positioned my hands at two and ten.

Dashiell blinked slowly, but finally put the belt on before me having to ask again.

Alvaro wanted us all to drive in his truck, but I wanted to have my car with me. I liked to have my own things with me at all times. But this also gave me an opportunity to have Dashiell alone since Alvaro took Lachlan and Vienna.

He was still parked in the street, even though I told him he should be using my parking space, so we said our goodbyes at the elevator, and Dash and I continued lower.

"It's good that we'll have this time alone." I started the car and the talk. "I wanted to talk to you."

He said nothing. I glanced at him as I went up the ramp to exit the parking lot and Dash was facing the window, avoiding me.

"Can we talk?" I asked again.

"You can talk."

Not the most enthusiastic reply, but all the encouragement I needed. I turned left as we exited the building, following my GPS to the first school we were going to visit.

"I noticed you do a lot for your siblings." I didn't wait for a reply. "I'm new at this, but I don't want you doing it anymore."

"Excuse me?"

I glanced at him to catch the angry expression. "I can learn."

Dashiell scoffed and looked at the window again.

"I don't want you to worry about it anymore."

"And you're going to do it?" he asked without looking at me.

"Well, yes. And Alvaro is here, too."

"We don't know either of you. Lachlan is not going to listen to you"

I held the wheel a little forcefully. "I'll get to know Lachlan. I want to. And Alvaro is your uncle."

"Who I don't know."

*"Turn right at..."* The GPS talked, giving me a moment to relax my shoulders. Moments of anger had no place in the car.

Alvaro made me believe he had a relationship with the kids. Caridad acted like he was something. I shook my head, turned right, following the instructions, and opened my mouth to talk, but Dash beat me to it.

"I wanted out of there. I couldn't deal with Tita hovering anymore, and at that school, everyone knew our business. I knew I didn't need to trust you to come over."

"I want you to trust me."

"I don't need to." He spelled it out. "You gave us a new home and now you're driving me to a fancy school. That's fine. I just need three years and then I can take care of them on my own."

I frowned. "You what?" I glanced to my side, waiting to see if it was a prank, but Dash was serious. "That's your plan? I said I can pay for college."

He shook his head. "I can take care of them by myself. That's what I am doing, right? I'll take care of them officially when I turn eighteen. I just need somewhere to be until then. Somewhere that isn't... there."

My mouth gaped open and then I closed with a snap. The GPS kept calling directions, and I followed, concentrating on that instead of what I just heard.

That was why the kids wanted to come with me.

They just wanted away from their grandparents.

# 9.
# Alvaro

Something skinny and quick pinched the skin of my upper arm, making me yelp. I had Lachlan in my arms when I turned to look over my shoulders at Logan's outraged expression.

"What was that for?" I wanted to know.

She looked at her side, Dash coming just behind her with an odd expression. He held his arms up to take Lachlan from me, but Logan stopped my hand, turning to Dash. "We got him."

I shrugged, a little worried about why she was acting so weird. We were in the parking lot of the fancy private school where she arranged a meeting. It was all going according to Logan's plan, so what crawled up her ass?

Ignoring her, I passed Lachlan to Dash. "Just give us a minute."

Logan's face fell like nothing I've ever seen when Dash took Lachlan and moved away, with Vienna on his heels.

"What's going on now?"

She turned her eyes from the children to me, narrowing them straight away. A gust of wind slapped me in the face, making me shake even if I was wearing my biggest jacket. "And say it quickly."

I was in no mood to stand outside more than necessary.

"You said you were close to the children."

"No, I didn't." I arched an eyebrow. "That's what this is?" I shook my head and moved away, but she grabbed my arm.

"I thought you were here because I was a stranger to them. It turns out you are one, too."

"I'm their uncle," I said, even as she squeezed my arm with those powerful fingers of hers.

"According to Dash, you are a stranger as much as I am," she told me, her jaw set, eyebrows meeting in the middle. "This is the last time you hide something from me. You got it?"

Done with this whole thing, I stepped closer, making her crane her neck up to keep eye contact. I let her sweat, dark green eyes widening as she took me in so close.

"I'm not responsible for whatever you think you know, Logan. I'm their uncle. I'm the reason my mother isn't here sniffing in your business. I'm sacrificing my time to play house with you so you and my mother don't end up in a legal battle."

"You know, the only person you are helping here is your mother. Any court would give me the children."

"Are you sure of that?" I tilted my head. "Because Dash is fifteen years old, he can testify and say you're a stranger."

Surprisingly, her reaction was the opposite of what I thought. Logan laughed, a bitter and horrible laugh. "No. To the court, he would smile and say he wanted to be with me."

"You trust so much he wants to be with you?"

She wasn't wearing a glove, I bet her fingers were freezing. She finally let my arm go. With a last look, she shook her head. "You really don't know shit."

It was surprising to hear a curse come out of her mouth but I didn't let it show. Instead, I shrugged. "I'm just the guy following orders, Jefa."

Logan turned and hurried across the parking lot and up the steps to where Dash and the kids waited.

Trying not to think too hard about what she just told me, I followed her after a beat. To them, I was a stranger. Yeah, I knew that much, and I wasn't trying to hide that fact from Logan. I just wasn't in the business of airing my mistakes everywhere.

"Finally. Can we go in?" Dash was asking as I jogged up the steps.

Logan was staring at Lachlan, holding on to Dash too intensely, her eyes like a blaze until she nodded stiffly.

Dash didn't seem bothered by the way she looked at him. He glanced up and snickered. "Lone Pine Academy?"

"It's a good school," she said, grabbing onto Vienna's hand as I made my way and opened the door for them all.

Lone Pine Academy, even though it had a funny name, looked expensive. Grand. It was in the middle of the school term, as my mother couldn't stop pointing it out, so the halls carried the buzz of a full school.

Pristine lockers and immaculate floors surrounded us. Logan led our group, with Vienna by her side. Her heeled boots echoing in the halls. After her was Dash, holding Lachlan, and I closed our group, my neck turning from one side to the other as I caught glimpses of the students.

It looked stuffy.

Real stuffy. But I liked living, so I wasn't going to point out to Logan that Dash wasn't going to adapt in a place like this. Vienna looked happy, practically skipping, making Logan turn her head and smile at the girl.

But Vienna had a mean streak. I knew that much. This school didn't look like the type to tolerate it.

I said nothing, following quietly until we reached a big mahogany door at the end of the hall with a small golden sign that read Principal Godwick.

Logan knocked, squeezing Vienna's hand and smiling. I scratched my beard and had a long look at Dash and Lachlan.

I could smell trouble.

"Miss Hart." The door swung open.

"Hello, Principal Godwick." Logan smiled, extending her hand to the principal.

The woman took Logan's hand, closing the other one over it like they were familiar to each other. Then she waved the formalities off. "Please call me Kendra. Karl called just to tell me about you."

Principal Godwick turned, leading us to her office of tall bookshelves in dark wood and right in the middle a desk with the comfortable leather chair she took, not before nodding for all of us to do so as well.

Logan sat, Vienna by her side and Dash with Lachlan in his lap, and finally I lowered down last. I looked at my youngest nephew. His big eyes looked all around the office before deciding he was not interested and cuddled into Dash once again.

"He told me they are very impressed with your work at Godwick and Sons," she continued.

Hmm. We all looked at Logan at the same time, making her ears pink. She cleared her throat and nodded. "Kendra's father is my boss."

"The boys run the company. I always liked education. I was never interested in their business," she said, now turning her head to look at the children. "Now, who do we have here?"

"This is Vienna Murphy," Logan promptly replied. "Dashiell is the teenager, and the little guy is Lachlan."

"Hello, everybody. It is great to meet you."

Godwick's smile looked genuine, even if her haircut looked severe and she sat with her back uncomfortably straight. Then again, we had a little robot in our party as well.

"And that's Alvaro Castillo, the children's uncle."

I extended my hand to the principal. "Thanks for seeing us."

"Of course."

"Logan emailed me your records and I have to say," she turned to Vienna, "what a brilliant little girl you are."

Vienna beamed, bouncing on her chair with a huge smile and not a hint of red in her cheeks.

"You both are bilingual..."

Dash snorted. I guess it took two minutes into this meeting until it fell apart.

"Something wrong, Mr. Murphy?" The woman asked, but I was on the ball.

"Nothing to worry about," I said at the same time Logan jumped. "What kind of extracurricular activities do you offer?"

But Principal Godwick had her eyes pinned on Dash. "Just a minute," she told us both. "I want to hear from Dashiell if he thinks something is amiss."

Dash tipped his head up, his gangly teenage body trying to appear bigger.

"I guess it's the first time someone thinks it's a good thing we speak Spanish."

Godwick opened a smile. "Here at Lone Pine, we value learning new languages."

"Here on this Earth, brown bilingual kids are the first to get stuffed into a locker."

I could bet my left arm he was talking out of his ass. Not that bilingual kids didn't have a rough time, but Dash had always been taller than anyone his age. He was a tough kid. I knew no one was stuffing him in a locker. Still, he wanted to make a point.

I saw Logan opening her mouth and then quickly closing it when Godwick took over.

"You're a smart young man, Dashiell." Breaking eye contact, she reached for a leaflet to the side and slid over him. "You'll do well in debate."

His eyebrows rose and the principal chuckled. "It is a good and valid point, but you don't know how to structure it and it comes off as aggressive."

I didn't point out Dash was being aggressive on purpose.

"You can get more flies with honey than vinegar. Have you ever heard that?" she continued, nodding to the leaflet. "It's not because you're saying the truth that you're allowed to be disrespectful."

To everyone's surprise, Dash reached out and took the leaflet. Godwick wasn't done.

"Logan is a Harvard alumnus," she said before glancing down at Dash's transcript in front of her. "You have good grades. You're bright and interesting. There's no reason for you not to go far, Mr. Murphy. But that's something you need to decide yourself."

Breaking eye contact, she clapped her hands and moved to look at Vienna. "Now, you little lady."

For the rest of the appointment, Dash remained silent. I caught Logan chancing a look at him multiple times, but he made a point to evade her gaze.

We walked the halls as the bell rang, students looking us up and down, making Dash close his expression even more. After that we saw the gym, the lab, and the library, we ended up on the other side of the campus where Vienna would be taking her classes.

It was a way more relaxed atmosphere. This building had artwork on the walls, and they offered dance classes after hours, which by Vienna's face, she was very interested in.

Finally, Godwick brought us to the door, a smile on her face as she shook Logan's hand and then mine.

"Thank you for having us," Logan said once again before we left the building.

"Just think about it," Godwick replied, making it obvious the opening was ours if we wanted. She peered at Dash, dipping her chin, and I opened the front door leaving the warm hall behind.

I WAS WATCHING LAKE Michigan, a towel around my waist while I put my thoughts in order, when someone knocked.

"Come in," I called before thinking better of it.

"Dinner is here an—"

I turned from the window to catch Logan standing at the door, her hand still on the knob and her eyes wide. It must have taken thirty seconds of silence until she made a strangled sound and looked away from my chest.

"Dinner is here, we ordered from that place you suggested." She cleared her throat, "And we have a meeting."

"A meeting?" I asked, trying to ignore how hot my skin felt with her eyes on me.

"Yeah, like a family meeting. We need to talk about the school thing."

"Just put them in the school." I sighed, going over to the duffle bag on my bed, since I never bothered to unpack.

"I don't want to put them there if they hate it." She forgot for a second I wasn't dressed and faced me, just to turn tomato red again and look away.

"Vienna loves the place. You saw it," I pointed out, taking my time on selecting a T-shirt. "And Dash... he's a teenage boy. He'll hate everything."

I heard her huff, and then a click. For a second there, I thought she was done with me and had let herself out. But when I raised my head, she walked in and closed the door behind her.

Without saying a word, I just arched my eyebrow and waited. The T-shirt I grabbed from my bag was still clutched in my hands.

"He said something to me in the car."

"The reason you were so angry when we arrived at the school."

Logan scowled and crossed her arms in front of her chest. "I was angry at you that time."

I tsked, moving my eyes back to the duffle.

"You can use the drawers, you know?"

I sighed. "Tell me what Dash said."

"He said he wants to be the kids' legal guardian."

That caught my attention. I threw the T-shirt on the bed and turned to Logan. "What?"

"Yeah." She chewed on her lower lip, stepping closer to me.

I couldn't stop myself from noticing she was padding with no shoes. Still in the clothes she was wearing this afternoon, but no boots. Logan's little pink toes wiggled on the cream carpet as she talked again. "He says he's waiting until he turns eighteen."

Darting my gaze from her feet to her face, I concentrated on her frown of worry. "That's a ridiculous plan."

"Of course it is, but that's what he wants to do. He wants me out of the way."

"And it's easier to push you around than my mom." I chuckled.

"I'm glad that this is funny to you, because—"

"You're stressing too much." I cut her off. "He's a fifteen-year-old. How is he going to provide for them? How's he going to fight for custody? That's a fairytale."

Logan blew out a breath, shaking her head and bringing her hands up to her temple. "I know. But he wants me out of the way. He doesn't want me to have my time with the kids. He doesn't want this to work out. And I bet it means he's not going to college, too."

"I don't know." I shrugged. "Godwick was doing a good job of dangling that Harvard keychain in front of his face. Do you think he could get in?"

She lifted a shoulder. "He is bright. And he has good grades. It all depends how he's going to behave for the next couple of years."

"Trying to become a legal guardian to his siblings isn't the way. That's what you mean."

"I don't care if he goes to Harvard." She moved away. "I care if he goes somewhere. Sofia always wanted to go to college. It was her dream."

That horrible feeling stepped in again. Just the mention of my sister was enough to break my heart into a million pieces. I never thought about her going to college, but why wouldn't she dream about it?

She was a smart girl. Of course, she had a bright future in front of her. But then she got pregnant and… things changed. Logan was the one who left for college. Sofia stayed.

"Things change," I said, clearing my throat. "He says that now because he's not thinking—"

"I started with this, knowing my losses. That was Caridad. I accepted I might lose you, too. But the kids… no. I had to have the kids. And now…"

"What are you talking about?"

She turned to me and blinked her eyes like she had forgotten I was there for a minute. Shaking her head, she headed for the door. "Come down for dinner."

She was gone before I could ask anything else.

# 10.

# Logan

"WHAT DO YOU THINK about the Lone Pine Academy?"

I wasn't really good at easing in on a subject. I hated tiptoeing around anything. We all had our plates loaded with lasagna, thanks to a quick delivery from Alvaro's favorite Italian restaurant. Lasagna was the best way to make kids and adults happy.

As I dished it out for everyone but Alvaro, I set Lachlan's plate by my side, using a pillow to prop him up in his chair and ignoring Dash's narrowing gaze.

"I love it. They have dance classes and art classes. I can be a ballerina." Vienna let us know her plans.

"Great," I said as I smiled. "What do you think, Dash?"

He shrugged. "It's your money."

"It is your education."

He mumbled something, leaving it clear he didn't care at all about his own education. His plan was ridiculous. One that would force him to sacrifice his entire future, just the way his own mother had done. My heart hurt to think about it.

That was what Alvaro wasn't getting. I wasn't scared if Dash took his siblings from me. I was fearful for *him*.

I served myself and sat down, taking a breath before turning to Lachlan with a smile. I reached for his plate and started cutting this lasagna into little mushy pieces.

The three-year-old looked at me like I was poisoning his food, but before he could cry or look at Dash, I sent him a smile.

"Do you like lasagna, Lachlan?"

He didn't reply. I needed to book an appointment with a pediatrician, but that could be done another day. I waited to see if he was going to start with his dinner, my face burned with the looks Dash sent my way. With a sigh, I took a spoonful of food and blew on it before offering it to him.

And he took it.

God bless lasagna!

Happy with my success, I kept feeding Lachlan and talking to the others. "Lone Pine is an excellent school. You're welcome to pick up any extra-curricular activities as long as they make sense with your schedule and I can drive you there."

"I can get the bus," Dash said.

"True. Once you get used to the city. For the first few weeks, I prefer to drive you."

Lachlan kept eating what I served him, getting a little more relaxed with each mouthful.

"I'm back to work Monday," Alvaro said.

"That's fine."

"Aren't you working?" Dash asked.

I shook my head. "Not until we're settled."

"What are you going to do while we are at school?" he snorted.

There were about a million things I needed to get done while they were at school, but that wasn't what I said.

"I'm keeping Lachlan here."

That had his attention. Dash's eyes flew from his plate to my face, his forehead creasing. "They have a daycare at Lone Pine."

"A good one." I smiled and nodded. Feeding Lachlan one more time. "But Lachlan needs time to get to know me. I think it's a good idea."

"That's your plan?"

I forced my gaze up, facing his accusing eyes. He reminded me so much of his mother like that. Sofia was passionate, full of heat, especially when something annoyed her. I was the quiet and uncertain one. She was a thunderstorm.

Sofia's son looked at me like I was the enemy, but I didn't cower under his Castillo stare. I faced him head on and nodded. "My plan is to make you all comfortable. And I think Lachlan will be—"

"You want him to bond with you, so we get stuck here."

I rested Lachlan's spoon on the plate. "I want to take the load off your shoulders."

"He doesn't know you," he spat and raised to his feet.

"Sit down, Dash," barked Alvaro.

But I waved him off. I didn't need him to defend me. I actually didn't need him at all.

"And how will he ever know me? I don't see what the problem is here."

"The problem is that I'm sick and tired of—"

He never said it. I was dying to know what he was sick and tired of, but that was the moment Lachlan chose to tip the lasagna plate off the table, falling into a messy splash, followed by a thud.

Tomato sauce made a painting on my floors, reaching even my toes. I looked down and then looked up at Lachlan just to catch the moment a switch turned on him and he opened his mouth and started to cry.

It was loud, but not so loud I didn't hear Dash's next words.

"She won't last a minute."

He made moves to go to Lachlan, but I held my hand up the same time Alvaro was leaving his chair, his face murderous as he snapped at Dash, "Go to your room."

The teenager didn't think twice. He stomped his feet and left, Alvaro going after him. Taking a calming breath, I smiled at Lachlan. "It's ok buddy, accidents happen."

I went for him, sure he was going to resist me, but to my surprise, he let me hold him and transfer him to my lap. I smelled his hair trying to make sense of the child in my arms. He was a three-year-old who wouldn't talk or feed himself. He sobbed like a much younger child, and I felt his pain right in my chest. I moved my body from one side to the other, humming something soothing. Still hiccupping, his cries subdued, so I took the opportunity to cut my own lasagna into small pieces to offer to him.

He opened his mouth and let me feed him. Exhaling, I wondered out loud, "What am I going to do with your brother?"

"This is a very nice dinner, Logan!"

Vienna's voice came out of nowhere, making me jump in my seat. She was eating it all up happy, unbothered by the mess this dinner became. She cleaned her plate and sent me a smile so bright it confused me.

Maybe I needed to book a pediatrician appointment for her as well.

"How's the first official day going?" Willa asked on the phone.

After dinner, I let them watch a little TV until Lachlan started rubbing his eyes. One of the parenting books said that was a sign they were tired. Tantrums were another. Scared of getting into that specific part, I told Vienna to turn off the TV and brought her and Lachlan upstairs.

I didn't need to be a genius to know rubbing your eyes was a sign of sleep, but at the same time, until the book pointed it out, I didn't think about checking.

The thing I had learned about children is that they didn't have any idea what they were feeling. Not at Lachlan's age. He couldn't inform me he was getting sleepy. He only felt the consequences when it was too late.

My shoulders were up to my ears when my phone rang and flashed Willa's name, relaxing me a little. Putting my shoes on and grabbing a coat, I closed the glass doors and stepped into the cold.

"Traumatic."

"Oh, I'm sorry, honey. What's wrong?"

I rubbed my temple, taking an icy breath as I looked at my view. When I bought this place it was because of this little garden. At the time I only had a couple of chairs. The previous owners didn't take care of it much, but I saw potential. I hired a landscaper who transformed my balcony to a green wonderland, a paradise in the middle of the city, with Chicago as my view it looked beautiful even during the winter months.

It brought me calm. A symbol that anything could work if I planned hard enough.

I hugged my mid-section and watched the city lights. Maybe some things were out of my control.

"Why do you think Sofia trusted me with this?"

"Lo... are you having second thoughts?"

I shook my head, "Of course not. I just wonder..."

"Because you tried to protect her," Willa responded. "Because you are an amazing person, and she knew she could trust you with them."

"I'm not a mother, Willa," I said. "I don't have the instincts. I don't know what I am doing."

"But you're figuring it out. You want to be there for those kids. That must mean something."

"Yeah..." I nodded, not so sure right now.

"Honey, do you want me to come..."

I sniffled a rough laugh. "No. I'm ok. I have to go now, I'll call you soon, ok?"

"If you're sure..."

I didn't let her finish the thought. "Don't worry, Willa."

She let me go, but I knew she didn't want to. What could be said to make the situation better? I was in over my head. And when I wasn't thinking about how over my head I was, I remembered that Sofia died. That she felt alone, and sad, and she needed help, but none of us were there to give it to her.

The next breath I took, made me glad it was cold, freezing my lungs. I needed something to concentrate on other than my racing thoughts.

"No one is their mother."

"Shit!"

I swirled around, hands on my chest while I faced Alvaro, who let himself out without me noticing. He wasn't wearing a jacket, which probably meant he was crazy. He was standing there with his arms crossed over his chest, a big frown on his forehead.

"What?"

He nodded to the phone in my hand. "You said you aren't a mother, and I'm telling you no one is their mother."

"But they could be with someone who knows what they are doing."

"Are you changing your mind?"

Second time in the last ten minutes I was asked that silly question. I rolled my eyes. "No. Let's go in. You're going to freeze."

Alvaro let me pass, but at the last second, he grabbed my elbow and yanked me closer. "I supported you because you cared enough to fight for them. I can change my mind if you're getting scared."

I shook him off, tipping my head up to look him right in the eyes. "And do what? The kids belong with me. You can't do anything. This is not a popularity contest. I don't need your vote. I thought I did, but you're not even close to them, are you? So, tell me Alvaro. What good is it to have you by my side?"

Not waiting for a reply, I left him in the cold.

"Hello. It's me and you now, buddy."

Lachlan looked at me for just a second before turning back to the cartoon on the TV.

Dashiell and Vienna were officially enrolled at Lone Pine Academy, a favor that I couldn't forget to thank Kendra with a basket of some sorts. No one understood how crazy hard it was to get accepted in a prestigious school like that in the middle of the term. They got dressed in their new uniforms and Alvaro drove them this morning.

Lachlan looked good today, even though he was still quiet and refusing to do anything on his own. I was learning quickly, that if I didn't, Dash would. But once he was fed and dressed, silence took over the both of us.

"What do children do all day?"

I knew I couldn't let him watch TV the whole time, but right now it was helping to keep him occupied as I thought about my next move.

All my early childhood books showed the stages of development Lachlan should be on. Not that he wasn't, but I couldn't tell. I had no idea about his motor skills, because someone always had to feed him. I didn't know if his speech was ok, because he never talked.

Nodding to myself, I got my laptop and opened two tabs. One to help me find a bed for him. Another to find him a doctor. I bit my lip as I scrolled down the search. I didn't want to tell Dash about it. I knew he was going to find a way to see me as the bad guy for wondering, but...

Lachlan had been through a lot.

Sofia reached out to me when Lachlan was just a baby. David had finally left, and she described it as coming out of the fog. She had time and energy to think of something that wasn't related to him.

For fifteen years, all that she thought about was his reactions to things. Things that she did, things that others did. The fucking weather.

Without David, she said she could see clearly, and she missed me as a friend. Now, I wished I pushed more, that I asked more questions. At the time, I didn't want to upset her. I thought it was better if I let things be breezy between us. Let our friendship rekindle little by little.

But Sofia was a single mother of three children. She was always working and when she wasn't working, she was with the children. We couldn't go to a bar and talk shit about her ex.

I wanted to know what happened in the years he managed to separate her from everyone.

That conversation was meant to be had face to face, I thought. One day we'd meet and I'd ask.

When you're an adult, one week turns into a month, and then a year... or two.

I blinked, and my friendship with her was online. We never met up. Our lives clashed. The things we talked about were superficial.

Did she like *Stranger Things*?

What about the newest Taylor Swift album?

Things that I wondered about her, things I wasn't so scared of asking.

And then one day, I opened my social media expecting to see a message from her and instead I found out Sofia was dead. The attorney's call came after, when I already had spent my day reading the sad messages left unread on her timeline.

*Time.* I thought I had time, but I didn't. I thought I understood what was happening, but I didn't.

I was determined not to make the same mistake with her children. I might think I understood what was happening to Lachlan. I might think he only needed time.

No.

With renewed will, I checked the credentials of the first two doctors in my search, deciding on one and calling to make an appointment.

"They give lollipops at the end," I mumbled to myself. "Kids like that."

# 11

# Alvaro

"Living in a fancy penthouse, and now he thinks he can roll in later than everyone."

Mike chuckled, making the other men follow his lead. I had barely locked my truck in front of the site and they were already on my case.

"Dropping the kids at school," I mumbled, not in the mood.

"Missus got you whipped?"

Mike was a good guy. He just liked to run his mouth, make people laugh.

"I'm still the boss, Mike," I reminded him. "Where's Dustin?"

Mike nodded to the building. "Up there, *boss*." I didn't care for the snicker that followed.

Without another word from them, I popped the hard hat on and went inside. This place should have been condemned, an old building with cracked walls, but a chain of hotels was paying us good money to put it back together. Disguising themselves as a small business, their plan was to build a cozy alternative to their expensive hotel just a couple of blocks away.

The crew was already in, nodding as I passed. I followed the path upstairs, ignoring the way the stairs creaked under my feet, and found Dustin in the second room, talking to the electrician.

"It's not looking good," the man was saying.

"Too early for bad news," I said as I walked in.

Dustin checked his watch. "Are you sure?"

I grunted, already tired of everyone pointing out I was late.

When I left my room, Logan was already downstairs, feeding Lachlan in that uncertain way of hers. Dash and Vienna were in their Lone Pine uniforms, Dash's eyes almost burning a hole into Logan's skull.

I ignored his stupid plans because I knew it was never going to happen. Even if he could become their legal guardian when he turned eighteen, even if he could get rid of Logan, my mother would never let that happen. His plans were so improbable, I dismissed them the second I heard them.

But Logan might have been right. The way he watched her feeding Lachlan like he was personally offended by it, I realized it wasn't about the plan coming to fruition or not.

I rushed to my truck and drove them to Lone Pine. Not before Logan had her time fussing over their lunches, promising to pick them up at the right time. Not that any of us had any doubts she was going to do everything perfectly.

Logan was as type A as they come. Back stiff, Ivy League attending, checklist making, little type A. I could see in her face when something went a hair out of what she had planned. Her little heart barely could handle it.

It was a bad combination. A woman who couldn't deal with the unexpected and three kids who did nothing according to a script.

Not that I was good by any measures. I was bad actually, as bad as Logan's shoulders were stiff.

I had no idea how to talk to kids. I didn't know what I should be doing for them besides not letting them die. That part was simple. The real question was, what was I supposed to do to keep them from talking about me in therapy?

"You can't avoid that," Dustin told me during lunch, after the electrician finished telling us how much everything was going to cost.

I took a bite of my chicken bacon sandwich. "Some people have no problem with their parents."

Dustin laughed. "Who? Who the hell? Nah." He shrugged. "Some of us don't care enough. But a parent's job is screwing up the kids."

"I know now why Alma loves co-parenting with you." I grinned.

Alma was the girl he knocked up when they were eighteen. They never got together, but Alma always tried her best to co-parent with Dustin. Until his last comment, I was certain it worked.

"You're an ass, but I'm going to give you advice, anyway."

"Great," I huffed.

Dustin dug into his pasta. "It's like building on uneven ground."

I pinched the bridge of my nose. "Tell me you're not going for builder analogies."

"Asshole. Listen. I have wisdom I want to share." I arched an eyebrow and for some reason, that seemed like enough to keep him talking. "We put our insecurities in the children, like our parents put theirs in ours. So it is inevitable."

"I don't have any insecurities."

None that I'd share with the kids, at least.

"Everyone is fucked up," Dustin continued.

"I hate you since you started going to therapy."

Instead of being offended, he puffed his chest. "It brings this horrible deep understanding."

I finished the sandwich and crossed my arms in front of my chest. "So you're ok knowing you screwed Austin up?" I asked about his kid.

"The way I see it, man, Austin is eighteen now. He's definitely a better eighteen-year-old than I was. I'm not perfect, so I'm sure I fucked up some along the way. But he's a better man than me, so that must count for something."

I grunted and had a drink of water instead of replying. The kids had already had too much trauma. Sofia was a good mother. I knew that in my bones, but the children's dad was a piece of shit.

*David Murphy*. All I cared to learn about him was that he was the same age as Sofia, so as much as I wanted to kill him when she got pregnant, I couldn't murder a kid.

Their relationship wasn't a fairytale, but I didn't expect much coming from the way they started. Sofia never married him, but they had lived together since she was eighteen.

When Sofia left David, I didn't think much of it. People separate all the time.

Not until she killed herself. Not until it was too late. I never stopped to ask if my sister was ever happy.

My family pressured Sofia to be with David because she was pregnant. Logan was the rich kid who, according to Mamá, never learned how to deal with the consequences of her actions. So when everything happened, Logan was called privileged to even suggest that maybe Sofia shouldn't be with the kids' dad. At the time, it didn't matter. It was just a comment here and there and I didn't pay much attention. Now? I grasped on to all the information I missed more than fifteen years ago.

Whatever people thought about Logan, she knew Sofia better than I did. She knew David better than any of us. And she was important because Sofia didn't leave with much of a goodbye, but the demand for the kids to go to Logan.

Mamá chose to be offended, thinking Logan was chosen because of money. Sure, money brought possibilities. It was true. The kids had their future laid in front of them because of Logan's wealth. But my skin felt tight on my bones, my ear itching, letting me know I was missing something.

Maybe all those questions could be answered in the letter Sofia left Logan. Mamá refused to let any of us read it.

Yeah, the kids weren't in the same place as Dustin's kid. Sofia's kids carried the trauma of too many adults. All of our mistakes.

"You can bring them to a child psychiatrist."

"Huh?" I asked, distracted.

Dustin wiped his mouth with a napkin. "If you're so worried. You can bring them for an evaluation."

I cringed. "They'll think we think they are crazy."

Dustin chuckled. "Or you can work on your internalized problems in therapy before bringing them to it."

I sighed, leaning over with my elbows on the table between us. "Who is she?"

"Huh?" It was his turn to not hear me. Expected, I was sure he heard me fine.

"Who is the nice piece of ass who taught you all these terms, Dustin? Because I might believe you're a fan of therapy, but it is really hard to believe you became Freud for anything less than a piece of ass."

"You wound me," he replied.

I waited.

"Delilah," he breathed out. "She's doing her masters. Man, she's fine. Smart... and her ass?" He whistled. "I'm telling you it is worth it to learn all these—"

I stood up. "You're a tool."

TAKING THE WRONG TURN, I cursed as I drove away from the site. I was still not used to Logan's penthouse. I've lived in my corner of Chicago since I left my parents. It was where my business was, my small apartment and the gym I used to go to everyday before I was responsible for the emotional state of three children.

I rolled my shoulders back, adjusting my route. I needed a routine in my new life. I needed to work out like I used to do. My old gym was too far, but I could use hers.

She converted a bedroom into a gym and while it didn't have all the equipment, it was enough for me to create some kind of normalcy. Wake up, work out, bring the kids to school and head to work. That could be my new normal.

By the time I arrived at the penthouse and parked on the other side of the street, I felt foolish. What was the point of holding back?

I was here. I was involved. It didn't matter if my truck was across the road or in the parking spot.

My life wasn't going back to what it was because I refused to accept I lived in this place.

Breathing out, I pushed the button for the elevator, still surprised each time the doorman smiled his good evening instead of asking me what I was doing going up to the penthouse.

Dash was spread over the couch in the media room, still in his uniform. He didn't even look at me when I came in and said hello.

His eyes were on the screen, completely ignoring the screams coming from upstairs.

"What's happening?" I asked, looking up like I could guess without going to see for myself.

"Vienna." He shrugged and then turned to me. "Logan can handle it."

He didn't smirk, but I knew what he was doing. Vienna was having a tantrum, and he was punishing Logan for wanting to be with Lachlan.

"We need to talk."

"Can't wait," he replied, already bored with me.

I couldn't remember if I was this obnoxious growing up, but I would bet my ass I was. At fifteen, almost sixteen, I was as tall as Dash but also big. Training every day, I was at the peak of my talent. MMA was it for me and everything that got in my way was the enemy, my parents included.

They were wrong. I got a career out of it. I was in the game until I got too old for it. Still, at sixteen, I thought I could do no wrong.

I wanted to compete in the sport I liked. Dash wanted to raise his siblings. As plans go, his sucked, but it was still his plan, and his heart was in it just like mine had been.

Before I lost my temper, I headed upstairs. I immediately wanted to go back down.

"It is not fair! Not fair!" Vienna screamed and went back to crying.

I walked right onto the landing, where it was all happening. Logan was sitting on the floor, her back to the wall beside Vienna's door.

She was wearing heels for some reason, when I knew she stayed at home with Lachlan, dark pants, contouring her shapely legs, and a simple top.

"What's going on here?" I asked.

Logan's head whipped up. She was chewing on her lip, but dropped it as she took me in.

We were so different, Logan and me.

She was delicate and soft. I was not. I was wearing my worst jeans and a stained T-shirt. My heavy boots weren't made for her floors. My temperament was not good for her life.

Still, the resistance came only from me. When Logan looked at me, she never stared at the stains on my clothing or the brute way which I moved.

It hit me like a ton of bricks that I wasn't very different from my mom. I decided who Logan was without ever asking her.

"Vienna is having... a day."

I sighed, coming over I knocked on the door. "What's going on, Vienna?"

"I WON'T EAT IT!" That was my answer.

I arched an eyebrow and looked down at the woman sitting on the floor.

"Broccoli." She shrugged. "And peas. Or anything I tried to negotiate. I told her she's allowed to have likes and dislikes, but she needs to eat proper food."

"I can't believe you tried to give her peas. You are an awful caretaker."

Logan blanched before she realized I was teasing. My lip curved and her shoulders relaxed.

"It's more than that, of course. I just can't figure out what."

Logan had her legs bent, her knees under her elbows, but as she talked, her legs stretched in front of her, revealing yet another parenting book.

Of-fucking-course.

"She doesn't want to eat vegetables that—"

Before my thoughts were even out, Logan was shaking her head. "Changes are hard for kids," she whispered, as if Vienna could hear us over her own wailing. "They have different ways of dealing with it."

My skin crawled, wanting me to walk away. I never stopped to overthink my actions. If I saw something I didn't want to deal with, I walked. I was a simple man.

At least I thought I was. Because right there, Logan watched me, blinking fast as she endured what Dash thought was her dues. And I wanted to walk away and have a shower, but instead, I sat down.

I had to force myself to crouch, taking a seat with my back to the wall too, only Vienna's door separating us.

"And you think that's what Vienna does? She has a tantrum to deal with changes?"

Vienna let out another stream of "I'm not going to eat it!" We both looked at the door and then at one another.

"Kids have a lot of feelings, but they don't know what each means," she explained, her hand over the book. "Sometimes it comes out in a burst. Of course, some children are just trying to test your patience, but in this case…" she trailed off, looking at the door.

I nodded, tipping my head back. "Dustin thinks we need to send the children to a therapist."

My head turned when I felt movement. Logan's leg folded under her butt, and she turned completely to watch me.

"I was thinking the same," she said quietly. "Especially for Lachlan. He's not talking." She frowned and gulped, her voice going even lower. "I have a name already."

My lip twitched, but I held the chuckle back. This woman. Of course, she already had a doctor's name.

We stayed in silence for a little bit, the only noise coming from Vienna's room when Logan asked, "Who is Dustin?"

I chuckled. "He's my business partner."

She hummed. "I thought you owned Castillo Construction."

It was right there in the name, right?

"I started it. It was right after I finished my last fight. I had money to start something, and I went for it."

"Did you know anything about construction?"

I nodded. "I'd been doing jobs for years. It was just not full time. MMA was my life. But this was Plan B. There's a clock over every impact sport athlete's head. You know one day your body won't handle anymore."

"So you were preparing for that?" She sounded pleased by my preparedness.

"I was."

"And how did Dustin get into business with you?"

I released a breath. "He's younger than me. When I met him, he already had a child and no way to take care of him, so..." I shrugged, "I taught him the trade."

"Like someone did for you. Passing it on."

I chuckled. "It's not that poetic. Dustin worked his ass off. He's good, he's reliable. Then five years ago he asked to buy in. He put money into the business and now he's my partner."

We stayed in silence for a little longer. And she talked again.

"I didn't want to bring up the therapy. I don't think Dashiell is going to like it."

I faced her. "Isn't anywhere in that book of yours saying teenagers aren't supposed to make the decisions?"

She sighed. "I don't want to make him angry. He's already..."

"I know." I nodded. "I'm going to have a talk with him."

She groaned. "Don't tell him his plans are ridiculous, please."

"Why? My parents never coddled me. Latino parents tell the truth in their children's faces and stuff them with food in the same breath. He's Cuban. He has to hear he's being a dumbass. Who is going to tell you if not your family?"

"As charming as that approach is..." I could almost swear she curved her lips a little, "he's a flight risk right now. He needs to trust us."

"And the only way for him to trust you is if he respects your decisions. You can't coddle him into respecting you."

"I'm not coddling him," she said, with a frown right on her face.

Something crashed inside the bedroom. I looked at Logan. "You need to make her stop."

Logan chewed her lip. "This is probably just the way she's processing her feelings."

"Tell her to process them quietly."

"Alvaro…" she groaned, throwing her face into her hands.

And something in me… broke.

Logan tried so damn hard. It was annoying to see. She wanted this so much, she wanted to master it in a day. We felt like strangers most of the time, but as she groaned my name into her palms, I couldn't stop myself from… feeling.

Shit, I was in this with her, wasn't I?

"Listen, it's good that you're not screaming at her and that you're trying to understand her point of view. But this," I pointed to the door, "it can't happen. You need to tell her to cut it out."

Frowning, she searched for a fault in my reasoning for a beat, but when Vienna wasn't showing any signs of stopping, I had to push a little more. "You said we fucked up when she did this in the car. Now it's time for the do over."

"I'm good at making people see the logic behind things. I'm good with numbers and actual facts." She looked at the door. "I don't feel like an eight-year-old will be easy to rationalize with."

"No. I don't think so." Suddenly, something came to me. "Where's Lachlan?"

Logan winced. "Having a nap."

I glanced down at my watch. "He's not going to sleep tonight."

"I know. I was just trying to..." She shook her head.

"How was today?"

"We survived." She breathed out. "He ate, he followed me around and let me hold him, but..."

"No talking." I guessed.

"It's ok if he's really upset and taking his time. But what if it's more? What if..." She took a big breath. "He's so little. Does he even understand Sofia isn't coming back?"

My guess would be... no. I struggled with that, and I was forty-six years old. I couldn't start guessing how a three-year-old felt. Actually, how any of them felt. It was a mind fuck to think my sister needed help and I couldn't see it. But as her children? Did they miss her too much? Did they feel abandoned?

"One thing at the time," I told her. "Just go in and bust her ass."

Logan made a face. "No, thanks."

"Go in and tell her who is the boss."

"Hm..." She thought about it.

"Just go in, Logan. I'm getting a headache."

With some kind of confidence, Logan got up to her feet, her hand closing on the knob. Surprisingly, she opened it at once. I didn't know why I expected it to be locked. I knew for a fact Logan took the keys to avoid problems like this one.

"Vienna, that's enough."

"I won't eat it!"

"No, you won't. Because dinner is finished now. But that's not what I want to talk about."

Suddenly, I could hear my own thoughts again. Just a simple sentence shut Vienna up. She was caught unaware. And the only moment of silence was when Lachlan padded from his bedroom, rubbing his eyes.

He found me sitting on the floor, and I put my finger over my mouth telling him to be quiet, and then I called him to me.

As Lachlan walked, I tuned back to the conversation.

"School was ok."

"Are you sure?" Logan asked. "Because I feel you're upset and lashing out at me."

Lachlan came and sat on my legs, his head turning to the side like he was listening to the conversation as well.

"Some girls are nice," Vienna said.

"And some are not?" Logan wanted to know.

Vienna must have shown some kind of body language, because I didn't hear an answer from her, but Logan tsked. "I met your mom on my first day at school. Did you know that?"

"No."

"She was the coolest. Everyone wanted to be her friend, and I was the weirdo. I was awkward and quiet and Sofia just... sat beside me and started talking."

Vienna still said nothing, so Logan kept going. "You don't need all the girls to be nice. You only need one, you get it?"

Silence, and then finally. "Yeah, I get it."

"Was anyone mean to you?"

"No."

"Would you tell me if they were?"

"Yeah."

"Ok..." Logan took a breath. "I get a lot has changed. But you can't be mean to me to make yourself feel better."

"I wasn't being mean to you," Vienna argued.

"You were screaming at me for hours. I'm exhausted. I bet you're tired, too." Without waiting for a reply, she kept going. "From now on, when something is bothering you, even if it is small, you come and tell me. We can talk, we can try to solve it, or I can just listen if you want me to. But this is unacceptable." Growing confident, Logan added. "And you're going to have to eat..."

"I don't like it!"

"So you're going to make a list of vegetables you like. You can't hate them all. You have to eat properly. That's not negotiable." Her voice grew hard. Lachlan in my lap turned his head to look at me with his widened eyes, like it surprised him too.

"I want to make things good for you, Vienna. I want to be... your friend. Can we be friends?"

The silence held for a while... we all held our breath.

"Yeah. I have no mommy, and you have no best friend. Makes sense that we stick together."

And my fucking heart shattered into a million pieces.

# 12. Logan

"No."

That was all that he replied.

On Wednesday, I thought I had it. I had a crazy day on Monday, an ok day on Tuesday, and I had high hopes for Wednesday. I got an appointment for Lachlan with a renowned children's psychologist. Alvaro said one hundred times I didn't need Dashiell's approval but bringing Lachlan behind his back felt wrong.

I told Alvaro I'd bring the kids to school today, so I could tell them before I drove Lachlan to the appointment.

"I'm not asking permission," I informed him.

"There's nothing wrong with him." He huffed.

"He doesn't talk anymore," Vienna helpfully pointed out.

"There you go." I nodded. "But anyway, something doesn't have to be wrong for him to see a therapist."

Dash shook his head. "He will talk when he's ready."

I turned right, following the road without glancing at him. "Maybe we should all go. Everyone grieves differently."

"Can I go to therapy too, Logan?" Vienna wanted to know.

I looked at her from the rearview mirror. "Of course."

"You just like to talk about yourself, Vienna," Dash interrupted.

"She's eight," I reminded him. "There's nothing wrong with anyone in this car. But I think a checkup is in order."

"So wait until I can go with him."

"Why?" I poked. "You can't go in."

"That's not good." He fretted. "Not good at all."

"You know what, Dashiell?" I just realized. "I think you're a control freak."

"Oh, yeah, you came to this conclusion after half a week of living with me?"

"That's how transparent you are," I sassed.

Looking at the road, their school approached. "There's nothing wrong with Lachlan," I told Dash. "There have been a lot of changes and I just want to know if he's dealing with them, ok? I want what's the best for him. Can you believe that?"

He took his time, but eventually nodded. "The problem is that you don't know him well enough to know what's best for him."

I parked at the school. "I'm going to start with fed and healthy and we'll go from there, what do you think?"

Dash mumbled but opened his door and then Vienna's. She said her goodbyes, waving animatedly. Dash never looked back, even the back of his head looked like it was sulking.

I released a calming breath and glanced at Lachlan in the mirror. "So, here we go buddy."

"Can Lachlan and I have a chat?"

Dr. Maya Humphrey was her name. I read everything about her before making the call, and if the tons of degrees decorating her walls were to say anything, she was more than qualified.

Her office was nothing like what you expected of a therapist, all soft tones and cheerful. Her desk tucked in the corner, while toys took up the majority of the room. Building blocks, soft mats made of big jigsaw pieces, and a small table with sheets of paper and arts and crafts filled the room.

She looked kind, had curly hair and a soft voice. She was waiting expectantly for my reply. I had no other option but to nod and go for the door. We had talked about what recently happened in our lives, not in depth, but I gave her as much as I knew and now she wanted a chance to connect with Lachlan on her own.

I glanced over my shoulder, Lachlan watched me go with his little forehead closing in a frown.

Of all the kids, Lachlan had more of his father's looks. Dash was the spitting image of Sofia, his frown was the trademark Castillo trait. Vienna didn't look exactly like Sofia when she was young, but it was more about how she talked. The softness of her tone, the warm smile.

But Lachlan had green eyes like David, and he hid his cards as well. He was only three, but a Castillo gave everything away with just one look. I knew it. I lived with four of them.

They couldn't help wearing their hearts on their sleeves, even the big bad MMA fighter. It was easy to read him like a book. But Lachlan?

I had no idea what that look meant. Was he upset I leaving the office? Or maybe to him I was a stranger as much as Dr. Maya.

I held my breath and waited for him to whine. He never did. I opened the door and let myself out, even waiting at the other side. After a full minute with no protests, my shoulders sagged and I stepped away just to face the receptionist.

"I know it's tough, mama."

I didn't correct her and sat in the waiting area. I watched the door like a hawk for any movement, but from time to time the receptionist smiled my way and I had to pretend I wasn't watching.

My phone chimed, MOM flashing on the screen making me forget the door watching business for just a second.

With a breath and a prayer, I took the call.

"Hey there, Mom."

"Hello, Logan," her pleasant tone greeted me. "I hope I'm not interrupting your work?"

"I'm not at work," I said without thinking, but then squeezed my eyes shut when I realized my mistake.

My head fell to my palm when she asked, "Why not?"

I was a big girl. I wasn't scared of my parents. I just wasn't in the mood to have this conversation again with them. They knew I got guardianship of the kids, and I knew all their thoughts on it.

"I asked Godwick for a leave," I explained. "So I could stay home for a while until the kids adapt."

All that she needed to do was to breathe, and I knew what was coming after.

"You're really doing this, Logan?"

"Mom, can we please not talk about this?"

"I have the right to know what you're doing with your life."

She acted like the kids would destroy my life. They wouldn't. Even with all the difficulties, even if Vienna kept screaming and Dash kept resisting my help. Even if Lachlan needed specialist after specialist. Still, I'd fight for them every single day.

"The kids live with me now," I updated her, omitting the man who came with them. "They are attending Lone Pine."

A hum of appreciation came through the line. Life in Chicago was what my mom wanted for us. For me to attend a prestigious private school and her to attend gala after gala.

Dad wanted to keep us away from it all. He thought that was the right way to raise a kid and decided the best school in our district was a public school. What a disappointing twist of fate for mom that her only daughter went to public school just like her.

Mom didn't come from money. Her parents were working class, but for some reason she decided to forget about that piece of history.

I was the princess she wasn't. Since her childhood dreams for me didn't work out, she couldn't have been happier when I was accepted to Harvard.

Living the dream, she would say. Whatever she decided the dream was.

Working with a big company, getting money and owning a penthouse, that was what she saw for me.

Taking in three kids my best friend left? Being mistaken as a teen mom every time I went to pick up Dash from school?

Yeah, that wasn't in mom's plans.

Lone Pine was good, though.

"Were they accepted?"

I snorted. "Don't be so condescending."

"I'm not Logan." She tsked. "Lone Pine is a good school. I'm impressed."

I wasn't telling her my boss' sister was the principal there. Keeping my mouth shut, I defended the kids. "They are bright kids with good grades, no reason they wouldn't be accepted."

And of course the big fat check I had to sign for a year's tuition.

"Are you sure that's the path you want to take, Logan?"

Mom made me hate my name sometimes. She said it so stiffly, like my nose had to be up to pronounce it.

"There's no other option for me," I replied honestly. "I won't give them up."

"Well, then I'd like to meet them."

My tongue must have gotten stuck in the roof of my mouth because suddenly I was coughing, an invisible lump in my throat.

"Don't be like this, Logan Magnolia."

I rolled my eyes. "I'm not being like anything, mom."

"If you're bringing these children into your life, isn't it normal I get to know them?"

Yes, it was, of course, the normal thing to do. They were part of my family, so it should be normal for them to meet my parents. But I really didn't want to do it.

"They are adapting," I told her. "I can't promise anything yet."

"Well, I guess that's to be expected. They've been through so much."

My eyes rose to the door where Lachlan was right now with the doctor. If I couldn't put my feelings into words, how could a three-year-old do it?

"I'll wait for a few weeks," Mom was saying. "But I want to meet them, Logan."

"You will. I have to go, talk to you later."

I let her go, already thinking about how long I could avoid the meeting. How long could I hide that Alvaro was living with me?

No more logs on this fire. That was all that I wanted. I couldn't deal with it anymore. Between Alvaro's parents, the kids' problems, and Alvaro himself, I couldn't add my mother into the mix.

I rubbed my temple in thought, my phone chimed yet again, and I almost cursed in public.

**Alvaro:** How was the appointment?

**Logan:** Still going.

**Alvaro:** What? The boy doesn't talk. How long could it take for them to see that?

**Logan:** I don't know. I'm outside now.

**Alvaro**: ...

**Alvaro:** And you're freaking out.

**Logan:** I'm freaking out.

**Alvaro:** This is the right thing to do, Logan.

Even though I wasn't hearing it, I remembered the quality of his voice when he called my name. I liked that a lot. Alvaro was older, bigger, his presence taking up the whole place, wherever he was. He exuded calm, and I needed that right now. So, I released a calming breath and texted back.

**Logan:** I know.

**Alvaro:** Breathe, Jefa. You're doing fine.

**Logan:** Will you ever stop calling me that?

**Alvaro:** No.

He wanted me to be annoyed at him, but a little smile slipped through. No one ever called me a nickname. Sofia called me Lo, just like Willa did, but it wasn't very exciting.

Never in college, definitely not at work. I was a little standoffish. I knew that. I was a woman in a male-dominated field. I had to keep a certain posture. I couldn't be fun, nicknamed Logan.

*But Jefa...*

I knew it wasn't a compliment, but it felt like something. Like we were more than two strangers forced to be around one another.

*Safe.* It made me feel like I wasn't in this alone, even though I knew I was.

Alvaro wasn't going to live in my house forever. He had his own life, doing his own thing.

He probably had a girlfriend who was somewhere out there unhappy that me and the kids were hogging all his attention.

I groaned to myself and tilted my head up. I was growing attached to co-parenting when I shouldn't.

Worse than that, soon I'd need to have better communication with Caridad.

It was only Wednesday.

I took a fortifying breath. They had been living with me not even a week, but it felt like a month.

I had a mountain of things to finish up. Get the apartment ready for the children because soon Alvaro was going to leave me.

And that was ok. I wasn't attached. No one could grow attached in less than a week. I did everything on my own. I could raise them on my own too.

I *was* raising them on my own.

"Logan?" the door cracked from the therapist's office. "Can you come here?"

Jumping into my feet, I dropped the bag resting on my lap. Feeling silly, I brushed my hair back and sent a smile to the receptionist, marching straight to the therapist.

Lachlan was right in the middle of the room, sitting on the mat and playing a game of Memory. He turned a card, seeing it was the image of a cow. After just a second, his hand went straight to the piece above, turning to find another cow.

"He has a great memory," Dr. Maya told me. "Here, take a seat."

By taking a seat, she meant on the floor close to Lachlan. I sat down, not taking my eyes off the boy, who was already going for another pairing, his little hand holding the ones he got right.

"He's doing well from a development point of view," she said. "He knows how to count to ten. That is very good. Right, Lachlan?"

He looked at the doctor for just a second, without replying, and went back to his game.

"Motor skills are also perfect for his age. And like I said, he has a really excellent memory. Look at him go." She nodded to Lachlan and yet another victory.

"That's good," I said. "That's really good."

"It is. But I think you should keep bringing Lachlan here once a week. And we'll see how it goes. What do you think, Lachlan?"

He looked at Dr. Maya and nodded. That was more of a reaction than I'd ever gotten. With a sense of accomplishment, I saw myself mimicking him. She must have noticed the tension rolling off me, because she gave me a sincere smile.

"He's fine."

"They say children deal differently with..." I cleared my throat, "change." I chose instead of grief.

She nodded. "Sometimes kids need a little reassurance after a traumatic event. That means he might step away from tasks he previously knew how to do on his own."

Not just talking. She meant feeding himself, walking around, things like that. He was acting younger than his age because he needed someone to take care of him.

The doctor noticed my eyes filling up with tears, because she quickly added, "Lachlan is healthy and developing well. You don't need to worry. He would benefit from coming over, though."

Bobbing my head up and down before she ever finished, I agreed. "Of course. He looks happy. Doesn't he look happy?"

If she could tell by my tone that I knew nothing about parenting, she didn't let it show. Soon, Lachlan finished his game and Dr. Maya was saying goodbye to us.

Lachlan was quiet as we left the office, quiet when I brought him grocery shopping.

I tried to talk to him, blabbing to see if I got at least one nod like Dr. Maya got so easily.

He gave me nothing.

I still talked as we made our way to Lone Pine to pick up Dashiell and Vienna and tried to ask him questions, even while his sister talked over everyone.

I'd keep trying. Didn't matter how many times Dashiell scowled at me like I personally offended him by being kind to a toddler.

My hands firmly on the wheel, I drove them back home and started with dinner the second we were all settled. Took convincing, but Dash changed from his uniform, and I kept going. Talking, cooking, and making a list of the toys I saw at Dr. Maya's office so I could buy them for Lachlan.

"I think I'm adding a little bit more garlic," I told him.

On the stove, I was mixing marinara sauce as he sat on the floor playing with a small truck. I was taking full advantage of the fact that Dashiell and Vienna were both having showers, and I could have Lachlan a little longer.

"Do you like garlic?" He didn't reply, but he looked at me. "Of course you do. Oh garlic bread."

I twirled to the freezer and grabbed a baguette, turning the oven on.

"Garlic bread is just one of those things you have to like. It is the best. This one has cheese too, just so you know. You can't go wrong with that. I'm making chicken parmigiana. Do you know what that is?"

"If he answers, I'm shitting my pants."

I stopped in my spot, turning slowly toward the voice with the frozen baguette still in my hands. Alvaro was at the door, his hand stretched high as he held himself by the fingertips on the molding.

"Put the weapon down, Jefa." He nodded to the baguette.

I rolled my eyes and put the baguette on the counter, pretending I didn't see that when he reached up his T-shirt rose a little, showing a sliver of skin.

Very tattooed skin.

Shaking my head, I smoothed my hands over my clothes. "I'm making dinner."

He moved from the door. Crouching over to Lachlan, he took his truck and played a little, pretending he was going to roll over his toes. Lachlan curled his cute baby toes to escape, and when that didn't work, he... giggled.

I inhaled sharply, the sound of his giggle enough to make me stop in my tracks. I threw myself on the floor beside Alvaro.

"Do it again," I urged, my hand clutching to his arm.

His eyebrows furrowed, but he did it. He even added a little truck noise with his mouth.

Lachlan giggled again.

It took my whole heart. Just there. That kid destroyed me with a giggle.

"Breathe, Logan."

I did like I was told, relaxing my hand over his arm but still holding on to him. I knew my eyes were full of tears. I just couldn't help it.

This was huge.

"How was the appointment?" he asked, opening his palm to me, giving me the truck.

"It was ok. She says he's developing well."

"That's good news."

I nodded, taking the truck. Both of them watched me as I took it in my palm, uncertain of what to do.

I didn't like rejection, even if it was by a three-year-old. I wanted him to like me, I desperately did.

"I can do the truck's noise for you," Alvaro offered.

I turned to him with a smile. What a goofy thing to say. But he did it.

"Vroom, vroom…" he said, like warming up the car.

I bit back a laugh and put the truck on the floor. Alvaro kept going with the soundtrack as I moved to Lachlan's little toes, bumping into his foot a little. As I made a pass over his foot, Alvaro screeched.

"What's that?" I wanted to know.

"You're going off-road." He bumped his elbow into me. "Keep going."

I chuckled and moved to pass over Lachlan's foot, my eyes on him when he opened the smallest of the smiles.

I gasped again, my hand letting go of the truck.

"You're the worst at this game," Alvaro complained.

Tsking, he took over, now running over the other foot and then Lachlan's leg. The boy giggled more, and I watched with one hand shaking over my chest.

"Now, come on, I bet you need a bath," Alvaro said to Lachlan.

The boy didn't complain when his uncle took him in his arms and stood up. I was frozen in place, my hand holding to my heart before it escaped.

I was still lost in thought when I heard the sigh over my head. "You did good today."

And it was so fast, I almost missed it. But before he left with Lachlan, he kissed my hair.

# 13.
# Alvaro

Throwing the budget on the table, I pinched my nose with a heavy sigh. "I liked it better when I wasn't the boss."

"They have money," Dustin argued, putting his feet on top of the table and reclining. "Electrical damage takes a toll. They know the drill."

"Yeah, yeah." I waved my hand away.

He was right on both accounts. It didn't matter how much the renovations cost, we were talking about people with deep pockets here. Cost didn't matter to them. Time, on the other hand, did.

"Hate dealing with bullshit," I said. "Being out there is easier." I nodded to the workers milling around and doing their jobs while we stayed inside an improvised office dealing with documents and unhappy clients that knew nothing about what made an old building like this up to code.

"Knock- knock?"

My eyes flew from Dustin to the doorless space and found Logan there. She was wearing skintight leggings, a t-shirt, a jacket, and a hardhat.

She never looked so casual.

The changes were noticeable now. At first she was dressing like she was going to the office every day, even if picking up after Lachlan was all she did. Now she wore leggings. Her hair wasn't so tight to her skull.

"Come in," it was Dustin who called when I didn't react.

She looked self-conscious, padding over us. Her brown hair fell into rogue strands over her face, and she quickly brushed it back. I let my eyes wander, from her rosy cheeks to her fitted t-shirt and her legs... shapely with full hips.

Logan looked good. Wholesome and...

Young.

My eyes zapped from her legs. I shouldn't have been gawking.

"They gave me this," she told me timidly, pointing to the hard hat.

"That's right, no one's allowed in without one. What are you doing here?" I asked, but it was obviously too harsh. Logan frowned, but Dustin saved me when he extended his hand. "I'm Dustin, Alvaro's business partner."

"Nice to meet you. I'm Logan."

She didn't say what she was to me. She wasn't mine, so that was that.

"I brought Alvaro something to eat."

Moving away from Dustin, she came to me. I rose on my feet, rolling my shoulders back, trying not to be an ass.

"I was grabbing lunch, and I thought..." She swallowed and trailed off, extending a paper bag to me.

It took me a second too long to take it, thanking her in the process.

"It's nothing. I just thought you might like it. Do you like Vietnamese food? It's my absolute favorite."

I'd never had it, but my mouth watered just from the smell.

"Where is Lachlan?" I looked around like she was hiding a toddler behind her back.

"Dr. Maya," she replied. "I decided to grab lunch as they talk. I already ate and I still have," she checked her smart watch, "twenty-eight minutes."

Something about the way she said it made me smile. That was so Logan, knowing everything so precisely. Scratching my cheek, I nodded in the direction she came. "Come on, I'll give you the tour."

I didn't expect to see the excitement in her eyes, but she bounced on her feet and waved goodbye to Dustin as I guided her out.

"I'll be back soon," I told him, but he just smirked and said nothing.

I hated the way he looked at me, that little smile on the corner of his lips like he knew shit.

Ignoring him, I brought Logan out.

"Here, let's start with the lobby."

"What's this going to be?" she asked, her eyes sweeping across the room.

"It's a guest house. A cheaper alternative to a hotel."

Logan scrunched her nose. "This is an expensive area. How cheap can it really be?"

I couldn't hide my smile. "Smart girl." I chuckled. "They own the chain of hotels down the road."

"No."

"Yeah, greedy fuckers. They get them coming and going."

"Hmm, show me more."

We walked around. I pointed out the changes, the walls we had to knock down, the room's positions, and the ideas for a common area. Finally, I brought her to a very barren back lawn.

She smiled. "I always wanted a big backyard."

"You live in a penthouse."

She hugged her midsection, lifting one shoulder. "I know. I liked the view, and it was one of those properties that when it's on the market you have to be quick."

I nodded. "I get that. But a house is what you want?"

"She sighed. "I think kids need space, don't you?"

She turned to me, her head a little tilted because of our height difference.

I really liked her like that. Her nose was a little red from standing in the cold, her cheeks rosy, too. Since Logan got a smile out of Lachlan, a weight had dissolved off her shoulders.

And relaxed, Logan was just...

Breathtaking.

I cleared my throat, looking away. "You can get a house, if you want a house."

She nodded but said nothing. Eventually, she ran out of time. "Thank you for showing me around. I'll see you tonight."

I kept my eyes on the barren yard, refusing to watch her go.

"Oh hey, Dustin, see you soon."

Of course, he was around. Knowing what waited for me, I turned to catch my business partner holding a disposable cup full of steamy coffee and that annoying smirk of his.

"What?" I made the mistake of asking.

He smiled. "You want to fuck your sister's best friend."

I LEFT THE JOB early.

*I don't want to fuck my sister's best friend.* I said it to myself while I started the car and negotiated the streets.

It wasn't just the memory of Sofia standing between us. Everything about this situation was unusual and difficult.

There were kids in our lives that weren't mine. My mother pressuring Logan and...

She was young.

Sure, she was thirty years old, but sometimes I looked at Logan and she seemed so fucking young. Happy, trying her best and thinking that was enough to prevent the world from chewing her up.

Maybe I was jaded, but I couldn't be that optimistic anymore. Logan could say whatever she wanted, but that girl was walking and talking hope. She wanted a happy ending, and I was everything but.

"How's it going Andrew?" I passed the doorman.

"Great, Mr. Castillo." He nodded and called the elevator before I could even make it across the atrium.

"I told you to call me Alvaro."

He nodded in acceptance as the elevator doors opened. I knew he was going to call me Mr. Castillo again tomorrow, but I was going to try until he could say it.

With a last wave, I used the keycard and ascended to the penthouse, my body still buzzing with something.

The house was empty, kids probably at school, and Logan was busy with something or other.

She always seemed busy these days. Getting a bed for Lachlan, organizing the kids' wardrobe. Calling a designer to plan a playroom. The woman was relentless.

Hopeful, annoying.

Beautiful.

I blamed the leggings and that smile on her face. The cute little nose, all red from the cold. I knew she was gorgeous, but her beauty wasn't for me, so I did the best I could to ignore it.

A switch was flipped on and tugged me, propelling me toward her even if she wasn't here.

My head ached, filled with reasons I couldn't be lusting after Logan Hart.

A humorless chuckle broke free. I was Alvaro Castillo. El Toro. Six foot three inches of pure mass, making me a fucking bull in the china shop of her life. She was a princess. Beautiful Logan Hart, with a fancy job and a penthouse.

I had tattoos covering all of my skin and calluses on my hands.

And Logan? She was all hope and bright green eyes.

Done thinking about impossible things, I headed to my bathroom, taking a pair of basketball shorts and tossing my T-shirt to the side. Logan said I could use her mini gym whenever I needed, and today was the day.

Crossing the hall, I went in. The gym wasn't much but had good equipment and speakers on all sides of the room.

She kept the obligatory cardio corner, an exercise bike, treadmill, and a couple of jump ropes. But she also had weights, bigger than I thought she would care to buy. A weight bench and a fucking freestanding punching bag.

That was all the invitation I needed. I warmed up a little, then went to the weights, taking a smaller one and going from there. I had a routine, but for some reason, this time around, my muscles needed more.

I tried to concentrate on pushing myself instead of thinking about everything going on.

My mother's calls asking me details of my life with Logan like I was really her errand boy. The kids resisting Logan. Fucking Dash and the most idiotic plan of the century and... Logan.

I moved to the punching bag, determined not to think about her. But as I landed the first punches, my mind drifted. Logan cooking. Logan's face when Lachlan smiled at her, like that was the biggest gift she was ever given.

The way her hair smelled like strawberries when I kissed the top of her head.

I wanted to protect her, I realized. Mostly because every turn of the way, Logan proved she needed no protection.

I punched the bag, keeping my stance, my knuckles bruising. I breathed slowly out of my nose and willed my mind to stop running amok.

Blame Dustin. He put the what ifs in my mind when they had no place there.

Even if she was just a girl in a bar, I'd never hit on her. I knew my hands weren't made for something so beautiful.

I cracked my neck and kept going, releasing that energy buzzing under my skin.

A laugh broke free, manic, making my own hair stand on end when I thought how ridiculous this all was. I was concentrating on the little things to forget the biggest issue of them all.

We wouldn't be here if Sofia hadn't killed herself.

Most days, I could ignore it. Maybe playing Mamá's spy was a blessing in disguise. I worried about the kids all day long and ended up forgetting why we were in this position in the first place.

Because I failed Sofia.

I was failing the kids, and I'd fail Logan, too.

A growl came out of me, remembering the moments when I tried to be good. Mamá saw MMA as rebellion, but in those years, I displayed the most discipline.

I followed a schedule my trainer made. I ate what he said I should eat, I trained, I built muscles, and I watched hours of footage of my own fights to catch my mistakes and correct them.

No one saw it, though. Mamá thought I was in Chicago, being a hooligan or whatever. She never even watched the fights and acted surprised when I came home for Christmas with a bruised face.

But the only person who tried to keep up with my career was the one I was too hardheaded to pay attention to.

I left Sofia alone, too angry with my parents to keep a relationship with her. And the only person who watched out for Sofia?

Logan Hart.

Shit, I punched the bag again and again, trying to make Logan sound less appealing.

But it didn't matter where my mind went, it came back to her in those leggings with a smile on her face, wanting a fucking back yard for the three kids she got after a shitty deal.

I stopped punching, holding the bag when it bobbed in front of me. Taking a breath, I rubbed my face, but the feeling was still there. *Restless.*

I shook my head, but Logan's smile was printed under my eyelids. She was the picture of wholesome and I wanted to eat her alive.

I shouldn't, I couldn't, but that was beyond the point.

Sitting on the bench beside the weights, I scratched my shadow of a beard as I regulated my breathing.

Fucking Logan, making me wonder. Those little gasps of hers. They got me twisted, even though they were never aimed at me.

I wondered if I could make her gasp. If her voice went soft when she was needy. If that blush rose up from her tits to her cheeks. If her nipples were pink like her lips.

*Shit.*

Before I knew it, I was hard as a rock, doing the opposite of what I should have been doing.

Instead of forgetting about this whole thing, I parted my legs and palmed myself over the basketball shorts.

Feeling my piercing on the tip of my cock, I thought about how I should stop and head for the shower, but the house was silent and the images of Logan spreading her legs to me were vivid in my imagination.

Glancing once over at the door, it was half closed, but no one was home, so it didn't matter. I had at least two hours before the kids were out of school.

I took myself out and promised it was only one time. I wasn't going to make a habit out of thinking about Logan. I needed it now, but then never again.

My mouth watered thinking about her. Those prissy little suits she wore. The severe ponytail low on her neck. She was all business.

I bet she wasn't all the time.

Before I could stop, I stroked. Slowly at first, playing with the barbell ring through the tip.

I flicked my wrist over, tightening the grip as I went down. In my dreams, Logan was finally relaxed. Her shoulders down, her smile playful. She was the same Logan, that cute little nose, the perky tits and hair smelling like strawberries, but I got to see the other side, too.

She came willingly, her eyes full of desire, her voice full of want.

I kept going, increasing my pace, as images of Logan ran through my mind. I dirtied up every single interaction we had.

I ate her pussy in the kitchen. I fucked her at the construction site. I threw her in the back of my truck, and she rode me like a fucking champion.

Dream Logan did all that with a smile, those rosy cheeks, and full of sass. She was wet for me, ready to give, and tasted amazing. And even in my dreams, even as I stroked myself harder and said I was never doing it again, I knew it was a lie.

I shuddered, ready to come with that image of Logan plastered in my mind. That fucking smile that shattered me into pieces, that taste of strawberries on my tongue.

I came like a train, my growl taking over the gym. I came so hard, I couldn't even feel shame for the fucking mess I made on myself. A forty-six-year-old, so horny I couldn't make it into the bedroom.

Shaking my head, I glanced at the door, but no one was there. Not even Dream Logan, wet and waiting for me.

# 14.

# Logan

Oh my god.

Lachlan was so heavy. He fell asleep sometime during the drive home after running errands and I didn't have the heart to wake him up. I knew he was going to be a pain tonight when he couldn't sleep, but I wasn't a good disciplinarian. I could admit to that one.

I always thought I had that part down, yet I was incapable of waking up a toddler. I couldn't ever say no to Vienna because when she blinked those Sofia eyes at me, I was a goner.

His head lolled to my shoulder as I made my way to the elevators in the parking lot, awkwardly pressing the button, too scared of waking him up from the nap he shouldn't be having.

When the doors opened, I had another problem—taking the keycard from my jacket pocket. Once I had that done, I propped myself on the wall and let the elevator ride up.

I was tired, and I had… an hour and a half until picking Dash and Vienna up from school. I needed a killer schedule in place before going back to work. I could handle right now, but my life was those kids, and I was barely sleeping.

I got into the apartment, tiptoeing even as I climbed the stairs, afraid of shaking him too much. When we reached the top of the stairs, I opened the bedroom Lachlan shared with Dashiell.

Gone was the king-size bed. Now Lachlan had a small bed, while Dash had a queen-size on the other side of the room. I placed him in bed carefully, promising he was only allowed to sleep for another twenty minutes before I woke him up.

Nodding to myself, I closed the door without making a noise, thinking I might need to order something for dinner tonight since I was completely wiped.

That was when I heard it.

The lowest of growls. A deep voice, a growl like from a beast trapped somewhere waiting to attack. I stopped in my tracks, turning my head to the side, watching the home gym's door where the sound was coming from.

Obviously, Alvaro was home and making good use of the gym.

My shoulders relaxed, and I went over to tell him we were home. But something made me stop.

*A grunt.*

It sounded so dirty my knees weakened. That was my warning. My chance to step away. The hairs on the back of my neck stood up and I stepped closer to that door, almost like an invisible hook was pulling me toward it.

I padded carefully, my hands shaking. The door wasn't completely closed, just a small gap, and I peeked inside.

And there he was.

I swallowed thickly when my eyes landed on Alvaro sitting on the bench beside the weights, stroking his cock.

My tongue felt thirty times bigger inside my mouth, my legs closing like my pussy was turning into butterflies that could fly to him.

Hmm, that wasn't good.

God, that was too good.

Alvaro had no shirt on and just like I imagined, he was packing. Perfect golden-brown skin, muscle upon muscle, peaks and valleys, and every single inch of his body had ink. His arms were wide, his jaw set as he kept a ferocious rhythm palming his cock that was one hundred percent not average.

My hand flew to my neck as I tried to swallow, but I seemed to be stuck in place. I should  have stepped away and let him finish, but I stood there, my eyes glued to him, waiting for his next move.

His hand went down. I could only imagine the tight grip he was keeping, and my mouth flew open when I saw the little sparkle of a jewel on each side of his shaft.

*He was pierced.*

He was pierced.

He. Was. Pierced.

My mind went into overdrive, incapable of forming a single thought that wasn't about Alvaro Castillo's monster dick or his piercings.

And it wasn't just the one that went through his cock, but the one at the top, too. A barbel in his pubic area that made me wonder what was there for.

God, my mouth went dry thinking about the possibilities.

When I realized how much I wanted to figure out about his piercings, I should have stepped away.

But my feet grew roots. I was there forever, watching as Alvaro tugged his massive cock up and down and growled like he could make me wet just with his voice alone.

Heart thumping in my chest, my ears blocked, but I couldn't take my eyes off Alvaro. His hands were so big, his arms powerful and that pierced cock.

*Lord have mercy.*

And it was only when he was finished, when he spilled everything, that I came back to myself. A silent gasp left my lips at the same time his groan reached me. Sweaty, my cheeks burning, and soaked. I was so wet it was criminal.

Before he caught me, I moved away, padding silently to my room. I leaned on the door after I closed it, panting, trying to regain any type of composure.

I saw that. He did that.

I rubbed my temple, trying to see if I could erase the image, but no, it was forever printed under my eyelids.

Alvaro used to be the action hero on the screen, but somehow he became the man in my gym.

Masturbating.

Was that normal? Has that happened to other people with roommates?

How the hell was I supposed to look at his face every day and not ask about his pierced cock?

Like a reflex, my head turned to my bedside table where my vibrator lived. I was stepping in its direction when I caught myself.

Nope.

That was a slippery slope. If I did that just once, I knew I would never stop. I couldn't become the woman that masturbates thinking about her dead best friend's brother.

To the kids' uncle.

To Alvaro Castillo.

And with that thought, I marched to the shower.

"THIS IS YUMMY."

"Good."

I tried to tell myself to relax, but the food on my plate tasted like cardboard. It didn't matter how many times Vienna complimented her meal. It was like she could feel my discomfort and was trying her best to lighten the mood.

"Shut up," Dash started.

Vienna opened her mouth to retort her brother, but I was quicker. "Don't say that to your sister." Taking a breath, I looked up and faced Dashiell. "How was school today?"

He shrugged and didn't answer.

"I made a new friend," Vienna informed us.

"Good." I nodded. "Tell me about them."

Vienna's long story about a boy at school who was very shy but agreed to play with her was a blessing in disguise.

She was sitting to my right, talking non-stop, and I concentrated on her. Ignoring the heat that came from my left where Alvaro sat helping Lachlan with his dinner.

According to my books, Lachlan should feed himself. Dr. Maya said his motor skills were developing well and he should at least try. I was trying to make him pick up the spoon at least once or twice per meal, but one of us always needed to be there to hand it to him, or he wouldn't show any interest. Today was Alvaro's turn.

But I wasn't paying attention to that side of the table. I was concentrating on Vienna and her little friend. They visited the chickens together.

Did I know Lone Pine had chickens? No. But they did, and kids visited them from time to time. I wasn't sure if I should be concerned.

"You know what we are eating right now is dead chicken, right?" Dashiell said, taking a bite off his dinner.

I sliced him a look. "Do you need to be that cruel to your sister?"

Dash was the epitome of a teenager. He was childishly pressing Vienna's buttons just for fun in one breath and claiming he wanted to raise her in the next. He thought he was all grown up when he couldn't even spend a full dinner without antagonizing her.

"It's not cruel to say the truth."

"It is," I cut him off.

"So we should lie?"

"Dash..." Alvaro growled.

My hand snapped up to stop him, and I raised my eyes to Dash, a smirk on his lips like he had just won the argument.

"You should always tell the truth when you're asked. Being deliberately cruel and hiding behind the idea of honesty is not ok." I breathed out, shaking my head and coming back to my dinner. "I know you're trying to make me look bad. That's ok. You're not the first and you won't be the last."

"What's that supposed to mean?"

When I looked back at him, it wasn't the same sneering the teenager. He had a frown between his eyebrows, his eyes softening a little.

"I mean, I work in a male-dominated field. I'm used to people trying to antagonize me."

He crossed his arms over her chest. "I don't dislike you because you're a woman."

Vienna gasped. "We like Logan!"

I chuckled. "I know you don't." I ignored Vienna's support. "But I'm used to having everything I say twisted to make me look bad. That's why I learned to..." I swallowed, "be careful about what I say and how I say it."

When Alvaro spoke, his voice was nothing like I was used to.

"You don't need to be afraid, Logan." His tone was kind and while I was trying to avoid his general direction until now, I faced him when he said, "We don't do that kind of shit here."

"You shouldn't curse in front of the kids," I said, but my mouth was curving into a smile.

Before I could stop myself I glanced down his arms, and my brain threw the memory back right in front of my eyes. I choked on my tongue and spun away.

Not a cold shower, not time and space, nothing was ever going to take that image of Alvaro and his cock out of my mind.

"Come on, Lachlan. Come on..."

He looked at me like I was a stranger trying to snatch him from his bed. Lachlan's face was red from his wailing, his pajama covered legs thrashing on the bed like he was in pain.

But he wasn't. I put him to sleep at the time he should sleep, but because of his long afternoon nap, I was being punished.

He was a good kid, though. Even as he wailed, even as he seemed to hate my guts, he stayed on the bed that I put him in.

I reached for his belly, settling my hand there and rubbing slowly as I used calming tones.

He cried, he thrashed, he wasn't happy. I even offered his pacifier that I knew I should have been more active in taking from him, but one trauma at a time. He was doing well during the days, using it only when we got in the car. I wasn't ready to tackle the fight for him to give it up at nighttime.

He moved so much and so brusquely, his little sock shot away from his foot, landing by the door. I followed the movement and caught Alvaro as he walked in and bent over to grab the sock.

"I see you have the night routine down." He smirked.

I brushed my hair out of my face, blowing a raspberry. "It's my fault. I let him sleep in the afternoon."

"Kids take naps, Logan."

"But the book said..."

"If you mention *the* book one more time, I'll think you're my mother."

I opened my mouth to complain but ended up giggling at his bible reference. Lachlan kicked again and reminded me he wasn't amused. I reeled back, trying to avoid a hit, and Alvaro tsked "That's enough," he said to Lachlan.

Without waiting for a reply, he took the boy and scooped him out of the bed. The child, with hopes things were going to work his way, quieted down at the same second.

"They said he needs to fall asleep in his own bed."

"Are you saying "they" so you don't say "the book" again?"

Guilty, I closed my mouth. Alvaro chuckled while Lachlan took up residence in those arms.

I hated to admit it, but there was something about a big man like Alvaro holding a child. Lachlan was even tall for his age, but in Alvaro's arms he looked tiny. His uncle's arm stretched as he held Lachlan against his barrel chest, all that ink in perfect contrast with Lachlan's yellow pjs.

Alvaro kissed Lachlan's temple. "Déjame mostrarte algo," he whispered to his nephew and took him out of the room.

I groaned to myself but followed them. Of course I did. Passing by Vienna's room, she was already in bed, with a book in her hand.

"Everything ok?" I asked.

"Yes." She smiled.

"You brushed your teeth?"

She nodded. And I nodded too. "Good."

I was letting myself out when she called, "Logan?"

"Yeah?" I turned.

"Can you give me a goodnight kiss?"

I didn't know why that destroyed me, but it did. I went inside, even a little nervous when she lowered in the bed, leaving her book on the bedside table.

I tucked her in, something I never did for another human in my life, and then planted a kiss on her forehead.

"Have a good night, Vi," I said.

She beamed when I called her by her nickname, it again stabbed my heart.

Before I started bawling, I moved toward the door, turning off the lights before closing it softly.

The house was silent, so it meant Lachlan never went back to crying. Even without invitation, I stepped into Alvaro's room.

Alvaro had Lachlan in his arms, both of them at the window, and he was pointing to things at a distance.

"Can you see the lake?"

I crossed my arms and leaned on the doorframe, watching. Lachlan said nothing, but he nodded when his uncle showed him something new in the distance. I had no idea how many minutes had passed since I stopped to watch them, but eventually Lachlan rested his head on Alvaro's shoulders and started drifting off.

Even as he did, Alvaro kept talking in Spanish, the soothing rumble of his deep voice enough to put the boy asleep.

Turning finally from the window, he caught me.

"He's asleep."

Alvaro moved quickly, putting Lachlan in his bed. He stirred a little, but never fully woke up. I closed in, my eyes on the boy and my face scrunched in question. Being careful, I sat down on the bed, my hand edging closer to his little hand.

"You're overthinking this," Alvaro said, almost like he was disappointed in me for doing so.

"Vienna asked me for a kiss," I whispered.

He arched an eyebrow. "That's good."

I flickered my eyes from Lachlan to him. "It never occurred to me. I thought about the proper time for them to go to sleep and what they should be eating. I never thought she might just want a kiss." I took a deep breath. "You think that's what your mother was afraid of?"

His eyes were somber, his shoulders stiff. Shaking his head like he couldn't believe me, he said, "Come on, lay down."

Doing exactly the opposite, my spine went straight, ready to bolt a moment's notice.

"Why?" I narrowed my eyes.

"Because you're talking crazy now." He nodded to the pillow. "Come on."

Lachlan was right in the middle. Slowly, I laid my head on the pillow. A second later, Alvaro followed.

Even if the bed was big, his shoulder hung out of it when he laid facing the ceiling, an arm under his head.

"My mother doesn't think you're unloving."

I tucked my hands under my chin, looking at him on my side. I watched as his chest moved, his Adam's apple bobbing when he explained. "She was just scared of losing the kids. Of you showing them something she couldn't provide."

I nodded. "You think that was why she never liked my friendship with Sofia?"

"Yeah," he croaked. "Mamá is proud. My parents are good people, but they like to do things their own way."

I wasn't one to pry, but I couldn't stop the words from falling off my lips. "That's why you came here for MMA?"

He never glanced my way, just nodded to the ceiling. "They didn't agree with me."

"Well, you showed them."

That made him turn, his arm falling. "You think?"

"Don't you?" I asked, surprised.

"I never went big or anything like that. I never was someone people knew by name."

"But you did it. You were a professional athlete. I don't understand why that's not a victory."

It was like I caught him. His eyebrows furrowed, his eyes focusing somewhere else. I kept going.

"It's hard for people to understand other people's professions. They don't know what milestone and goals—"

"Anyone can see you're successful," he interrupted me.

"Mmm," I hummed. "Sure. Because of money. But success isn't always measured by money or fame. You got to do what you loved, right?"

He grunted.

"Don't be like that," I actually scolded. "I watched a lot of your fights growing up, Alvaro. I know you're good."

He looked me right in the eyes. "What do you do you know about MMA, Jefa?"

I bit my cheeks not to smile at him. "I know you're the big dude who won the fight."

He tsked. "They are all big dudes."

"You were the biggest. Is that what you wanted me to say?"

He, honest to god, grinned at me. "Well, it is always lovely to hear."

I couldn't deal with serious MMA fighter Alvaro Castillo grinning at a dick joke. One, because he was gorgeous when he smiled. Two, because I knew for a fact he was right.

He was so goddamn right. He was the biggest I've ever seen. And the piercings...

The blush came from between my breasts, burning its way up my cheeks. He noticed it, looking confused for a second before he cleared his throat and faced away.

"You should stop worrying so much."

"Mmm, sure. Done," I replied sarcastically.

"It's been only two weeks." He turned back to me.

Yeah, it was only two weeks, but I still felt like I was failing somehow. I feared the kids telling his mom, who they were visiting this weekend, everything I did wrong. Arguing with Dashiell, messing up Lachlan's naps, and forgetting to kiss them goodnight. Caridad would be horrified. What cold and horrible woman was I, denying kids the simple comfort of a kiss?

"I can see the wheels turning in your head," he said, almost in a whisper.

I gulped, afraid of crying. "I don't want to fuck them up."

His lip twitched. "You never curse."

"That's how much I don't want to mess it up."

"You're not messing anything up," he told me in a firm tone. "You've got this. I don't know how, but you do."

"It's not enough," I whispered, like I could make it a secret between us. "There are so many variables to being a guardian and it's like when I figure out one thing, another comes up."

"And then you fix that part. It's ok."

I blew out a breath. "It is not enough."

Surprisingly, he chuckled. "That's the kind of thoughts that go through that mind of yours?" He reached over, his thumb grazing my temple and smoothing over the worry lines.

"It is hell inside."

"So, tell those voices to shut up," he told me, looking serious. "You're ok. You're enough."

I almost laughed, "Says who?"

"Are you contesting my authority?"

A smile tugged the corner of my mouth. "Only every day."

"You should respect your elders."

That made me giggle. "You're too old to ask for respect, Alvaro. You have to demand it."

My words unlocked something in him, and he turned completely my way. Going up on his elbow, his eyes locked on me. I felt myself grow hot again, and I swallowed a lump in my throat. His warm whiskey eyes traced the curve of my neck before fixing back on mine.

He was holding himself back. No reason why I should know that, but I could see perfectly the effort it was taking for him not to reply to my comment. I was dying for him to let loose.

Just the thought made my cheeks burn. He noticed my tomato red cheeks and smirked. He said nothing, just looked at me and unknotted all the knots of my existence. With just one burning look and a smirk.

My mouth was dry. I would have fallen onto my knees if I were standing, but I was in bed… with him. I rubbed my thighs together, making his eyes go that direction and like a pull between us, we moved closer to one another.

And Lachlan whined.

Alvaro and I stopped in our tracks, looking down at the toddler's head between us. Gulping, I put distance between our bodies, chuckling to myself, trying to change the mood.

"But anyway, maybe I just need a couple of days to rest. You're bringing the kids to your parents straight after school?"

It took him a second to reply, his eyes glossy, watching me. Eventually he nodded, and taking a breath he moved away too, rubbing his head. "Yeah, right after school."

# 15.

# Alvaro

Logan blinked at me with those innocent eyes of hers, mouth opening in a smile when she took me in. Those cheeks getting red straight away.

A laugh, rolling her eyes before she straddled me, her center right on top of my cock. My hands were on her waist. I was so much bigger than her, I could just move her whatever way I wanted.

I rolled us to the side. Her back was now to my front, even though I wasn't sure how I got there. Her scent was all up my nose, soft hair tickling. I couldn't resist. My hand went up to her chest. She was naked before, but now I had to go under her clothes to take a tit into my palm.

Her back arched when I flicked a nipple, my mouth salivating when I pushed myself against her ass and I heard a whimper.

In a need that made me dizzy, I tugged a nipple and ground on her. She took my breath away, so fucking perfect in my arms, wriggling and needy.

This was a good dream.

This was the perfect dream. To have Logan like this without feeling guilty about it.

Except that now I knew it was a dream. I felt a little guilty.

But I pushed into her ass, and my hand went slowly from her tits down to her belly and then I cupped her pussy.

*"Alvaro..."*

My eyes flew open when the voice that begged for me wasn't in the dream.

It was the real Logan.

My cock stuffed between her cheeks, my hand right on her pussy and, like an uncontrollable ass, I moved my finger, making her moan.

Fuck, even her moan was pretty.

Delicious and delirious, I knew I had to get out of that situation.

I never closed the blinds. I squinted as my eyes got used to the light and bits and pieces of the night came back to me.

After a while of talking, I put Lachlan in bed, but he woke up a little, and I stayed with him until he fell asleep again. When I came back, Logan was sleeping in my bed.

I could have carried her back to her own bed. But I didn't. I told myself the bed was big enough, and she looked comfortable even though she was still wearing her full clothes.

"Alvaro..." she called again, her voice rough with sleep, and I knew I was in deep trouble.

My hand was right there. Even though we had pants and underwear between us, I could still feel how hot she was. She was within reach of my fingertips.

I squeezed my eyes shut, breathing through my nose. Slowly, without bothering her, I moved my hand away throwing my whole body to the side trying to get away from her.

I almost got away with it.

*Almost.*

She woke up in a gasp—thank god I wasn't cupping her anymore—and I quickly schooled my expression to pretend we both woke up at the same time.

She turned around, putting even more distance between us, her eyes wide like a deer caught in the headlights.

"Good morning," I tried, ignoring the hard on I was still trying to control.

Something went through her, like electricity through her body, as a reaction to my voice. Whatever it was, she hid it pretty quickly, brushing her hair out of her face.

"I fell asleep here?"

"Yeah, no problem."

When I sat up, I leaned forward to hide everything from her, but she wasn't watching me like I watched her.

"What time is it?"

I checked my watch. "Not six yet."

She nodded. "Ok, good. I have time for a shower before Lachlan is up."

Right to business. Logan stood up, smoothing her clothes like she needed to be presentable even in her own house. She moved to the door, but suddenly stopped to turn to look at me.

Her toes curled on the floor, and she bit her bottom lip. "Thank you for yesterday. For the help with Lachlan and for," a big breath came out, "the talk."

She looked uncomfortable. Maybe her family was too stuck up, but whatever we talked about wasn't a big deal.

I wasn't one to share my shit with anyone, but that was a far cry from sharing. I just asked her to relax for a minute.

Not here to antagonize her, I simply dipped my chin, willing her to leave so I could have a shower myself and try to forget how she felt in my arms.

It was only when she was padding away and I released a calming breath that it came to me.

*It was my name she called.*

She moaned my name. She was dreaming about me, too. That realization made me smug, bold even.

I straightened my back. "Hey, Logan?"

"Yeah?"

I had to train my face not to give anything away, but I asked anyway, a frown between my eyebrows trying to fake concern. "Were you having a nightmare?"

Her face was priceless. Eyes as big as they could get, her knees even buckled.

"W-why are you asking?"

"You were moaning and—"

"No, no nightmare," she cut me off and bolted for her bedroom.

I only laughed when I heard her door slamming shut. Lachlan whined somewhere in the other room. Now I needed to push my shower for later.

It didn't matter.

Heading to the boys' room with a smile on my face, I couldn't stop thinking it was going to be a good day after all.

IT WAS AFTER I dropped the kids at school that my phone rang. That number on the screen was enough to make me rethink if it was a good day that I was having.

With a snarl, I accepted the call. "Who do you think you are to call this number?"

"Hey, hey," Paddy's slimy voice reached me. "Is that how you talk to an old friend?"

"Who gave you my number, Paddy?"

"I have friends who know people."

"Well, delete it." I was ready to hang up, and he heard it in my voice.

"Alvaro, come on, man. Let me tell you what I have, alright?"

I'd arrive at work in five minutes, so I gave him thirty seconds.

"Remember the kid you fought last year? Little blond kid from Muriel's gym. You ended him."

I grunted. That was enough for Paddy. "He has been training like a maniac since. Muriel is up my arse, saying her kid wants a chance."

"No, thanks." I went to end the call again.

"Hey, come on. You're El Toro. Everyone wants a chance to defeat you. The kid wants to prove himself."

"I'm not in the business of helping anyone's self-esteem."

"You're not in the business at all."

"Exactly. Don't call me."

"Shit, Castillo, it's like you're a happy man now, huh? Life is that good you don't come over to work frustrations out on another man's face?"

I didn't want to give in to Paddy, but with one sentence, he messed me up. My hands strangled the wheel, my teeth ground into one another like I needed them pulverized.

No.

I wasn't a happy man. I couldn't be ever happy because Sofia was dead. I was a guilty man, a shitty man. I was a shitty brother and a bad influence for her kids.

Slamming the wheel, I cursed under my breath.

There was no happiness for me for as long as I lived. Everything good in me died the same day as Sofia.

"I'll think about it," I growled out. "Don't fucking call me anymore, Paddy."

I hung up before he could say one more fucking word. The heaviness in my chest staying with me the entire day.

# 16
# Logan

I WAS GOING TO kill him.

That was all I could think while I drove through the streets of Chicago, my knuckles white and my heart full of rage.

"I can't believe he would do that. Two weeks, you get that? Two weeks."

Lachlan didn't reply, not even when I made eye contact through the rearview mirror and I knew he could understand me. In the last two weeks, I learned a lot with the littlest Castillo. He was quiet, but the kid was smart.

I got a bunch of memory games for him since our first visit with Dr. Maya, and he was amazing with them. Not just good for his age. I played with him enough times, never letting him win, and still Lachlan was cleaning the floors with me every week.

He also disliked certain foods. He wouldn't tell me what they were, but by trial and error, I knew if I put a pea on his plate, he would refuse to eat it.

So, I had to accept while he wasn't talking to me yet, he was listening.

Lachlan was a superb listener. I kept rambling, telling him how many ways I'd kill his brother. Not my best parenting moment, I knew I could do worse.

"A fight. Can you believe that?" I glanced at Lachlan, but he looked so cute dangling his little legs from the seat, my heart melted. "Of course you don't. You are a sweet boy, aren't you, Lach? You are never going to fight and get me called to school."

I parked at Lone Pine, my pits sweating and staining the blouse under my jacket. I hated being in trouble. Even though I wasn't directly in trouble, I was responsible for the teen in trouble. Which made me in trouble by association.

I opened the door and then got Lachlan, undoing his seat belt and helping him out of my BMW. He left his pacifier behind, but not before sending me a look like he wanted to bring with him.

"You know the rules, buddy."

He knew them, so he left it in his car seat, giving it a longing stare before grabbing my hand. Poor child endured my sweaty palm and my brusque walk without complaining. I opened the front door, forgetting for a second that school was still in session.

Lone Pine Academy was full. Kids in front of their lockers talking and messing around in the halls. I turned and took Lachlan into my arms, afraid he wouldn't like cutting through the crowd.

I was steaming. Everything I did was to make life easier for them. Dash tried again and again to antagonize me, and I turned the other cheek. But fighting at school?

No, I couldn't deal with that.

I blew a hair out of my face as I marched straight to Godwick's office. When had teenage boys gotten so big? Dash was tall, but Alvaro was so large sometimes I forgot Dash would look intimidating if his uncle didn't make him look like a little boy.

Regardless, anger took over. I stomped through the hall, ignoring everyone in my way until I reached the end and turned right and there, sitting in front of Godwick's door, was Dashiell.

He only looked up when the heels of my boots scratched the wood. His mouth closed in a line, like he was upset to see me and not the other way around. I cut him a look and then checked my watch.

Only half an hour until the end of school.

"Go get your sister."

He nodded and then extended his arm to grab Lachlan, but I shook my head.

"Just go do what I said."

Maybe he knew he was in deep shit with me, because the only attitude I got was the raise of his eyebrows to my tone before he got his backpack and turned to do what he was told.

I watched him go, his shoulders down, dragging his feet. He had the shirt folded up to his elbows, and of course, the uniform jacket he forgot in the chair. I sighed and took the jacket, repositioning Lachlan on my hip. I took a long breath and knocked at the principal's office.

"Come in," Kendra called, and I opened the door a little. "Oh, hey, Logan."

I left myself in, shaking in my shoes. "I'm so sorry, Kendra." The words had to be said.

God, even my butt cheeks were sweaty. Getting the kids in Lone Pine sounded like a great idea before, but now, as I sat in front of her with Lachlan perched on my lap and Lake Erie under my arms, I wondered if I didn't make a mistake. In my work life, I could control how the Godwicks saw me. But here?

I couldn't control Dashiell. That much was obvious. I had nothing under control, and I voluntarily mixed my personal and work life.

Letting a breath slowly go, I faced Kendra head on. "What happened?"

"Relax," she said with a slight smile. "He had an argument with another student and things escalated."

"He punched him?" I guessed.

On the phone, the secretary only told me things had gotten physical when I pressured her to talk. Nothing more than that.

"Yes. He knows he did wrong."

"That's not enough." I swallowed. "That's not going on his permanent record, right? Will it hurt his chances for college?"

"Breathe." She only talked again after I breathed deep. "There's no permanent record."

"I remember there was," I said.

"No, there isn't. But that's not what's going to hurt Dashiell's chances for college."

So *something* was hurting his chances.

"I'm still waiting to see if he wants to be here," she said. I opened my mouth to tell her we were still in the early days, but she interrupted me. "I know it is still early. But maybe changing Dashiell's mind is what you should worry about."

I swallowed. "He told you he doesn't want to go?"

She smiled sadly. "I've been a teacher for a long time. I can tell."

I sighed, letting my head rest on top of Lachlan's head.

"How are you doing, Logan?"

I gulped and lied. "I'm ok."

"You're young. And you have three children in your care, so I'm going to ask again." She leaned over the desk. "How are you, Logan?"

Taking a breath in Lachlan's hair, because even at three, he still smelled like baby and goodness.

"I'm ok," I told her. "It will be ok."

Almost looking disappointed I didn't spill my guts, Kendra nodded and looked down at the paperwork in front of her.

"We don't tolerate violence here. Dashiell is suspended until Monday."

It was Thursday. That was just a one day suspension.

"I couldn't just let it slide, even though I understand."

Did she? Because I sure didn't. It didn't matter how many books I read on the subject, or how many trips I took to Dr. Maya's office. I still couldn't begin to understand how the kids were feeling.

"Thank you, Kendra." With a little smile, I stood up with Lachlan on my hip and extended my hand to her.

"You look tired," she said.

I swallowed the sarcastic reply and shrugged. "The weekend is almost here."

I winced as soon as the words were said. The kids were going to their grandparents when I knew Caridad was salivating for an excuse to take them from me. She was going to find out about Dashiell's suspension.

Exhausted. I was beyond tired now.

Kissing Lachlan's head, I left myself out. He didn't need the kiss, I did. I opened the door to Vienna, smiling at the bench beside Dashiell, her cute uniform askew.

"Hi, Logan!" She was already hyper, jumping to say her hello. Vienna hugged my midsection like a baby koala. I smiled and hugged her back as I shot daggers at Dashiell.

"Let's go."

"What'd she say?" he asked.

"Let's go."

I didn't wait for him to reply. I turned on my heels, holding Vienna's hand, and marched through the hall.

When I got into the car, I immediately rang Alvaro.

"Hablame, Jefa."

"I'm at the school," I blurted. "I was called here by Principal Godwick." I glanced at my side. Dashiell had already his seatbelt on facing the other way, actively ignoring me.

"What happened?"

"Can you come home?"

The words escaped from my lips and I knew I couldn't bring them back. My voice was softer, my shoulders relaxed because I asked him to come home.

It wasn't his home. I actually had no idea where he lived. But he had a room in my house, one he loved the view.

I wanted him home.

It was one thing to spy on him masturbating. One thing to have a dirty dream or two. It was completely different to feel this safe when I heard his voice.

And my heart thumped like an idiot when he said, "Meet you there."

Just like that. He didn't push, he didn't ask for anything more. He was going to meet me there.

Shoving those feelings deep inside, I started the car, checking once again if everyone had their seat belts on, and we headed home.

I WAS PLAYING BLOCKS with Lachlan and Vienna when Alvaro arrived, only twenty minutes after me.

"I had a shit—" He eyed the kids. "Sorry."

"That's ok." I stood up, brushing myself off.

His eyes went down straight to my legs. You couldn't convince me otherwise. He took his time ogling all the way down the black leggings to my bare feet and then back again. I licked my lips and remembered the bomb I had in my hands.

"Principal Godwick called today."

"Dash fought a boy," Vienna informed her uncle with glee.

I flashed her a look, but she just shrugged me off and kept playing with Lachlan.

"Dash," Alvaro roared. "Come here."

I shifted on my feet, biting my cheek. I oozed anxiety when Alvaro turned to me with a frown on his forehead. "You're not the one in trouble."

*Ugh. Whatever.*

Dashiell came to the living room, still in his uniform, his jaw set.

"You got into a fight?"

"I guess."

Crossing my arm in front of my chest, I tried to look like a disciplinarian when all I wanted was to cry and ask why couldn't he just be chill? Why do we need to do everything the hardest way?

"You're not even a month into this new school. You can't just start fighting," Alvaro was saying, his voice like thunder. I started respecting Dash a little more for not physically flinching.

"He's suspended, too." Again, from Vienna.

"Well, I'm going to take these two for a bath," I said, nodding to Vienna.

Her running commentary was only going to make Dashiell annoyed and at the end of the day, I wanted to know what happened.

Up we went, and I helped them to get clean as quickly as possible. First Lachlan and then Vienna, trying to hear something from downstairs, but I just caught the occasional rise of Alvaro's voice but nothing concrete.

When everyone was finally clean, I brought them to their improvised playroom, where I was keeping their toys and a TV for movie nights and pressed play on something they both agreed on.

"I'm going downstairs, but no peeking," I told my girl specifically.

"Pinky promise," Vienna agreed.

I twisted my pinky with hers and nodded at once, leaving them to rejoin the fight.

I padded downstairs and I heard Alvaro saying, "It's not ok. That's not enough of a reason."

Dashiell was sitting on the couch, his mouth still in a sneer like we did him dirty.

"He told you what happened?" I joined beside Alvaro.

"Yeah..." Alvaro nodded and scratched his buzzed scalp.

I was a controlled person. *Controlling, actually.* I hated emotional displays and shouting. But the second Alvaro told me what the other boy called Dashiell?

All that went out of the window.

"He called him what?"

"Logan..." Alvaro shook his head, but my attention wasn't on him.

My eyes on Dashiell, I asked. "Did Principal Godwick know?"

His eyes meet mine and he nodded slightly.

"That fuck—" I cursed.

"Logan, it doesn't matter."

"Doesn't matter? He's suspended, but I never even asked what the other boy got."

"Nothing," Dashiell offered.

I pointed at him and looked at Alvaro. "We need to go to the school. We need to talk to Godwick..."

"Logan, listen to me. He's still in the wrong."

"How can he be in the wrong?" I turned to Dashiell. "Did *you* call him any slurs?"

Dashiell's lip twitched. "No."

"Well, so there you go." I moved to grab shoes, my bag and—

"Logan." Alvaro caught me by my shoulders. "Listen to me. He can't punch every asshole in his way."

"Well, that's true." I nodded and turned to Dashiell. "Did you hear that? Next time call Alvaro, he can do it for you."

This time I saw it. He chuckled.

"I definitely can't punch teenagers, Logan."

"I don't care," I told him. "That's not acceptable behavior. Dashiell can't be suspended. He's the victim."

Alvaro argued, "It's only one day."

At the same time Dashiell growled, "I'm not the victim."

I ignored them both. "The talk with Kendra was too easy. She was talking shit about Dashiell going to college."

"I'm not going to college."

I pointed at him. "You don't start with me." Turning to Alvaro, I kept going. "She never told me the entire story. She talked about not tolerating violence..."

"He was violent."

"For a reason." I narrowed my eyes at Alvaro.

"I don't think that holds up in court."

"We'll have to agree to disagree."

"Isn't self-defense a thing?" Dashiell asked from the couch.

I smiled triumphantly. "Well done. It is a thing."

Alvaro scoffed. "Yeah, the boy is a genius. Harvard law."

My smile opened even further, but Dashiell was quick to destroy it. "Don't give her any ideas."

"What I am trying to say here," Alvaro started again. "Is that the world is full of idiots."

"You guys are great at this. Keep going," Dash mocked.

"Do you know how many shitty names I was called?" Alvaro continued. "We can't beat up every idiot."

"I don't see why not." The teen shrugged.

I flinched. I was on his side, but I didn't want him to think punching people was ok. I just felt... stupid. I trusted Godwick's judgment on this. She told me Dash was in the wrong and I believed her.

Alvaro tried again. "Because brown kids get punished for existing, you start punching every idiot and it's not college where you're headed. It's jail."

"Rich coming from someone who made a career out of punching." Dash raised an eyebrow.

Alvaro sighed. "So you should listen. And next time some ass calls you shit, you come directly to me, alright?"

Dashiell moved from the couch. "Can I go now?"

We both nodded and watched him go.

"The kids upstairs?"

I faced Alvaro. "Yeah."

"I'll have a look."

He left me alone and without even thinking about it I put my boots on and grabbed a coat, sliding the double doors for the outside open area.

Hugging myself, I watched the lights of Chicago from one of the most beautiful buildings in the city with a checklist running through my head.

I could never keep up. It never ended. I breathed through my nose, trying not to shake and it wasn't from the cold.

The double doors slid open, and I closed my eyes knowing my time was up. He came after me.

"Logan," he said my name with a sigh.

"I'm ok."

He breathed out and joined me at the city vigil. "It's only one day of suspension."

"It's more than that."

"Tell me what it is then."

I rubbed my eyes. "It's... I can't keep up."

"You're doing fine."

“I don’t understand why Sofia thought I could handle this. I clearly suck.”

“Jefa, help me out here.” I felt him shifting at my side. “How did you go from that fire in your eyes wanting to burn Godwick’s office to this?”

“I can’t believe someone called him that at school.”

“So it’s your fault because you registered them at Lone Pine?”

“It’s stupid,” I muttered.

“It is.”

“I’m not a martyr.” I thought he needed to know. “I know not everything is on me. But it is just one more thing I need to pay attention to, isn’t it?”

He hummed without a reply for that one, so I talked again. “And your mom is going to eat this up.”

“Let me worry about my mother.”

I snorted. “Have you met Vienna? She’s spilling the beans the second she sees your mother. And I know—” I rubbed my temple, but suddenly he took my hand in his and lowered it between us.

His rough fingers were warm, making me shiver from the contact.

“I said let me worry about that. When was the last time you let someone do something for you?”

I opened my mouth to say plenty of times, but he interrupted me.

“No,” his voice was low. “When was the last time you took the worries from your chest and really put your trust in someone?”

My fingers looked so small in comparison to his. I distracted myself from the question, watching my neatly manicured nails look tiny beside his.

"I'm not really good at trusting people," I confessed.

"That's something we need to work on."

He caught me off guard with a smile, my heart beating fast when I realized how much I wanted to trust him. I kept running scenarios in my head, but they always ended the same way. Alvaro wasn't here to stay.

I took my hand from his, in need of breathing space. Alvaro noticed the change and stepped back as well, grabbing the back of his neck and turning his eyes to the city once again.

"What I mean is that I'm here to help."

I nodded, more to myself than to him. "I know."

*Until when?*

I had no idea. I wanted to ask, but fear clogged my throat. He wanted me to say when was the last time I completely trusted someone?

*Today.*

When I called a man that did not belong to me to come home.

Trust was something hard to build. And for the first time in my life, I was paralyzed with the fear of failing.

I learned from an early age that failing wasn't an option and now, I had the most important task in my hands.

There were no do overs when it came to the kids. It was the biggest risk I'd ever taken and right when I needed to be perfect, I let myself trust.

I took another step from Alvaro. "I'm going to go..."

"I'll order something for dinner," he offered.

I nodded and hurried away.

*Trust.*

The word kept running through my mind, demanding definition. I went to my office and clutched that checklist I started the first night with the kids.

Practically running, I only spared a glance at the kids to see they were entertained enough and went to my room. I scribbled down everything I needed. Not only physical things, but what I needed to learn, what answers to seek.

Again and again, the knot in my throat wouldn't ease even as I wrote everything down and told myself I just needed a plan.

I said I was doing this myself and I was. It was just a bad day and there will be no bad days if I plan enough.

Taking a breath, I wrote pages upon pages and then kept them on my bed, watching them, adding to them.

Still shaking, still feeling weak.

But I had a plan.

And all a woman needs is a plan.

# 17.

# Alvaro

"Tell me again."

"We are not telling Tita how many times we ordered in food."

I nodded. "What else?"

"Not telling what her house looks like."

"Right, and the most important?"

Vienna took a breath, and for a second I thought she had it. I really thought she did. But her mouth closed in a line, and she refused to talk.

"Can't tell Tita I got suspended, dumbass." Dash shook his head, exasperated. I couldn't even complain about his impatience with his sister. I had been hammering that point since we left Logan's. We were close to my mother's and the information wouldn't stick in Vienna's brain.

"Language, Dash." I sighed. "Vi, this is very important," I tried again.

Vienna shrugged and looked away. I breathed in while holding the steering wheel.

"Vienna." Dash turned on the seat. "I'm in trouble with Tío, already. And the school. But if you tell Tita she'll blame Logan, you get that?"

"Why would she blame Logan? It was all your fault."

I took over before a fight started. "Because it is Logan's job to take care of the three of you. Tita is going to assume Logan is not doing a good job."

"Well, we tell her Logan is doing good." Her nose went up.

I opened my mouth, but Dash beat me to it. "Risk it then. If we end up back with Tita, I'm sure blaming you."

A switch flipped. Vienna found me through the mirror, her eyes full of tears. "Logan won't let that happen, right?"

I blew out a breath. "Of course not, kid. Logan won't let anyone take you from her. She's scrappy."

"Tita is mean," Dash grumbled under his breath.

"Excuse me?" I turned.

He shrugged. "To Logan. I like her. She's nice to me."

He wasn't wrong.

"It's better if they don't fight, Vi," I told my niece. "Just don't tell anyone Dash is suspended. It's a secret, ok?"

This time, she nodded. "I like having secrets."

Odd, but I nodded and kept going, closer and closer to my destination.

Logan needed a break. That much was obvious. She kept going with rare fierce determination, but she needed a minute to remember the world would keep on turning even if she relaxed a little. This morning she said she wasn't feeling good, a headache. I brought Vienna to school and took Dash and Lachlan to the office with me.

The office was just the small room I had under my apartment, but I needed admin work done for the company and I wasn't letting Dashiell stay at home playing video games the whole day after getting himself suspended.

The kids changed my life completely. I thought about them constantly. What did they need? How could we make their lives easier? And when I wasn't thinking about the kids?

I was thinking about their legal guardian.

I couldn't think of anything that wasn't Logan. I thought about her and her little prissy clothes and severe ponytails. I thought about her ass when she was wearing those leggings. I imagined her in ways I shouldn't imagine, but my biggest crime was that I still felt her tit in the palm of my hand.

I told myself a million times I should forget about that morning. I shouldn't be touching her, even if it was my name on her tongue. We were sleeping. It was *accidental* humping, as juvenile as that sounded.

But nothing, not even the devil himself, was going to erase the memory of her soft skin on my rough palm.

I reminded myself she was sixteen years younger and my dead sister's best friend. She was the kids' legal guardian and the woman my mother saw as the enemy. The reasons were plenty. At the end of the day, it didn't matter. Nothing mattered.

I needed a break. A full weekend without Logan, putting much needed distance between us. I was going to fill my nights with whatever used to be enough for me.

When I parked in front of my parent's house, Mamá was already in front, swinging the door open to hug Lachlan like it had been years since she had seen him.

Dash and I exited. He went straight to the house without looking behind, and I opened the door for Vienna. "How's it going?"

"He looks pale." She gave her an assessment of Lachlan.

"Yeah, not many outdoors activities this time of the year," I told her.

She joined me on the sidewalk, her hands now on Vienna. She made noises in the back of her throat as she took in the girl's perfectly good ponytail.

"You're staying for dinner." She told me rather than asking.

"Can't, Mamá." I was already circling the car and going for the driver's seat.

"What do you mean, can't?"

"I still have to drive back and do a few things." I cleared my throat to sidestep my lack of reasons. "I'll be back to pick them up Sunday, ok?"

I never gave her time to agree. I got myself in the car and drove away before she was even inside the house. It was nothing against having dinner with my parents. I actually missed Mamá's food more than I missed not paying my own bills.

It was Friday, I was exhausted, and I had to stop by Logan's to tell her the kids were delivered and we all would be back by Sunday.

I drove in blissful silence and reached the city quicker than I thought possible. I hopped out of my truck, said my hellos to the doorman, and went up straight to the penthouse.

Right as the elevator dinged and the doors opened, I knew something was wrong.

Everything was dark. The living room area looked exactly the way I left in the morning. Even the T-shirt Lachlan spilled orange juice on during breakfast was still laying on top of the table exactly how I left it.

"Logan?" I called out but got no reply.

Starting from the kitchen, I tidied up things a little while I cursed under my breath every time I found a new pair of shoes tucked in a corner.

How many shoes do these children have?

Once everything looked back in place, I dared to go upstairs.

She could have left. It was Friday night. Maybe she was on a date or something.

I rolled my shoulders, pretending that wouldn't bother me, and brushed the idea off. Logan didn't have time for anything. She wasn't swiping right on Tinder when I wasn't looking.

Inching closer to her bedroom, the door wasn't closed. I only had to push. "Logan?"

Something small moved between the sheets, but it was hard to see. The room was still dark, stale air like the door had been left closed for the whole day.

I got inside. "Logan?" I called again.

She moved in the bed, facing my way. I could only see the tip of her head. Everything else was covered by a blanket and darkness. Her dark brown hair was unkempt, her green eyes dull. I went to her, sitting on the edge of the bed. The first thing I did was to bring my palm to her forehead.

"Are you sick?"

"I'm ok," she whispered.

"You don't look ok, Jefa."

"Aren't you charming?"

I wanted to chuckle, but I couldn't summon the humor. She wasn't hot, but her skin was damp to the touch.

"What are you feeling?"

She didn't reply, moving her eyes away from me and rubbing her chest.

"Logan?" I tried again. "You're clearly sick. Tell me what's happening."

"Nothing is happening." She moved to sit up. "Are the kids with your parents?"

I stopped her mid-action. My hand closed on her arms. She had to be sick because I didn't even need to push hard to get her to lie down again.

"Tell me."

"Alvaro..." She sighed. "Go home. Let me be."

"Not happening."

She had black under her eyes and her clothes were the same as she was wearing last night. Not even pajamas. Something wasn't right here.

"If I tell you, will you go?" she bargained.

"Sure." I lied.

Rubbing her forehead, she avoided looking at me.

"I sometimes get a little overwhelmed. It's nothing. I'm not sick."

My eyes narrowed at her little shitty explanation. Clammy skin, rubbing her chest.

"Did you have a panic attack?"

I didn't need to be a doctor to know Logan suffered from anxiety. Anyone could see she accepted nothing but perfection of herself, and if I learned anything in my forty-six years on this earth it's that wishing for perfection left you a disappointed wreck.

My hand came to the curve of her cheek, angling so she couldn't escape my eyes.

"Yes," she replied.

Nodding, I stood up and left the bedroom.

# 18.

# Logan

The second Alvaro left the bedroom, I could breathe in peace. I hated feeling like this, and I wasn't in the mood for an audience. It was one thing to be vulnerable, but to allow myself to do it in front of someone else was inexcusable.

In the back of my mind, I knew I needed a shower and food, but I couldn't move. Each time I tried, I fell back to the bed with a stabbing pain in my chest.

I called it an early failure. When failure was coming for me, and even though it didn't happen yet, my body felt it. My tongue could taste it.

That feeling left a weight over my body and a spear in my heart. My vision was fogged, my arms too weak to move. I stayed in the same position the whole day, allowing twenty minutes to feel sorry for myself and then I'd have to move on.

Time after time, my heart hurt too much to move.

I worked on breathing slowly, letting the air come through my nose and work its way through my body. I needed a plan. That's what I said. I wasn't even giving myself time for a plan.

I squeezed my eyes shut and lied, telling myself I was going for a shower as soon as I dared to open them.

I had no idea how long my eyes stayed closed, but when I opened them again Alvaro was back.

With tea.

"Here." He put the cup on the bedside table.

"What's that?" I peered at the cup.

"Peach tea," he said.

My gaze went for the cup back to him. "What's happening?"

He sighed. "They say herbal tea helps with panic attacks."

I took the tea in my hands. The mug was warm enough to make me feel better, and I took the smallest sip. "Who are they?"

"The internet." He avoided my eyes.

Another sip. "I thought you were leaving."

"I lied."

"Mmm."

I closed my eyes as the warmth spread through my chest. My toes curled in satisfaction when it felt like a blanket over the part that hurt the most.

"Better?" Nodding, I opened my eyes to him. "Tell me what else I can do."

"Nothing," I said too quickly.

"What do you usually do when it happens?"

I hated how eager he was to help. Alvaro was large, built with muscle and tattoos, but it was his soft side that was the most dangerous.

"Shower, change my clothes, change my sheets."

"Ok, so finish your tea and we can do all of that. And I'll order something to eat. What about that Vietnamese place you like?"

He was already moving, fishing his phone from his pocket, and checking on places for delivery.

"It's the weekend. You should go home."

He frowned at my suggestion. "Finish that."

With that order, he left the room, phone in hand.

The tea helped, but I was scared his presence helped more. My shoulders relaxed the second I heard his voice, just like I promised myself wasn't going to happen. Moving the blanket, I found the pile of paper I scribbled on last night. My plan.

I shook my head, placing the cup on the bedside table and hiding it all again under the pillow.

"Done?" he asked, coming back to the room. "Food is coming."

"Thanks." I sat up, getting comfortable, and he arched an eyebrow, making me ask. "What?"

"We are going for a shower."

I rolled my eyes. "It's not a magical solution. I don't have to do all the things and—"

"But it might help, right?" he pushed. "And a shower will be good for everyone."

I blanched. "What do you mean?"

"I mean, you're going for a shower."

There wasn't any room for discussion, especially when he came closer and took me in his arms with impressive ease. My mouth fell open when he stepped away from the bed and I had to lace my hands around his neck.

"What are you doing?"

"Shower, Logan. You're slow when you're sick."

I wanted to correct him to say I wasn't sick, but I felt my muscles melting. His arms were hard but felt heavenly, and before I could think too much about it, he entered my bathroom and dropped me gently on my feet.

The lights were brighter here, but instead of worrying about how I looked, I concentrated on him.

Why did he have to be so hot? Why couldn't he just be a normal guy? Better yet if he was married or something.

I really didn't have time to keep fantasizing about Sofia's big brother. I craned my neck to give him a proper look, and he placed his hand on my cheek. "Do you need more help?"

I should have told him I had it from here, but the words never formed in my mouth. The next thing I knew, he was arching an eyebrow, stepping away from me and turning on the shower.

My knees faltered, feeling wobbly after a day without eating. I held on to the cold tiles beside me and then Alvaro was turning back to me, leaving the shower running. Without a word, his fingers hooked under my blouse and lifted it over my head.

*It was reflex*, I told myself. The reason I raised my arms and let him take my clothes off. My eyes followed the blouse as it fell in a heap on the floor, watching it all like it was a dream. Blinking, I looked at the man in front of me. He smirked as he reached for the claps of my bra around my back.

"I promise I won't look."

My arms out of the way, I let him unclasp my bra, and helped to take the straps from one shoulder and then the other.

*Cold air woke my nipples, not him*. I lied again.

We stood frozen in time for three exact seconds. And then… he looked. His eyes burned, something flashing over his face when he took me in.

"You're a liar," I whispered.

His gaze back to my face, he smirked. "I'm too old to feel embarrassed. Hold on to me."

He took my arm and hooked over his shoulder, bending over to help me out of my pants. His skin was warm and smooth. I had to hold myself back, not to trace the tattoos on his shoulder. The side of my breast brushed against him, and I would have missed his reaction if it wasn't for the strain on his neck.

And it was that vein in his throat and the tautness of his jaw that I was looking at when he helped me out of my pants and underwear. I moved my feet to let them pool under me, now completely naked in front of him.

Alvaro went up to his full height, and this time, he looked me in the eye. I wished he didn't. It was too intense, a million feelings going through them. My skin felt on fire, my toes curling over the cold tiles.

Prepared to turn around and get into the shower by myself, he surprised me, circling his arm around my waist. My hands landed on his chest when he walked us to the shower.

T-shirt, jeans, working boots and all. Water ran over us, my naked body in his hands and he never—not even for a second—let his eyes wander anywhere. They stayed on mine the whole time.

Steam filled the bathroom, and I couldn't think beyond the feeling of Alvaro. The roughness of his jeans against the sensitive parts of my legs. The damp t-shirt on my chest, tickling my nipples every single time I took a breath. His hand carved on my waist and then he let me go, my legs unsteady on their own.

He only moved for a second, reaching to the side to grab my shower gel and applying a generous amount to the palm of his hand.

Lathering it over my stomach, I looked down in nothing but complete shock as his rough hands served as a luffa. Over my navel, up to my ribs and closing on my back.

"You're all wet," I managed to croak.

"I bet you are too."

My flush came with vengeance. I couldn't hide it even if I wanted to. My cheeks warmed, and he groaned.

"Jesus, every time you blush, Logan."

"What?" I asked with my mouth dry.

"I want to eat you whole."

The hands lathering soap over my back, fell to my ass. He brought me closer. My legs fell open when he positioned his thigh right between them. His jeans were in contact with my clit and I couldn't hold back. I whimpered, and he followed, his head falling down, his breathing coming out ragged.

"Be a good girl and ask me to check if you're wet, Logan."

My head tilted back. He looked down at me with his jaw set. I could tell him the truth. I was. I couldn't stop thinking about his piercings and I barely held it together when he looked at me.

Now in his arms? I was melting. Something unraveled deep inside and all that heartache and the need to be the perfect Logan Hart was nowhere to be found.

"Alvaro?" I rasped.

"Tell me." His voice was a whisper, low, so deep it vibrated within my chest.

"Check if I'm wet."

In one quick move he pinned me against the tiles, shock leaving my body in the form of a gasp. Alvaro took my chin between his fingers angling me up like he was going to kiss me, but instead, he smirked. His thumb swiped across my bottom lip, and then he went on his knees.

This mountain of a man, the MMA fighter, kneeled in front of me. He pulled my leg over one shoulder, my hand holding to the other when I felt like falling.

My head bumped back with an audible thud when I felt his mouth taking me. Like he needed no invitation. He was Alvaro Castillo, after all. His tongue circled my clit just once before he sucked and my knees gave out completely.

Holding my leg with his palm, Alvaro chuckled between my legs. "Hold yourself together, Jefa. I'm just starting."

A moan ripped from my throat as he kept working. Slow torturous swipes of his tongue, his arms built in muscle under my fingertips and my brain couldn't connect I had Alvaro Castillo there.

It was the man from the tapes, the power in the MMA cage. He was older, stronger, and a force of nature. I watched a man three times my size last less than a minute against Alvaro.

And it was that man kneeling for me, making me moan like I never have for another man.

His mouth rested, taking a break from undoing me. He brought his thumb over my clit. "You taste so good, Logan. Tell me I can have it. I can drink from you as much as I crave."

I wanted to tell him all that, but it only came out a whimper of his name, "Alvaro..."

"You're pink everywhere." He opened my pussy with his thumb and forefinger and slowly licked me. "That blush of yours makes me crazy. I want to see it on your cheeks, on your nipples." He sucked again. "Look at you. Not so in control anymore, are you?"

That I could answer. I shook my head desperately. It was the furthest I've been from control. I couldn't even talk or move if it wasn't for him telling me what to do.

"I want you to let it go," he said, teasing my clit. "I'm going to tell you what to do and you'll just do it."

I moaned louder. He licked me so good, and I couldn't hold myself up when I felt his finger edging inside. He put two in at once, and I shuddered.

"Come on, Logan, trust that I have you. I know what you need. You can relax. You can let me take control because I've got you."

No one ever had me. That took the breath out of me, and I looked down facing him with my eyebrows scrunched in question and he nodded, answering my silent question.

"I've got you. I'm going to make you come so good. I know what you need. Just trust me."

Trusting was a dangerous game. I didn't want to do much of that if I was being honest. But I never wanted to trust in something so badly in my life. My eyes pinned on him. I jerked a nod.

His fingers worked faster than ever, inside and out, as his tongue licked my clit in an unforgivable pace. Alvaro added another finger, making me cry out loud. Impossibly delicious. His fingers curved, hitting me in the right place, and I felt my throat scratch as I called his name.

"Logan, fuck..." he murmured between lavishing me with his tongue. It was like he needed to say my name.

I kept calling for god, calling for Alvaro himself. My hand moved to his head, taking the buzzed cut under my palm. I shoved his head over my pussy and fucked his mouth.

Having Alvaro like that felt like take and release. In control because he kneeled. Out of it, when he asked me to trust.

My voice failed and I came, my hips moving and looking for friction, making Alvaro groan as he kept licking me.

"Tell me, Jefa," he growled. "Who owns you?"

My head hit the tiles, eyes opening with the irrevocable truth. "You."

# 19
# Alvaro

I REACHED QUICKLY FOR the towel, bringing it over her shoulders, covering her up. Her taste was on the tip of my tongue, my cock impossibly hard against my zipper. It took everything in me not to throw her against the tiles and fuck her within an inch of her life, but that was a bad idea.

Everything was a bad idea. Fucking up my relationship with Logan wasn't an option. Not only because she was the kids' legal guardian, but because I wanted to help.

I truly fucking wanted to help, and that realization slammed against my chest. And by helping her, I didn't mean with my fucking dick.

Taking a step back, I nodded to the room.

"Go ahead and get dressed."

She blinked at me. Her fingers gripping the towel, it didn't cover her completely, it had a gap right in the middle showing me her navel and down to her pussy.

*Shit.*

"I have more towels under the sink," she told me, her voice far away.

Maybe I fucked her pussy with my tongue so hard, it changed something in her because this wasn't the Logan

I knew. Her voice was softer, her eyes unfocused. Seeing that she wasn't turning away, I sighed and got moving.

I peeled off my soaked T-shirt, toed off my boots, and dragged down my jeans. I looped my fingers over the band of my underwear and looked up, catching her eyes while she watched me.

"Logan, go get dressed."

She tilted her head to the side, curious eyes still unblinking, zoomed in on the bulge in my boxers.

Groaning, I wrapped a towel around my waist and grabbed her shoulders.

"Come on, Jefa..." I practically begged her.

I guided her back to the bedroom and thank god she followed without complaining. I made sure to wrap the towel securely around her body, afraid to catch a sight of anything that made me change my mind about being good. Right then, the intercom chimed.

"Get dressed," I told her once again. "I'll get our food."

Before she could react, I turned and went to my room, throwing the wet underwear to the corner and grabbing sweatpants and a t-shirt. I jogged to the elevator, only letting the air out of my lungs slowly as it made its descent to the ground floor.

Rubbing my face on my palm, I cursed. I barely had time to count the ways this was a bad idea, and the doors were opening again. I met the delivery man and paid him, my mind still on Logan upstairs.

She was feeling like shit and yet her body melted in my hands, and it wasn't just because I made her come. She needed someone to lean on. Even if made me feel like a fucking king, I couldn't be that person to Logan.

I grabbed knives and forks, water, and a couple of trays so we could eat in bed. I was sure she wasn't up for anything else right now.

My theory was proved correct when I arrived back at her room and she was still in her towel, sitting on her bed and looking at the wall.

"Logan..." I sighed and went to her, leaving the food and utensils on the top of the dresser before kneeling in front of her. "What's going on?"

"You regret it." Her voice was small. "The second it ended. I saw you regretting it."

"That's not it." I defended myself.

Logan made a noise from the back of her throat, something ugly and self-deprecating I didn't like. She took her hands from mine and tried to put space between us.

I was quicker, taking her in my arms and flushing our bodies together, I stood up. Her legs parted and I fit between them. She held on to my shoulders as the useless towel fell on the floor, and I sat back down with her straddling my legs.

"You think I'm regretting what just happened or that I don't want you?" I asked, causing her eyes to narrow and her back to stiffen.

Tsking, I brought her hips down, making her feel how hard she made me. "That's not it."

"It's ok." She tried getting up from my lap. "The food is getting cold."

I gripped her thighs, not letting her move. "That's the thing, Jefa. You always have all the answers. But tell me you didn't love when I took control?"

The blush took over her cheeks. She shook her head. "Alvaro..."

I couldn't hold back the chuckle. "Don't make assumptions about me. If you want to know something, ask."

Slowly, she faced me. Her eyes narrowing with distrust like I talked shit for sport. Logan lowered herself back, her tits grazing my t-shirt, and I regretted this damn game I started.

"So why didn't you let me suck you off, Alvaro? Wasn't it something you wanted?"

She killed me by keeping eye contact. My cock jumped and begged for her mouth. I didn't go for it though.

"Yes..." I confessed. "But—"

Logan's eyebrows lifted to her hairline. "You think this is a bad idea."

"I *know* it's a bad idea."

She blew a breath, making her tits jiggle. In the next second, she was nodding. Fucking agreeing with me.

"It's a very bad idea." Her leg moved so she could roll away from me, but I held her in place once more.

"It doesn't mean it's not tempting as fuck."

She laughed, and this time I couldn't keep it to myself. I took a nipple in my mouth, groaning when I had it. Logan rasped a moan and before she could recover from the surprise, I took the other nipple.

"You're giving me mixed signals."

"I'm having a snack because I know I can't have the full serving."

"I really should point out how flawed your reasoning is," she told me. "But I don't want to."

Instead of stopping me, she held my head to her tits, letting me lick them as I pleased. Her hips worked on top of me, her pussy rubbing against my cock to a point I was ready to spill in my sweatpants.

The material was thin, and Logan was hot and needy. I licked between her breasts, nipped her shoulder and she worked me, riding, and letting me imagine how delicious it would be if I were buried inside her.

With all my strength, I held her hips, stopping her mid-action. "I'm not coming in my pants," I growled.

"But in my gym is ok?" she cocked an eyebrow.

Momentarily out of words, my face showed my surprise, making her smirk and lower her mouth to my ear. "I watched when you fucked your hand in my gym."

My hands clutched to her, the smooth skin under my palm. She moved again, and I let her. "Did you like what you saw?"

I raised my hips, letting her feel a little more, and she moaned her answer. "I loved it."

"You watched it all?"

"Until you finished."

"I bet you were so wet for me."

Logan picked up the pace, using the bed for purchase to keep an unforgivable pace. The muscles in my lower stomach tightened. I worked my hips up and down, fucking her even with my sweatpants between us.

"You're pierced, Alvaro." She moaned.

"I am, Jefa. You like it?"

Like I asked for something impossible to reply to. She tilted her head up, rotating her hips, looking for friction. I took her chin between my fingers, angling her head to me. The other hand I brought down and between us, my thumb over her clit, but unmoving.

"Tell me how many times you imagined my pierced cock inside you."

"Alvaro please..."

I didn't move, waiting for the answer. "Talk," I barked.

Logan's green eyes were never so pure. I thought I knew everything about her, but that smile was a promise she had secrets of her own.

"I think about it constantly. You're not giving it to me, so I have to imagine it every single day."

"I'll give it to you when I think it's time."

No. I should have said we were never crossing that line. But I made a promise to the wind, something that made her breath catch. Taking pity on us, I moved my thumb over her clit and she rode faster and faster, undoing me from the bottom up.

When she came, head thrown back and my name on her lips, I followed her just after.

Keeping my hands to myself was going to be impossible.

"You should go home," she said with an arched eyebrow and a mouthful of eggs.

"Big words for someone who is eating the breakfast I made."

Last night we ate the food I ordered and watched something together. Logan didn't take long to fall asleep, and I went back to my room.

I woke up this morning with a raging hard on and wondering why I didn't stay with her in bed. We did it once. And we did it well. If I had, I'd have woken up with her body all over me and not alone and frustrated.

Logan tried the toast. "I'm fine. It's Saturday. Don't you have stuff to do?"

"I'm usually working or at the gym." I shrugged.

The mention of the gym had her blushing like crazy, and I liked that far too much. The idea Logan was spying on me was the best thing I heard in a long time. I loved that she confessed to watching until the end.

"All I'm saying is that I'm ok. Everything's fine."

"Sure. No one said it wasn't."

"Alvaro." She set her fork down.

"What do you do on the weekends?"

She frowned. "Meet up with Willa or read. It's not very exciting."

"No. What do you want to do today?"

Yeah, it would be wise to go home. Look what happened the first time we didn't have the kids as chaperones?

It didn't matter how many times Logan kept saying she was ok, I didn't quite believe her. After she fell asleep, I found a pile of paper under her pillow.

She was making a checklist of impossible things. An unattainable plan to be a better guardian for the kids.

I appreciated all the effort, but she was killing herself. An overachiever was never truly done. She'd need a lifetime to finish everything she wanted to perfect.

It wasn't my place, but suddenly it was my mission. I wanted to take the burden off her shoulders.

"Have you ever learned self-defense?" I asked, finishing up my plate.

Logan brought her knees up and hugged them. "No."

"What do you think about that?"

"You want to teach me self-defense?" She looked surprised.

I didn't like how surprised she sounded, so I played safe. "Yeah, why not?"

In reality, I knew anxious people like her could use self-defense. Even if she never needed it, and I hoped she didn't, it was a way to feel powerful.

She nodded quickly. "What do I need?"

"Just comfortable clothes."

Logan jumped to her feet and disappeared upstairs to change.

At least today, I'd do something right.

I cleaned up as she changed her clothes and headed upstairs as well.

Logan came in with leggings, sneakers, a high ponytail, and a Harvard sweatshirt. To distract myself from watching her ass, I snorted. "What's up with people and the Ivy League sweatshirt?"

She looked down at it with a frown. "I got this during freshman week. It's the comfiest thing I own."

"Of course it is. Come on, show me how you stand."

She blinked at me and moved her hands like saying *ta-da*. Ok, that was how she stood.

Chuckling, I rubbed a hand over my mouth. It was getting annoying peeling back the layers of her personality. She was cute as fuck, standing there being sassy.

"I meant your stance. Legs apart, left foot in front of right foot." She did what I said straight away.

It wasn't bad. She had strong legs and good posture. I circled around, holding her hips and pressing them down a little. Strong on her feet, I asked next, "Show me the hands?"

She brought her hands up closed in a fist, and it was as bad as you could imagine. If she ever punched someone, she was going to break her own thumbs.

"You have a punching bag in here. How come you can't punch?"

Logan lifted a shoulder. "I asked for a home gym. I didn't exactly choose each item."

I hummed under my breath, not sure what to do with that information. If it wasn't for the penthouse, I'd forget how rich Logan was. She acted normal. She never mentioned money at all. But I guessed, money wasn't something constantly in your mind when you had it.

She paid for the kids' tuition, dropping fifty grand in one rip of her checkbook without batting an eyelid. She never cared about the status of them going to Lone Pine. Never bored the kids telling them what kind of friends they should be making. Not that being friends with the right people was something Dash would do, but for a rich girl born and raised in money, Logan didn't seem to care about it at all.

I fixed her fist, and she punched the air. Looking happy, she faced me with a smile.

"Not bad," I told her with a twitch of my upper lip.

"How did you get into MMA?"

"I tried once at the gym after school."

Logan tilted her head. "And then you fought your parents for it?" She snorted. "There's more to it. It's something you love."

"Come on, try hitting the punching bag." I tugged her hand and brought her to the other side of the room. "Have a go."

She punched the bag. Not bad, but I made a few corrections and nodded so she would try again. As Logan punched, I let myself talk.

"I wasn't good at school or any other sport. I tried football because everyone thought I'd be great."

"Cause you were truck sized even as a teen?" she asked, blowing a strand of hair falling in front of her eyes.

I smirked. "Of course."

Logan punched the bag again, much better this time. I stopped her, afraid she'd hurt her hands since she had no gloves.

"Just one more?" she asked.

It was becoming obvious I couldn't say no to her. I nodded my permission.

She tried a couple of times more.

"Football wasn't for me. Nothing was for me, but when I got my ass inside the cage for the first time?" I couldn't stop the smile. "It felt good to be good at something."

She punched the bag again. "I know what you mean."

I arched an eyebrow, looking straight at her Harvard sweatshirt. Logan stopped punching and followed my eyes. Brushing her hair back, she shrugged.

"That was my MMA. I never had many friends besides Sofia. I wasn't pretty, and I was my mother's disappointment."

I laughed. "I know you're pulling my leg. You couldn't be a disappointment even if you tried hard."

"Now, that's the sweetest thing you ever said to me." She stepped away and reached for the bottle of water by the weights. "My mom is the head of multiple clubs. She plans events for charity. She's... she's likable. Everyone loves her. And her only daughter is..." Logan blew out a breath.

"Academics were the only place I felt like I could manage. Maybe I wasn't as smiling and likable as my mom wanted me to be. Maybe I didn't care about the same things, but I was smart, and I could handle school."

I nodded. "I guess you do know what I mean."

"Was it worth it?" she asked next.

I wondered how much she knew of the situation. I never stopped talking to my parents, and they didn't exclude me from the major holidays. We were Cubans, there was no escaping your family. But Mamá was always clear how good I could have turned out. A career as a professional athlete and a business of my own wasn't enough.

"At times. What about you?"

"I regret."

"Regret being smart and going to Harvard?" I snorted. Why would she regret that?

"I should have stayed and insisted on Sofia leaving him," she told me at once, her jaw set.

I hated Sofia's ex as much as the next guy, but I doubt her shitty relationship was enough to throw Harvard out the window. "Logan—"

"No." She shook her head. "Your mom always wanted me out and my mom thought I could have better friends at Harvard. Everything fell so perfectly into place for him. He wanted me away from Sofia, and he got his wish."

I swallowed something bad, my skin prickling with raised hairs as I asked. "What do you mean by that? Why did David want to end your friendship with Sofia?"

"Because that's what they do, right? They isolated their victim and they..."

"Stop right there," I urged her.

Logan stepped closer, tilting her head and looking at me like we were seeing each other for the first time. “How much do you know about David and Sofia?”

I knew enough. He was a piece of crap. Bad partner, shitty dad. Two years ago, she finally left, and he disappeared into thin air. Never came to visit his children. He barely knew Lachlan. He wasn’t at the funeral and wasn’t interested in taking the kids to raise.

“Tell me what you mean by that?” I asked instead of answering her.

Logan hugged herself. “David, at school…” she closed her eyes for a second. “I never liked him.” I nodded. I suspected that much. “He was always bossing Sofia around, telling her what she could do or how to dress. At first, she would listen to me and ask him to shut up. But she was a teenager. She was in love. And then…”

Then she got pregnant.

“She was scared and he… he was happy.”

I reeled back. “What do you mean?”

“He said they were going to have children together anyway, so why wait? She wasn’t sure at first, but David was so freaking happy.”

“They were children,” I said. “There’s no way they were happy.”

“I tried to talk to her, but David told her I was jealous. No one wanted to be my friend but Sofia, and I didn’t want to share her.”

Logan let out a sad chuckle. “He was right. David changed her. Sofia was my family. She told me she believed David about that and I… believed too. We were still friends until graduation. I stepped back and let them be a family. Your mom… we all knew she was grateful. To everyone, I was poison. I was the one filling Sofia's head. When I got accepted to Harvard, I don't know. My parents were so proud, so happy. I had to move away and..."

She stopped herself, rubbing her forehead. "I don't know why she wanted me to have the kids, you know? I should have stayed with her and trusted my instincts. I fucked it up."

This was the moment I was waiting for. The truth I was so scared of asking. In a flash, I stepped in. "What did David Murphy do to my sister?"

Logan parted her lips. I hated how she looked at me right then. Like I knew nothing. I assumed Sofia was depressed. I assumed it was my fault because I wasn't around to help her through it.

It was still my fault. But now, it was my fault for not killing David Murphy.

"I'm not sure exactly. She never told me the details. We drifted apart when I left for college. She stopped answering my emails. I don't know if she was getting them. Two years ago, when she left David, she found me on social media. We started talking. She told me I was right. She said David wasn't right in the head." I growled. Logan went to touch my chest, but I moved away. "Alvaro? I thought you knew."

"I knew he was a piece of shit." My words tasted sour.

"I don't know if he ever hurt her," she said, and I knew it was to make me calmer, but it didn't work.

"Something happened if she killed herself, Logan!" I exploded.

"Two years after she left him," she said. "That's not—"

"You said it yourself, you regret leaving for Harvard."

Why would she, if not to prevent Sofia's death? She blamed herself because she was the only one who saw how bad the situation was when none of the adults truly understood. I was one of the adults.

To me, Sofia was just a teen that got herself in a bad situation. I never spared a thought about David Murphy besides him being an ass.

Blood was pumping through my veins at a worrying speed as I stood there in the middle of my worst nightmare. Logan bit her lip. I could almost taste how uncomfortable she was for being the one who gave me the truth. But she was the beacon of fucking light.

Coming back to her, I gripped her chin, angling her up to me so she stared right back into my eyes.

"You did good. You were the only one trying to protect her. I don't want to hear it. You were the only one who tried."

Her face twisted as fat tears rolled down. I cleaned them with my thumb, my hand shaking with the grief, anger, and everything else that washed over me.

"I guess I was right," I whispered to her. "You couldn't be a disappointment even if you tried."

I wished I was man enough to stay behind and hold her while she cried from guilt. But I bolted after that, unable to carry the weight for a second longer. My skin burned, stretched over my bones like it didn't fit me right.

And I found myself at Paddy's gym.

# 20.
# Logan

He left Saturday after breakfast and never came back.

I tried not to be upset. After all, I told him he should leave. I was fine. It wasn't my first panic attack and, unfortunately, I knew it wouldn't be my last.

I curled further in the bed, my eyes on the TV forcing myself to watch the movie.

Alone.

I checked my smartwatch. It was past six. I wondered if he was staying at his mother's, and they were going to have dinner together. They might even spend the night. Maybe he was bringing them to school directly.

I brushed off that thought. I knew he wouldn't do that without letting me know first.

My whole body shook with a shiver that wasn't due to cold or sickness. I just felt so… fragile.

I had a panic attack, and then I came twice at the hands of Sofia's older brother. And if that wasn't enough to shake me… I spilled my guts about David.

No proof, just like fifteen years ago. Sofia never confirmed my suspicions, she just said David wasn't the person he appeared to be. That could have meant a million things. I knew nothing, really.

Nothing about family life, like Caridad suspected.

Nothing about people. I had no friends, like David once told me.

I just had Sofia.

Now, I had Sofia's kids.

The phone in my hands, I wondered if I should call Willa and let her cheer me up, but I didn't have the courage to dial her number. I just looked at my phone, waiting for a text from Alvaro that never came.

Finally, after seven, the door opened downstairs. I froze in my spot, noticing I was still wearing the Harvard sweatshirt from yesterday and cursing myself for not looking more put together.

The kids were loud, and my heart relaxed when their noise filled my house once again. Dash ran up the stairs two at a time, waving at me over his shoulder when he went straight to his room, barely looking at my opened door.

I sat up, a smile on my lips. Then Vienna barged in. She didn't even say hello, never said a word. She just jumped on my bed and held me in a powerful hug.

"Vienna?" I asked, confused.

"Tío said you were sick," she said, her head buried in my chest.

I relaxed in her hands, hugging her back. "I'm ok, Vi."

She never let me go, like her little arms could bring me closer to her than I already was. We stayed like that for a full minute, but it was my hand on her back that felt the little tremors in her breathing.

Slowly, I brought us down to the bed. She let me lay with her. I kissed her hair and whispered, "Vi, tell me what's wrong."

It took her a long minute to let me put space between us so I could look straight into her red-rimmed eyes.

"I don't want you to be sick."

"I had nothing serious." What the hell did Alvaro tell them? "I'm ok."

"I don't want you to be sick, ever," she told me with the determination of a Castillo.

I couldn't help but chuckle. "I'll be sick sometimes. Everyone gets sick sometimes."

"Mom was sick a lot and now she's not here."

"What do you mean, your mom got sick a lot?"

Vienna let me move, my hand over her cheeks, brushing the hairs back from her damp face.

"She told me once she was sick on the inside. She had a bunch of scars, but they were all invisible." She frowned. "Are your scars invisible, too?"

Yes. Our worst scars weren't visible to anyone.

I didn't say that to the crying eight-year-old in my arms, though. I just shook my head and brought my pink finger between us.

"What if I promise you I'll never leave you?"

"Can you promise that?" She wasn't sure.

I shook the pinky at her. "I'd never break a pinky promise. Come on."

Vienna looped her finger into mine, a small smile already blooming.

"I'll never leave you. I'll always be here to protect you."

"Tío Alvaro, too?"

I opened my mouth to say I couldn't make promises in his name when he appeared at the door. Lachlan in his arms. He looked different from when he left.

"What are you girls doing in bed?"

As he asked, Lachlan squirmed in his arms to get free. Alvaro lowered him down and the boy zoomed across the bedroom and hopped on the bed.

He was on my side, so I helped him up and he came to my lap quickly. I kissed his cheek. "How are you, buddy?"

Lachlan didn't answer, but he leaned back, getting comfortable on my chest and making me shake differently now. Alvaro must have noticed my expression, because when I glanced up to see if he caught that, he was smiling.

"What about pizza?"

AFTER THE CUDDLE FEST, feeling more like myself, and pizza I poured a generous glass of wine. His firm steps coming down the stairs made me glance up.

"Wine?"

"I'll grab a beer."

Coming behind me, Alvaro opened the fridge. I heard the can opening as I placed the wine bottle to the side, taking a long sip with my eyes closed.

"Lachlan?" I asked.

"Sleeping."

"Vienna too?"

"Yep."

I turned to face him. "Dashiell?"

"Playing video games, but I'll kick his ass to bed soon enough."

We stood one in front of the other, him holding his beer and me with my wine. I said nothing until my eyes landed on his knuckles.

They were hurt. I moved closer to him by instinct.

"What happened?"

Alvaro practically jumped to his feet, his eyes glazing over the hurt and shaking his head. "Don't worry about it."

I wanted to worry, but I had to respect his privacy. Instead of poking in his life, I took a breath and directed us to something away from all the topics we had to discuss.

"Do you want to watch a movie?"

He smiled slowly. "Yeah. That sounds good."

I was always direct, but this time around, I didn't want to ask him where he went and why he was coming back with bloody knuckles. The questions were on the tip of my tongue, but instead, I moved to the media room with Alvaro on my heels.

He helped me choose something to watch, a movie everyone was talking about. I finished my first glass of wine and filled up again, stopping by the fridge to get him a beer.

We were halfway into the movie when he moved, turning his body to mine and stretching his arms over the back of the couch.

"I saw your face when the kids were in bed with you, Jefa."

I smiled. "I know."

"You were so fucking happy. You really want this, don't you?"

Maybe it was the wine, but I looked him dead in the eyes and nodded. "I really want this. Even if—"

"Tell me."

I brought my legs up and hugged my knees. "Aren't you tired of my secrets?"

"Jamás."

Before I could laugh it off, he reached over, his arm on my back dragging me to his side of the couch. Like it wasn't a big deal, he moved me completely, like I was a little doll he was allowed to play with.

My legs over his lap, my whole body was beside his.

"Tell me," he asked again.

Warmth spreading over my chest, I tilted my head with a smile playing on my lips, "You're going to miss it, you know? It's easy to see people as a cardboard version of themselves. But you keep prying me open and I'll be a complete human. And then what, Alvaro? What are you going to do when I'm just completely flawed, like everyone else?"

His eyes traced my features. From the curve of my cheek to one eye and the other. "I don't know what I am going to do with you, Logan."

I sensed vulnerability in his tone, raising all the hairs on the back of my neck. The words flew out of me.

"I always had a lot of pain." I swallowed, deciding to just rip the band aid off. "I spent my twenties in and out of surgery until they took it all from me. The doctor said it was endometriosis."

"What does that mean?" A crease formed between his brows.

"I can't have children."

I stopped for a second, not sure how I could connect the dots of my convoluted thoughts.

"Growing up, my home life wasn't... Caridad always hated me because she thought with my influence Sofia would want things she couldn't give her, but the truth was—I was the one wishing for things I couldn't have." An empty chuckle left me. "I wanted love, a warm family. I always wished for a family like Sofia's. Like yours. I thought I was going to get the chance by making my own family and then..." I took a big breath, preferring to look down at my lap instead of at the man in front of me. "I just wanted to be somebody's mom. I wanted to be the family for a child who needed one as well so we could be there for one another. I wanted it so bad that sometimes I feel like my envy..."

I squeezed my eyes shut. That part was hard. Embarrassing. It wasn't like I did anything. I didn't. But all the feelings were so messed up inside.

"I loved her with all my heart, Alvaro," I tried to explain. "She was the only person who ever loved me for who I am. My parents like the idea of who I could be, not the real Logan. My dates liked my last name, my status. Sofia didn't give a crap about any of that. She knew me. And I feel so guilty, because I want the kids. I want them so bad."

The tears rolled down my cheeks and, taking all the courage I had, I looked up and faced him. "I want to care for them. I want to love them. But Alvaro..." I hiccupped. "I feel so guilty because it feels like I took them from her. I know she asked me to take care of them, but still. I just want them so bad sometimes I don't know if it was my will who got them to me. Now I have everything I've ever wanted, but Sofia is dead."

# 21

# Alvaro

Logan was right. Life was easier when people were just a cardboard version of themselves. She was complete in my eyes now. All those little parts of her were transparent, even the ones she didn't want to show.

She looked at me with eyes full of tears, hands trembling, and I did the only thing I could. I brought her to my chest and kissed her hair.

My guilt mixed with hers, the poisonous vice gripping our hearts and bringing us together.

Feeling sick to my stomach, I thought of how badly I let my mother treat Logan, even when she was the only one who tried to be there for Sofia. Logan gripped my T-shirt, pulling herself closer, her face buried in my chest.

The woman in my arms was all goodness, and I wanted to rip the world apart for her. End every person who ever put the idea in her head that she was unlikable.

This girl?

No.

"I don't know who the hell told you're not likable, Logan Hart. You're probably the only thing about this goddamn earth I like."

On Wednesday, she asked me to pick up Vienna and Dash because Dr. Maya rescheduled the session with Lachlan and she was going to be late.

Vienna bawled the entire way back. Dash snapped at her. And while I wanted him to be nice to his sister, I understood his frustration.

She was crying and neither of us knew what to do.

"Can't wait for you to have this problem on your own," I told him over the wailing.

He was in the passenger seat, his eyes on the window, but he spun my way. "You know about that?"

"That you're a dumbass?" I chuckled. "Yeah, I know."

"She's not like that all the time."

"No," I agreed. "Sometimes is enough, though." With a sigh, I looked in the rearview mirror. "Vienna, can you tell us what's wrong?"

She shook her head and looked away and cried the rest of the way home.

Her cry became a sniffle as we rode the elevator up, but Dash and I were too skeptical to trust it was the end. When we arrived, Logan was playing with Lachlan on the floor.

He was laughing.

"Hello, there," I announced my arrival.

She looked up from the game with the biggest smile and fuck if she wasn't beautiful.

I didn't know what to do with Logan anymore. I couldn't keep going down this road. I was damaged goods.

I couldn't give her the life she wanted with the happily ever after and the picket fence.

It was getting harder to resist, though.

Before I replied, Vienna ran to Logan for a hug.

"Are you crying?" she asked and turned her attention to us. "Why is she crying?"

"That's a great question. We forgot to ask." Dash rolled his eyes.

"You're rude *and* dumb?" I eyed my nephew. "You have to pick one, man." By his narrowing eyes, he didn't like it so much when someone else was being a smartass.

Logan ignored us both, concentrating on Vienna. "What's happening?"

"Lilah told me I can't sit with them anymore."

"Why?"

She shrugged and cried again. I pinched the back of my neck. That was the reason we were tortured the last half an hour? Some snotty little b-witch called Lilah didn't want to sit with my niece, and now I had to deal with it after a full day of work? Again, I turned, smiling to Dash. "Good luck. Why don't you take this one?"

"Shut up," he mumbled.

"Hey," Logan called out. "What's up with you two? Why is everyone in a bad mood?"

"Because Vienna cried our ears off." Dash shook his head.

Logan took Vienna's face in her palms. "You don't need lots of friends. You just need a good one, remember? If Lilah doesn't want to sit with you, that's her loss, got it?"

Vienna nodded.

Logan looked around at everyone's face. "I was waiting for you all to get here to see if you wanted to go out. I want to celebrate."

We all groaned.

She put her hand on her waist. "That won't do."

"Why did you want to celebrate?" I asked as she moved away, grabbing her phone.

"I don't want to spoil it with your bad mood."

"Maybe it's not a reason to celebrate at all. Tell us first," Dash argued.

She looked away from her phone and came to him with her hand extended. "If I'm right and you agree with me that it's a reason to celebrate, then you'll do it. My way."

Dash scoffed. "Sure, what if I don't?"

"I bring them to dinner, but you can order in."

Deciding that being alone was enough of a bargain for him, Dash shook Logan's hand.

Turning to everyone, still with that unbreakable smile, she announced, "Lachlan talked today!"

Everyone lost their shit. Vienna stopped crying right away, jumping to her feet. My mouth opened and even Dash had no words.

"How?" "When?" "What?" We all talked at once.

She shook her head. "It was only a word, and it was in Dr. Maya's office. We were building up to this for a long time. She said it's big that he's starting to trust. It's a long process though." She shook her head. "But it was a big deal." And turning to Dash. "Right?"

He couldn't say anything else. There wasn't an answer but to nod and agree. It was a huge deal.

"Dinner then?" he said, blowing out a breath.

"Well, that too," she said, going for her phone again.

Without a word, she pressed play on a song and looked at us expectantly. Moving her hips awkwardly, she chuckled. "Come on."

The kids moved straight away, Vienna and Lachlan on their feet holding hands, they started dancing. I looked at Dash, expecting to see that annoyed teen expression, but he wasn't wearing it.

He had his mouth opened.

"That's mom's screaming song," he said, almost in a whisper to himself.

"Well, *Let's get Loud* is Sofia's and my screaming song. But I'm glad she passed along the tradition."

"Come on, tío!" Vienna grabbed my hand to dance. "You just need to dance and scream when the music says..." She screamed mid-sentence. My guess was the cue arrived before she finished explaining the game.

Lachlan was doing a toddler jump, where they just bend their knees trying to leave the ground, but it's not quite there yet.

"You have neighbors, you know?" I smirked at Logan.

She shrugged and when the cue in the music came around again, telling everyone to get loud, we all followed at the top of our lungs. Even Dash.

He wasn't necessarily dancing, but he was there, screaming in the right places, laughing at Lachlan's baby jumps.

Logan sang in Spanish with the same enthusiasm she sang in English, egging on the kids to dance. And when the music died out and they were all out of breath, her smile was the biggest.

"Everyone, go change," she called. "I'm bringing you to my favorite restaurant."

Not needing another incentive, Vienna raced to the stairs.

Dash took Lachlan without complaining, and they all moved to their respective rooms.

I turned to her; her cheeks blushed. Another song was playing in the background, softer this time.

Reaching for her, Logan let me take her hand in mine, her eyes following the movement while the other curled around her waist.

We swayed together, her skin feeling so smooth under my fingertips.

"That was a huge win," I told her. "What did he say?"

"Hi." She giggled.

I smiled, dancing with her in my arms when I promised myself so many times I was going to stay away. The woman had enough problems.

Logan's fingers came to my temple, smoothing the lines. "I love when you laugh."

"I like to see you happy, Jefa." I told her the cleanest of my truths.

"Today was a good day. I want to make it last."

"So we go to your fancy restaurant."

"How do you know it'll be fancy?"

"I'm just guessing."

Instead of being offended, she laughed, throwing her head back. "I'm tempted to bring you all to a taco truck just to see your face."

I shook my head, twirling her around with the soft song. "Instead, where are we going?"

"It's not that fancy. A tapas restaurant." But she giggled. "We deserve today."

"You deserve every day, nena."

Her big green eyes watched me with a mix of innocence and dare. This woman was my undoing. That much was obvious. Before I could catch myself, my thumb grazed over her lips.

"We've never kissed," she whispered.

I nodded. I didn't have an explanation for that. Maybe if I avoided kissing her, I could walk away. Maybe if I didn't give her this one thing, she would understand we weren't meant to be.

I watched the different colors inside her emerald green eyes changing. The dark shades mixing with the light. I had no business feeling this protective over this girl, but all I wanted was to hold her close and fix her damn life. Take care of her.

And before I remembered I was a mess, I took her mouth.

Soft and warm, like I knew it was going to be. My hand angled bringing her to me, and even though I wanted to make it sweet, I pushed further, licking her bottom lip and groaning into her as she opened her mouth. Soon, her tongue was touching mine, twisting, tasting. Her hands gripped the front of my T-shirt like she needed me. My hands fell from her face and down her shoulders. One took her hips, bringing her closer, and the other stopped under her ribs.

The taste of her alone was incredible. Sweet, minty, and all Logan. She let me lead the kiss, turning and moving her and being perfect like she always was.

She laced her hand around my neck, bringing me down and biting my bottom lip, pulling a growl out of me. My need for her was bigger than I ever experienced.

I had never wanted someone like I wanted Logan Hart.

I wanted her splayed out on my bed. I wanted her riding me and being mine in every way. For a second, I let myself imagine.

Pretended we weren't two fucked up souls who were attached to each other because of a tragedy.

In that moment, she was mine to keep. And I wanted to keep her.

Fuck, I *had* to keep her.

# 22.
# Logan

"Why not?"

"Because..."

"You don't have a reason."

I didn't. I cut the sandwich and put it in Vienna's lunch box for the next day, avoiding Dashiell's exasperated gaze.

Vienna wanted to take drama after school. I was happy she was taking an interest in extracurricular activities, but it meant I'd have to go back to pick her up an hour and a half after Dash.

He wanted to get on the bus.

"You're new to the city." I grabbed a peach to finish up the lunchbox.

"It's just a bus." He blew out a breath as Alvaro came in, finding a bottle of water in the fridge. "Tío, you tell her."

I turned to him, knife in hands and arching my eyebrow. Putting his drink down, he took the knife out of my hands.

"Maybe I shouldn't get involved."

"Maybe you can pick him up." I smiled.

"Sorry, Jefa." He shook his head. "Project deadlines are cutting close. I'll be late most days."

I shrugged to Dashiell. "You heard him."

"I heard him saying he can't pick me up. Logan, it's just a bus. What's the big deal?"

I bit down on my lip and frowned to myself. It was only when I felt a warm hand cupping my shoulder that I realized Alvaro came to stand beside me.

"Let me talk to Logan for a second, Dash."

The teenager growled but left the kitchen. I blew out a breath, rubbing my temple before Alvaro captured my fingers between his and made me look up. He didn't like something in my expression. I could tell by the soft noise from the back of his throat.

Quickly, he took me in his arms and propped me on top of the counter, spreading my legs and standing between them.

"It's just a bus," he said.

"Not you too."

Alvaro shook his head. "I'll go with whatever you decide, Jefa, but explain it to me, ok?"

"I don't know," I told him the truth. "I don't know what to do with Dashiell, and it feels like if I give him a little freedom..."

"Ah." He nodded. "He'll just go."

I bit down on my lip. "I know he isn't running away. I know that."

"Still, you fear him being independent."

I frowned. "I don't want to give him any ideas."

"The ideas are already there."

I nodded. He was right. I was scared of letting Dash go, like getting a bus was going to be enough proof he could do it all by himself. In my heart, I knew they needed me as much as I needed them. But I wanted him to know that, too.

Alvaro hummed under his breath, burying his nose in my neck. "You think so loudly."

I dropped my head onto his shoulder. "I guess he can get the bus."

His palm came behind my head, massaging my scalp slowly. "There you go, you can relax."

"You keep saying that."

"And I'm never wrong," he added. "Don't worry about Dash. He'll only be alone for a while. He won't wreck the house."

I raised from his shoulder to flash him a look, making him chuckle.

"And I can cook tomorrow."

That caught my attention. "Really?"

"Don't look at me like that. I can cook."

A small smile spread over my lips. Alvaro's palms covered my legs and slid up to my waist.

"I've gained weight, you know?" I told him.

He made a face, not sure how to reply to that, and I laughed at his confusion.

"That's good. I struggle with eating when I'm not..." I cleared my throat. "Well. I can't eat much, and I just feel even more tired, incapable of the simple of tasks."

His eyebrows pinched together. He took my chin between his fingers and kissed me softly on the lips.

"I feel stronger and... a little less like Logan Hart."

He hummed, one hand cupping the back of my neck. "If you're not Logan Hart, who are you?"

My smile was small when I whispered, "My middle name is Magnolia, after my grandmother. She was soft and kind. She was nice."

I hated how easily I cracked when I was with this man. It wasn't just him reading me like a book, it was me who let him collect my truths without even stopping to protect my heart.

Alvaro's eyes scanned my kitchen, zooming in on the magnolia vase tucked in the corner. I knew what he was thinking. I always kept fresh flowers at home. It was the only thing I couldn't do without.

"Magnolia..." he hummed. "That's sweet."

I bobbed my head up and down. Yeah, having a flower for a name was sweet and wholesome. It was for nice girls with sweet voices. I liked that idea of being someone who people were drawn to.

"You're sweet," he said, reading my mind. "Your lips." He took my lips in a slow kiss, making me tremble. Nipping my jaw, he said in my ear, "And your pussy tastes sweet, too."

I was ready to ask why he wasn't taking me right here on the kitchen counter, when a piercing scream interrupted my thoughts.

I quickly jumped from the counter, running to the living room.

"Look what he did!" Vienna screamed at the first sign of me.

My eyes darted from the wall to the crayons Lachlan was gripping. He drew all over my wall up to the height he could reach. A sun, a couple of stick figures and something else. I wasn't sure what it was.

My mouth tried to break into a smile, but I schooled my expression. Alvaro came to the living room on my heels, taking the crayon from Lachlan's hand and telling him it was wrong.

I stood there, in the middle of the room, looking at those bright colored drawings on my crisp, perfect wall. At that moment, I knew.

I had the life of my dreams.

WHEN ALVARO TOLD ME to relax, he probably wasn't thinking I'd go back to work.

I wasn't good at relaxing, but I decided to act natural. Accept that being myself was enough.

And the Logan I was really liked her job.

I only had Vienna to pick up after drama class, so I took Lachlan with me to the office. I needed to collect a few documents and check out if everything was going according to plan with my clients. Maybe give them a call. It wasn't anything I couldn't do with him, but it still felt odd when I went through the glass doors with a toddler.

No one said anything as Lachlan and I crossed the atrium, sending a wave to the receptionist.

I waited for the elevator, talking to Lachlan without waiting for a reply, like I always did. A few people said hello, looking down at the boy like he was a wild animal. I'd laugh if they weren't looking at me in the same way.

Maybe I looked different. My hair was down. Lachlan managed to take the hair tie out of my hair and I never found it again. I was wearing jeans, a T-shirt, and a jacket. I bet they didn't even recognize me.

Without stopping to talk, I went straight to my floor, sending a hello to our receptionist Heidi. “I’m just popping in for a second, ok?”

Lachlan and I headed to my office, closing the door behind me.

“Now, buddy, this won’t take long.”

I got him paper and a couple of crayons I usually kept in my bag for emergencies like this.

“Only on paper, ok?” I said, holding the yellow crayon out.

“Ok,” he replied, making me smile.

He was talking more each day. Dr. Maya said selective mutism came from anxiety and even though he was able to talk before, now he physically had trouble overcoming his fear.

I could understand that. He was only little, and more had happened to him than to most adults. I understood why he felt too anxious to talk, and to be honest, I didn’t mind.

I wanted him to feel safe, first and foremost. Dr. Maya said it was important to include him in the conversation, so babbling non-stop was quite literally what the doctor ordered, good for me.

He laughed more. He responded more, even if it was with a nod of his head or by squeezing my hand.

And he was now being disobedient. Drawing on walls for crying out loud.

For a child that a few weeks ago only curled up on his big brother’s lap and refused to engage with the world, I’d take his drawing on my walls every day of the week.

I brushed his soft hair out of his face with a smile, and then turned to my computer, letting him play at peace.

On my third email reply, Godwick senior opened the door saying the obligatory, "Knock, knock?"

"Come in," I said, pressing send on the email before smiling at him.

"So this is the little man who stole our brilliant Logan?"

"No one stole me. I'll be back after—"

"After your maternity leave." He nodded, not noticing my wince when he called it that.

"This is Lachlan." I changed the subject.

My little guy didn't look up from his page, but that was ok. I knew he wasn't very interested in meeting new people. He was cute as a button. People tried to talk to him every time we went for groceries, but he barely acknowledged them.

"Are you thinking of coming back earlier?" my boss asked, giving up on Lachlan.

"No." I chuckled. "But I thought I could check on a few things."

"Nelson is taking care of your clients."

I tried to hide the contempt I felt for Nelson. He was a big guy, full of smiles and good at golf. If you asked me, he didn't deserve the clients he had. Much less mine.

Holding my tongue, I nodded. "I just want them to know I'm not abandoning ship."

Being a woman in business was shit. Everyone assumed I gave everything up to be a mom now. Not that I didn't love my days with Lachlan and the kids. I did. I knew we needed all the weeks I had off to strengthen our bond and create a home together, but I was allowed to want both. I happened to want it all.

I chatted with Godwick a little longer and finished replying to my emails right on time when Lachlan was done drawing and ready to go.

When we picked up Vienna from drama, she promptly told me everything that happened at school, not leaving room for silence. She loved her new class.

Feeling quite happy once again, nothing prepared me for the scene waiting for us in my living room.

The odd cologne smell hit me while we were still in the elevator. I brushed it off, but when the doors opened to my living room, all the hairs on my arm stood at attention.

The house was still, even though it hosted a teenager. I expected to find Dash playing video games still in his uniform, spoiling his dinner with snacks.

Instead, the house was silent. And that goddamn cologne followed us inside.

A kid on each side, Vienna was still talking, unaware of how my heart was thumping inside my ribcage.

A couple of steps later, before my feet pressed on the floor for the third time, his body stretched to his full height, standing up from the couch.

My couch.

He looked older than the last time I saw him, of course. Older, meaner, in a battered leather jacket with that insufferable smile of his.

My blood ran cold when Vienna stopped talking and whimpered, hiding behind my body. Lachlan followed her lead.

"Hey, princess aren't you going to say hi to Daddy?" David Murphy asked my kid.

Vienna wasn't interested. My eyes left David for just a second to find Dash on the other side of the living room, his face pale, hands closed in a fist.

"David, what are you doing in my house?"

"What are you doing with my children, Logan?"

"They are mine." No room for questions.

It was probably a bad idea to antagonize someone who got into my house without my permission and looked as deranged as they come. Vienna whimpered behind my legs, and I didn't want her to think she was anything but mine.

"He followed me here from school," Dashiell said from his corner.

"Are you ok?" I asked him, ignoring David for a second.

Dashiell nodded.

"Get Lachlan and Vienna and take them upstairs. I'm going to talk to David."

"Yeah kids, time for the adults to talk." He smiled at me like it was all a big joke.

Dash moved to my side, grabbing Vienna, who didn't want to leave me and Lachlan in his arms.

"Are you sure?" Dash leveled me with a look.

"I'm always alone taking care of you, right?" I arched an eyebrow, praying he heard my odd phrasing.

Before I saw it in his eyes, David chimed in. "Go now, Dash."

The kids left, my eyes following them as they went upstairs. When they were far enough, I let the air out of my lungs and looked at the poor excuse of a man in my living room.

I've hated David Murphy since we were kids. I hated the way he treated Sofia and how she was too in love to see he wasn't worth it.

I hated him more when he told everyone at school I was in love with her, and when that didn't shake me, he changed it up and made fun of me for my lack of friends.

"You did well for yourself, Lo." He smiled, using Sofia's nickname for me. "Is this Daddy's money or yours?"

"Who wants to know?"

He chuckled. "It doesn't matter, you're right."

"I'm going to ask again, David—"

"I'm just impressed," he cut me off. "Here in this penthouse all by yourself, and then suddenly you have three kids. Maybe you don't want them to cramp your style."

"I want them. Now leave."

"Lo, don't be like that."

"Stop calling me that."

That was enough ammunition. He smiled like the Cheshire cat. "Do you miss her, Lo? I bet you don't. What's the difference between dead or alive when you left her so many years ago, anyway?"

"I never left her."

I kept making mistakes, falling for his game, letting him take a piece of my soul every time he opened his mouth. I shook my head, trying to wake myself up.

"What are you doing in my house, David?"

He crossed the room, stopping right in front of me. He smelled like tobacco and that cheap cologne, his eyes pale green like Lachlan's.

"I'm wondering how much the perfect life cost you," he said. "The perfect house. The perfect kids. You've got it all, don't you?"

I snorted, not even a little surprised. "You want money."

David waved me off, turning and looking around my house again in a way that was beyond nerve wracking.

"I mean, the house is yours. The children are mine."

"Sofia left me as their legal guardian."

"And I came in her cunt to bring them here."

I practically gagged.

"Don't be such a prude, Lo. I remember when you wanted her cunt, too."

"Don't be so homophobic, David. You have enough sins."

Whatever reply he had to that, it was missed. The ding in the elevator only left me a second to turn as the door opened and a blur came raging through the door.

A shadow in the shape of Alvaro jumped on David, taking him by his neck. I blinked and Alvaro had the man pinned to the wall. David's head tipped back, his neck looking fragile under Alvaro's powerful hold.

"How dare you?" Alvaro growled.

His neck strained, a vein popping in his temple. He was going to kill David.

I rushed to Alvaro's side, touching his arm. "Alvaro..."

"Are you ok?" he asked, turning from David for the first time.

"I'm ok. Let him go."

"No." Another growl. Instead of letting him go, Alvaro's grip tightened around David's neck.

Despite how hurtful it probably felt, David proved once again he wasn't smart. A hollow chuckle came from him, his eyes darting between Alvaro and me.

"And you're fucking the big brother? You took everything from her."

His laugh turned into a groan as Alvaro shut him up by pounding his head into the wall. My eyes widened as I saw the blood trickling down David's neck.

"You have to stop."

"What are you doing here?" he asked David.

"You're going to kill him," I pleaded.

This time it was Alvaro's turn to smile. His eyes were full of rage, the smile without a trace of the wholesome man I knew.

"I am."

David's smile disappeared at the same second. I knew that was the moment he understood Alvaro wasn't joking. He wanted to kill David and the man just delivered himself on a silver platter.

As much as I wanted David gone from this earth, Alvaro wasn't a murderer.

I touched his arm again. "The kids are upstairs. Just make him leave."

Alvaro's arm relaxed under my touch and a second later, he dropped David, who fell in a disgraceful heap on the floor.

"Out," Alvaro said coldly, not leaving room for discussion.

David got up, narrowing his eyes from me to Alvaro. He wiped blood from the back of his neck and finally left.

"We have to leave a picture of him with the doorman," I said the second the doors pinged closed.

It felt crazy to let him leave like that. Just walking out like he was our guest.

I watched the elevator when Alvaro turned me to him. "Are you ok?" He checked me from top to bottom, looking for invisible injuries.

Nodding, I tried to swallow down the lump lodged in my throat when the three kids raced downstairs.

Vienna and Lachlan were crying. I kneeled and had them both in my arms in a flash. Each one took a side of my neck as they cried. I looked up to Dash hovering above us, brushing his hair out of his face.

"I called tío," he told me. "You said you were always alone, and that's not true. You're always with tío, so I thought that was a code for me to call him."

I nodded, happy he understood my meaning. "You did good."

Dash let out a breath, nodding to himself.

I moved to sit on the couch, Vienna still on my side and Lachlan on my lap. Alvaro remained standing, and Dash took the place in front of us in an armchair.

"What happened?"

Dash swallowed. "He was waiting for me when I got off the bus. Said he was watching us and wanted to have a word with you. I... I didn't know what to do."

"I can't believe he came up here," Alvaro said.

"I'm sorry." Dash's shoulders went down. "He said I had to do it. I didn't know what to do. Mom always said to just follow because it gets worse when we say no."

Dash broke my heart in a million ways. And even though he was taller than me, and told me to be out of his way, I couldn't stop seeing him as that little boy Sofia once held in her arms.

He looked young today, confused and hurt. I put Lachlan to the side, and I went to him. Sitting on the arm of his chair, I just took him in a hug.

"You did great. You called Alvaro. You protected your siblings."

*"Dumbass,"* Alvaro whispered.

I shot him a sharp look, but he sighed and shook his head finding Dash's eyes. "Vienna once said you only got a black eye when you were being a dumbass."

Dash winced, and I rubbed his back until he started to talk. "He was always mean to mom. He called her names, and he changed the house rules all the time. She told me to just go with it. It was better not to fight." He swallowed a lump, looking away from his uncle. "Sometimes I fought back."

Words died in my throat, I couldn't say anything to make it better, so I hugged him with all my might like he was just small as Lachlan.

And he let me.

"He's here to take us, right? That's why he came. He wants us to go live with him. You can't let him."

"Logan!" Vienna exploded in a cry, Lachlan following her, looking frightened.

The kids seemed frenetic. All the Castillo's did. Alvaro was pacing, rubbing his face, his hand closed in a fist like he wanted to break his own fingers. Dash's eyes were wide as saucers. He looked pale and ready to vomit.

And both kids were crying. The most horrible cries I've ever heard from them.

"Stop. Stop all of you," I started, and when they didn't follow quickly, I asked again. "Stop. No one is taking you from me. No one. Ever."

"He's our dad," Dash reminded me.

"Do you see this house?" I asked them. "Go ahead, look around. I'll sell everything I own before losing you."

"He wants money?" Alvaro talked for the first time.

I flashed him a look. “It doesn’t matter.” I turned back to Dash. “No one will ever take you away from me. I’m stubborn and I’m annoying, right? You know me well enough to know that Dash. So tell me if I’m going to let that piece of shit take any of you from me?”

The boy blinked as I spoke my piece. I hoped he saw the determination in my eyes, but I kept going, whispering something only to him.

“I shouldn’t have left you and Sofia. I should have stayed and showed everyone who he was. That was my mistake, and you both suffered, but I’m here now. You’ll always have me by your side. Even when you don’t want me. I’m here.”

It took a second, but Dash slowly nodded, absorbing what I told him. Believing it. I wasn’t letting David intimidate me again. Never again.

Dash’s eyes were glassy with tears he refused to let fall, so I saved him the pretense of being strong, and held him once again.

It took time until everyone stopped crying. Vienna was shaking, but when she fell asleep, she did it quickly, mouth opened with soft snores.

Lachlan fell asleep in my lap, his hand on mine as I hummed. Alvaro brought them to their beds, and as I tucked Lachlan in, Dash came and sat on his bed.

I kissed Lachlan and smiled at Dash. “Goodnight.”

He nodded. “Goodnight.”

It was when I was almost leaving, Dash whispered. “I’m sorry. For everything.”

I squeezed my eyes shut, holding myself by the door. He grew up with a lot of shit, and then his mom died. He didn’t trust adults. If I learned anything from Dr. Maya it was that kids delt with their sorrows in their own way, but they didn't have the emotional maturity to understand that was what they were doing.

Dash was trying to find a way to defend his siblings. To him, I could be a new David. It was only up to me to win his trust. Today we took a step forward, but I knew it was going to take time. Dash would see soon that I didn't mind working for it.

"Have good dreams, Dash," I replied.

# 23.

# Alvaro

His beard was drenched in blood after I punched, split his lip, and broke his nose.

He was as big as a tank, but the problem was… so was I.

With the rage brewing inside me, I knew I wasn't going to lose. And he knew it, too. As I made contact, blow after blow, never stopping for a second, never wavering, my hands split into a dozen unforgivable cuts. I'd destroy myself if it meant I could destroy him, too.

I was quick. He didn't have time to even graze his fist on me.

I never ended an adversary like that. Any other night, the fight would last longer.

It had been a week since David Murphy came to Logan's house. One week and the scene replayed in my mind in a horrible symphony that left me standing on shaky ground every day.

I couldn't sleep. I only existed in rage, shame, and guilt.

Logan talked to her cousin the day after. Sofia was smart, she made sure David wasn't registered as the kids' father on their birth certificates. She knew what was happening and even though the news he had no parental rights made Logan breathe in peace, it was just another nail in my coffin.

I hooked a fist into my opponent's face, my bare knuckles ending the fight once and for all as he stumbled back and fell into himself.

The air in my lungs was heavy. It didn't help.

None of this helped.

I beat him up to a pulp, and the words of Dash saying how Sofia told him to never disagree with David were still there, hammering in my head.

The people cheered for El Toro, their voices loud, but the ones in my head were louder.

I stood there, legs apart, breathing deeply as I dripped sweat from my torso and blood from my knuckles. And still, in the end, Sofia's life ended tragically because of me.

I couldn't find any other reason. I couldn't see anything else but my baby sister enduring years of domestic abuse while all of us ignored the situation.

For days I looked for signs, for reasons, for moments during a Christmas dinner when she looked different or could have asked for help.

By the third day, I started to wonder if he was physically abusing her as well as the kids. I burst in Mamá's house and took her pictures to check for bruises we might have missed at the time.

Refusing to tell her what I was doing, I could barely look at my mother's face. Mamá was against Logan, and so ready to make her a villain because of her own ego.

I could see it perfectly now. Logan had everything my parents couldn't give Sofia. She was so scared of money that she never asked herself if Logan was happy living like that.

Logan wanted a family. She found in Sofia someone to love her, since her own parents were missing. But Mamá denied her when she judged a child by her parent's wallet.

Once the pictures were insufficient, and my memory didn't show anything to confirm Sophia was in trouble, when my skin crawled every moment of every day, and I spent nights watching over the city instead of sleeping…

When everything failed, I called Paddy and scheduled a fight.

And now this failed, too.

Paddy's clammy hand reached my wrist and pulled up for a victory stance. I let him do it to trigger the crowd into a wild frenzy, El Toro being chanted in every corner.

I wasn't hurt, but I was in my forties, and my muscles were pulled tight with tension. Pulling my wrist out of Paddy's hand, I stepped away, barely looking at the man I left beaten in the middle of the ring.

Pulling the cords apart, I left them behind, and the crowd parted for me. Maybe it was my blood-shot eyes, my pissed off attitude, or the fact I just destroyed a giant of a man in less than five minutes. None of them dared to talk to me.

They called my name, they celebrated me. They never dared to touch me.

I parted the seas like fucking Moses and entered the locker room at once, slamming the door behind me. My things went straight to a duffle, a T-shirt stretched over my naked torso, and I put on my working boots.

I couldn't bother to shower at the gym. I was just going straight to my apartment. I would use the time to grab a few things before returning to Logan's.

Cursing, I looked down at my knuckles, knowing I'd find them tore apart. Stepping to the sink, I washed my hands, watching the blood run down the drain, controlling my breathing for the hundredth time this week.

And now what? I didn't have in me to ask Dash for details. A fucking coward, that was what I was, trying to understand a mystery I didn't really want to solve.

I couldn't hear from Dash's lips how fucked up their lives were, so I never asked. I just looked for proof that Sofia hid well enough.

That was the worst of my truths. Every time I looked for evidence, I looked for absolution. I wanted someone to tell me it wasn't my fault. I couldn't have helped.

Bile rose as I leaned over the sink, my hands clean but the cuts still open.

Death kept happening. Every day when I opened my eyes, I lost her all over again.

The scene outside was almost the same as I left. But instead of calling my name, they were cheering for whoever was fighting next. I didn't bother to look at the ring to check, or to find Paddy and ask how much money we had made in this fiasco.

Avoiding everyone once again, I negotiated the crowd. As I approached the exit, my eyes fixed on the prize, something moved.

His black hair was combed off his face, a smirk tugging his thin lips and those eyes.

*Lachlan's eyes.*

David Murphy was just at the door, leaning against the wall, watching everything like he didn't fear for his life. I stopped, my hand gripping on the handle of my duffle so forcefully I could feel the cuts bleeding all over again.

He should have been scared.

I tried everything to make this pain go away, and nothing helped. Killing him might.

It was the only thing that made sense. Killing him the way he killed my sister. Destroying every bit that made him human, like he did to her for years. Dragging him somewhere and taking my time as I slashed his skin slowly until he begged for mercy.

That possibility felt so good, so vivid in my brain it was enough to spread a demented smile over my lips. And right when he should have bolted from the sheer image of me, he smiled.

My blood boiled, my vision darkened, and before I could think much about it, I was moving people away and going after him. He moved quickly for someone who didn't seem so scared. He turned on his heels and left at once.

I pushed someone to the side, barely sparing them a glance as I stepped over and reached for the door. I could only see David.

I needed revenge to survive my next breath, the satisfaction of ending him. For the first time, I knew what I had to do.

It was so clear... so fucking clear.

He had no claim to the kids. He was no one. I knew his parents weren't close because they weren't involved with the kids at all.

No one was going to miss the fucker.

Actually, this was a public service. Life would be better without him, I was sure.

Cold wind bit my skin. I couldn't give a fuck. I turned from left to right, trying to guess where he went. The parking lot in front of the gym was full. He could be anywhere, but I chose left toward the alleyway.

When I turned, he was there. With a cigarette hanging from his lips, he looked me up and down with a smile.

"What are you going to do, El Toro?" He snickered. "Kill me?"

"Sounds like a great idea." My bag dropped to the ground, and I stepped toward him.

He took a drag, the smoke coming out of his nose slowly. "Think about the kids," he mocked.

I chuckled, shaking my head. "You don't have parental rights." I gladly informed him. "What did you have planned with that visit? Extort money from us?"

David whistled. "Not from you. You have nothing."

"Logan is their legal guardian," I said again, coming even closer. "You are nothing. And you won't be missed."

I was ready to pounce, have his neck in my hands and bash his skull into the brick when he moved his coat to the side, showing off the gun.

"I chose wrong." He continued smoking. "Logan is loaded, but she was so annoying at school. Too frigid. Sofia was softer."

I growled under my breath and did not think twice when I advanced. He was quick too, taking the gun into his hand and pointing at my chest.

"You're going back there and getting my money."

I laughed.

"I just want something for my emotional distress. Logan has it. Go back there and get my money and she'll never hear from me again."

"Or what?" I shrugged. Refusing to give in. Even if he was the one holding the gun.

"You can keep walking and die here," he listed. "You can walk away, not give me my money—"

"You have no money."

"Now, interrupting isn't good. Maybe I don't want you to raise my kids," he said. "Then again, I don't want someone involved with illegal fighting raising my kids."

For the first time, my eyes tore from the gun to his. He was smiling.

"Logan is the legal guardian," I said for the last time.

"Yeah, and she wants you with the kids. I don't blame you for staying with her. She's a piece of ass that comes with a penthouse."

My feet moved before I could think better. I just couldn't deal with her name on his lips. David held the gun against my chest, the cold metal carving on my skin, separated only by a thin T-shirt. I was much bigger than David, but his smirk never faltered.

"Don't look so angry. I'm complimenting the girl. Go home. Get my money."

"Fuck you," I snarled.

He pressed the cold metal further into my chest. "There's no point in doing this, Alvaro. Sofia is gone. But you can protect Logan. If you die here, what good is that to her? You can pay me, and I'll never breathe the same air as your ice queen. Isn't that what you want? Isn't that why you are here playing superhero? Trying to protect them from the big bad wolf?" he mocked. "Here's your chance."

I wanted to kill him. I shook from it, my hands closing in a fist, begging to just end his miserable life. I couldn't see reason.

I just wanted to end it. Him and I.

"I'd do you a favor. I'll walk away." He stepped back. Flicking the cigarette, the sparks dying over the wet pavement.

"I have proof, Alvaro," he said, putting his gun away. "What you're doing is illegal, and you just damned those kids. Tell me again who the big bad wolf is, huh?"

With a smile, he left, leaving me paralyzed in the alleyway.

Life turned up again, cars passing by, drunks watching the fights. A streetlamp flickered in front of my eyes, but I remained unmoved.

The reasoning for killing him was still there, but in my head, I could only replay his words. I put the kids at risk. Logan gave me her trust, and I threw it in the garbage by coming here.

David was a con artist, but it wasn't hard to prove I was here. If not for whatever proof he had, I just exited a gym full of people who were sketchy enough to be bought.

Paddy himself, even though the venue was his. I could see him betraying me to the highest bidder.

I fucked it up.

# 24.

# Logan

"I CAN'T LISTEN TO this anymore." Dash groaned as he pressed pause on the last song from *Encanto.*

"Shush!" I hid a giggle. "And grab Lachlan."

Vienna fell asleep in the first twenty minutes of the movie, even before her brother. I tried to move her, but her body was heavy with sleep.

"Mmm, Logan?"

"What?" I asked, trying to gather the girl in my arms, blowing a rogue strand of hair from my eyes.

"Maybe you get Lachlan and I take care of Vienna?"

I eyed him up and down. Sure, he was lanky, but taller than me and easily stronger.

"You're a twig, Lo." He smiled.

And it was the *Lo* coming so easily out of his mouth that made me step away from his sister, lowering my arms beside my body.

"Well, she's heavy."

Dash chuckled, rolling his eyes at me. For the first time, he was... messing with me. His eyes were light and not full of daggers. My heart squeezed and it took all in me not to jump on him and hang from his neck. He was a teenager, and I couldn't mess with our relationship that quickly.

Dash took Vienna, and I moved to Lachlan, but he was heavy too and I almost didn't make it up the stairs.

"Don't stay up too late," I whispered, tucking Lachlan in. Dash had made his way to their room after dropping off Vienna.

He shrugged. "I'll read a little first. Is Tío back?"

I shook my head. I knew our run-in with David messed with Alvaro's head. I could see the guilt consuming him every second and not even Willa's guarantee that he had no claim over the kids helped with his mood.

I wanted to push and make him talk, but at the same time... I was afraid to open my mouth. Afraid he'd say our time was up.

It was time to make that room for Dash. Time for Alvaro to go back to his own apartment. We never put a timeline on this little cohabitation game, but it felt like the end. The kids were fine with me. We found a rhythm. Dash was opening up, Vienna was adapting, and Lachlan was talking more and more at each session with Dr. Maya, who started seeing Vienna, too.

Our lives were clicking together. Didn't that mean that it was time for Alvaro to move on with his life?

Sure, he was still the kids' uncle. He'd still see them, but it was going to be different.

I wouldn't see him every day. Not hanging out on the couch, not sharing my biggest fears after dinner.

And... there would be no kissing anymore. I knew Alvaro and I were complicated. More than that, we were impossible. With the kids, and his mother hating me...

Being together was a bad idea.

He was their uncle. And if something went wrong between us?

I couldn't afford to feel awkward around the only person in their family within driving distance.

"Goodnight, Dash." I smiled tightly.

"Goodnight," he replied, already opening a book.

He was good. They were all good kids. I breathed in and out. David couldn't take them from me. Nothing could take them from me, Willa guaranteed. All I had done since they arrived in my home was give them the best I could.

Their teachers only had praises to sing. They were eating better, their behavior improved. I nodded to myself. *Nothing could destroy this.*

I tiptoed downstairs, the house dark and my heart lurched, feeling his absence above all else.

It was ridiculous to miss him. He lived here. I saw him this morning. Still, the man I saw wasn't Alvaro. There was no spark in his eyes, no smirk over his lips. He was a shell, and I was standing there watching as the waves took him away.

Deciding it was a great time to drink, I reached above my fridge, where I kept a cupboard with a small selection of bottles. I poured my favorite Cabernet Sauvignon in a glass and took a sip, releasing a satisfying hum when the sharpness reached the back of my jaw.

Swallowing slowly, my fingers danced over the glass as I heard the hopeful ping of the elevator.

I glanced down at my watch, just shy of eleven at night. Not bad. He didn't owe me anything. He could come and go anytime. It was me who was addicted to his presence.

Sipping again from the wine, my eyes fixed on nothing as I leaned over the counter and counted his steps in my mind.

Instead of going upstairs, I heard the approach, my hand shaking a little when he came closer until I could hear him in the kitchen. I didn't turn to see him coming through the door. My eyes were still cast down on the wine.

"The kids?" he asked low.

"Sleeping."

He came closer, the heat from his body took over, his scent making me drunker than the wine as he leaned over me. My knees wanted to buckle, to give in quickly when I felt his chest brushing my back.

"I love you in that skirt," he whispered in my ear.

I trembled, looking down at the silk black mid-skirt I paired with a simple sweater and the boots I took off the second I arrived home.

I cleared my throat. "Are you hungry?"

He chuckled darkly, raising all the hairs on my arm. "Famished."

His hands lowered to my shoulders and down my arms. Even with my sweater, I felt his heat on my skin. Slowly, he reached down, one arm curling around my waist.

"I'm really hungry."

He wasn't talking about food, and I knew it. My head tilted to the side, and I felt his mouth close over my skin peppering me with open-mouthed kisses.

He was hot and sinful, moving the glass of wine away like he knew we couldn't be trusted around something fragile. Without asking permission, his hand went up, taking my breast at the same time his teeth grazed my neck.

I muffled a cry. My eyes went down to see his tattooed arm taking me.

A gasp flew past my lips. "What happened?"

My fingers tried to take his bloodied hand off mine. He looked like a mess, but he shushed me.

"Just an accident. Don't worry."

I opened my mouth to argue that it looked much more than an accident, but his other hand was now on my ass, kneading so forcefully I stumbled, using the counter to hold myself together.

"Logan," he rasped. "Be a good girl and ask me not to stop."

The need in his voice tore my chest apart. It was his timber, his unexpected vulnerability, like he was crumbling without me.

His bloodied hand closed around my neck, tilting my head to rest under his chin as I whimpered, "Don't stop, Alvaro."

A growl that was more animal than man came from him and brought goosebumps all over my skin. He turned me around, making me look at him for the first time.

Eyes dark with want, he looked sweaty in a T-shirt and basketball shorts. He looked like he came from the gym, but the questions died on my lips when he took my mouth. Big, delicious, impossible. I tried to touch as much skin as I could. Down his arms, under his T-shirt.

He took me by the waist, putting me on the counter. I desperately brought my skirt up so he could fit between my legs.

"I'm addicted to you, Jefa," he told me between kisses. "How did you do it? How did you make me like this?"

I had no air to tell him it wasn't me. It was him who barrelled into my life, who made me need his presence and crave his company.

He was more than I ever dared to wish for. And yet he was all over me. His hot hands on my legs, his mouth on mine, his scent all over my house. I bit his lower lip, and that was all it took.

Alvaro growled, and then took me from the counter with only one arm, my hands laced behind his neck. Mirroring the desperation I felt deep inside, he asked when we reached the stairs, "Your bedroom or mine?"

"Let me down here." I wiggled in his hold.

"Rubbing on my cock isn't the best way to make me let you go, Jefa."

I drew a sharp breath. No one ever talked to me like that. I had sex, I went on dates, but I never felt consumed by the idea and the need to be with someone. He took my breath away, his rough words, hands, and personality.

"Dash might be still awake," I told him.

For a second, I thought he wasn't going to let me go. His hands gripped my ass like he wanted to leave marks, but then he let my feet touch the floors.

I swallowed and fixed my skirt, taking his hand and ignoring the overwhelming flare of questions that arose every time I glanced at his knuckles. The rest of him looked ok, though. He looked untamed—feral—but not hurt.

Unstable on my wobbly legs, I went up the stairs. The only sound was from my beating heart, hammering inside my chest, weighing my decisions.

I relied too much on Alvaro already. I told myself again and again that we were a bad idea, but still, I led him to my bedroom and closed the door behind me.

In the same second, he was on me. I craned my head up to face him, but his hand was already tipping my chin up.

"Take your clothes off," he ordered.

A shiver ran down my spine.

"Quick, Logan," he said when I didn't jump to his command. "I've waited too long."

Did he? Did we? Even as he asked me to do it myself, I felt his hand helping my sweater up, tossing to the side as he grabbed my face and came in for a torturing kiss, my body melting into his.

The camisole went next. I couldn't help the smile when I noticed Alvaro's staggering expression when he noticed I had no bra on.

"Killing me..." he rasped but never finished the thought as his mouth was taking a nipple. I whimpered, holding on to his shoulders.

"That fucking blush kills me every time." His teeth grazed a nipple as he went up to his full height.

He reached to his back, bringing the T-shirt over his head, and he tossed it to a corner of the room. My eyes took a second to watch him from one shoulder to the other. Smooth brown skin, tattoos everywhere my eyes could see. I licked my lips and pushed my skirt down at the same time as my underwear. I ignored my heart when I found myself naked in front of Sofia's big brother again.

His thumb went to my chin, opening my mouth as he claimed my lips, his tongue invading, twirling around. A moan escaped when our skin touched. He kissed me slowly, and I felt his erection rubbing on my stomach, begging to be let out.

His arm came around my waist, lifting me up. I never stopped kissing him until he dropped me on the bed. I watched from the edge, his breathing coming out shallow from his lungs.

I rose to my elbows and waited.

"Hair down, Jefa," he commanded.

I tugged on the hair tie and let my brown hair down over my shoulders. He swore softly in Spanish, making me smile.

It took one look, my eyes going down to his shorts and then back to his eyes. Questioning. He pulled his shorts down, showing himself to me.

I saw him before, but the air got stuck in my lungs, anyway. Close to his tip, a piercing went through it, one ball on each side. And at the base, over his cock, another barbell.

"Stop looking at my cock like it is going to ruin you for other men," he growled, taking himself at the base, a shudder going through his body.

"I didn't think we were supposed to lie to each other." I smirked.

He stopped, his Adam's apple bobbing, jaw ticking. For a second I thought I said something wrong, but he shook it off and came to me.

His body covered mine, his hand on the back of my neck bringing me up for a kiss full of everything that was missing in my life. Alvaro was it. The air in my lungs, the power, the desire. He was a storm taking over.

"Condom." He bit my shoulder hard enough to make me moan.

I reached for the bedside table, one handed, as he kissed me, rubbing his cock on me again and again, the friction driving me wild.

When I had the foil package between my fingers, he sat on his knees. "Put it on me."

He looked like a Greek god sitting on his legs, his powerful thighs apart, his cock hard, waiting for his demands to be fulfilled.

I scrambled to sit up, ripping the foil with my teeth. I reached for him, unable to stop myself from touching his piercing.

Alvaro hissed, his head thrown back. "Jefa."

I loved that quality in his voice. It undid everything tight inside me. Watching for his reaction, I lowered my head and took his tip to my mouth, my tongue playing with the piercing.

His hand quickly came to the back of my head, holding me in place. Feeling confident, I licked him from root to tip, drenched when he groaned my name.

His fingers twitched, gripping the hair away from my face. I felt his eyes on me as I bobbed up and down his length.

"Look at me, Jefa. Show me what you're doing."

My eyes flew to him. He smiled in approval, humming under his breath. "Look at you. Open that mouth, Logan. Take more."

I took as much as I could, his piercing banging in the back of my throat. I went back to his tip, twirling my tongue, he growled almost displeased. "Enough now."

He lifted my head by my hair and nodded to the condom still between my fingers, his jaw tense.

When I used both hands to sheath him, his hand left my hair taking the curve of my cheek.

"You blush for everything, but not for this?" he asked.

As I finished, my hair making a curtain around my shoulders, I peeked at him with a smile. "That's what you do? Try to make me blush?"

He tsked, his tattooed hand closing on my neck. "Jefa, I'm going to make you come so hard all your blushing will belong to me from now on."

Alvaro advanced without another word, his arm curling under me, taking me on his lap, my legs falling open with him between them.

"You know what they used to call me?" he whispered in my ear.

I sucked in a breath. "El Toro," I repeated his MMA nickname.

"So ride me, baby."

I nodded, my hand gripping on his shoulder. He moved us to the edge of the bed, his feet touching the floor as I held onto my knees and positioned him right in my entrance.

"Go down slow," he told me, kissing my head softly like I was something precious.

He kept breaking me and putting me back together. I looked right at him, his intense whiskey eyes on mine and I lowered down, feeling his head spreading me apart, dying for the noise that strangled out of his throat.

The piercing fit inside. I threw my head back on a moan.

"Keep working, Logan." He gripped my waist. "Come on, take it all."

I whimpered as we kissed. He took my lower lip for a long pull between his teeth. I lived for his eyes on me, his smirk each time he teased me.

We moaned when he was buried to the hilt, my head lolling to the side. His hands on both sides of my waist, he told me, "Work for it."

I could hear the smile in his voice. Placing my hands back to his shoulder, I used my knees and started to ride. Up and down, taking all those delicious growls that made me wet in a second.

"Keep going," he said, manipulating my body to take a nipple to his mouth.

The whimper broke free, and I worked harder, like he asked, taking him fully just to go up and drop down again. My skin burning hot. I was dizzy when he turned me around in one go, laying me on the bed as he ended up on top without taking himself out of me.

At this angle, he went deeper. I bit my bottom lip trying not to scream. But he was there, his thumb pulling my lip free. "Scream for me," he demanded.

Shaking my head, he thrust deep making me realize what the piercing at the top did. Between the barbells, my clit fit perfectly. My mouth opened in a silent scream as he thrusted relentlessly, a knowing smile decorating his lips.

Alvaro's hand took my legs, holding them apart, baring me to him as he pinned me to the bed, that piercing massaging my clit with every move of his hips.

"You're strangling my cock, Jefa," he growled.

I nodded. He was impossibly thick. Inside, I felt his other piercing on my walls and I took it all and craved more.

Another push. His mouth found mine even while he held my legs up and I screamed on his tongue, my orgasm ripping me inside out.

Alvaro's eyes rolled to the back of his head. He came down, licking me from neck to ear, biting my earlobe before he came.

With a feral growl, a vein on his neck popped. My toes curled, and I tensed up, milking him. With shallow thrusts he rode his orgasm, making it last.

His hands eased off my legs. They were shaking as I let them down. He looked at me, his eyes darting all over my features like he was seeing me for the very first time. His thumb grazed my lips, and he opened them for his mouth.

He licked me, kissing slowly, taking my breath away.

"You, Logan Hart. Fucking *you*."

# 25.
# Alvaro

She was fidgeting, her hand on top of her lap. Logan bit her bottom lip so forcefully, I was sure she was leaving a mark. Sighing, I reached over and took her hand in mine.

"Relax."

Her eyes left the window, falling on my hands on top of hers. I just kept driving, trying to look calm and feeling anything but.

It was my father's birthday. Me and the kids were driving to my parents, but last week when I informed the kids of our plans, Vienna asked why Logan wasn't coming and then Dash asked the same. Suddenly, it felt like Logan wasn't part of the family. They all looked at me with big eyes full of questions and my heart broke when Logan just snorted a laugh and said she wasn't wanted.

Soft. I was getting soft because one look at those dark green eyes and I declared she was coming with us. She was part of the family.

If I was going to rationalize this, yeah, Mamá needed to get over her problem with Logan. She was the kids' legal guardian, and they loved her.

It was obvious and growing stronger each day. Vienna was a fan from the beginning. These days I wouldn't find

Logan without Lachlan hanging off her neck, on her lap, or holding her hand.

And even Dash, who fought bravely, couldn't resist Logan in the end. He joked more, listened to what she said, and I even caught him asking for help with his physics homework.

When Logan explained the material brilliantly, like not a day had passed since she was in school, I took her hard on the kitchen counter after everyone went to bed.

We were all captured by her. Mesmerized, eating out of the palm of her hand.

And I'd be feeling like an idiot if I wasn't busy feeling so good. The foreign sentiment grew in my chest every day. It even eased the guilt.

I was ready to ignore everything and just stay with Logan, if it wasn't for the contract I had to finish at work and...

David Murphy.

My grip on her thigh intensified, like she was sand running through my fingers. Logan traced my knuckles, unaware of my internal struggle. "You should wear gloves next time at the gym."

My Adam's apple bobbed, and I nodded. My old friend guilt coming out to play once more. I told her I busted my hand on a bag at the gym and not at someone else's face. The fight was so quick, so unfair. It didn't leave any bruises on my face to raise questions.

But even if I did. I used to say to people I had a split lip from training. Fighting for fun or accidents at the site.

Those lies came easily to my mouth because I never regretted them.

Logan, though?

I hated lying to her. Hated that she cared enough to get cream for my cuts and applied it gently one night. I looked at her, at my hands, at the kids, and thought about David and the countdown he put on my happiness.

She slept with me every night that week. And each night I held on to her, knowing I had no right to.

How many times did I tell myself to keep my hands off Logan because she was all dreams and goodness?

How many times did I remind myself nothing good came out of me? I was damaged, selfish, and riddled with guilt and still... I couldn't help myself.

She was soft and delicious, patient and full of smiles. Every night I promised myself to pay David off and step away from Logan before fucking it up. Every morning I woke up with her hair fanning over my chest, her shy smile whispering good morning, and when she ended up riding my cock, gasping and gripping on my piercing?

Well, then I said I could have one more day.

Just one last day in paradise.

Again and again.

The days passed, and I never had enough. I ignored when Paddy called to give me my share of the fight and tell me David wasn't someone I should be messing with. I didn't bother to ask how he knew David. They both could go fuck themselves.

I just wanted...

Shit, I wanted another day. One more hour.

"We are here," I said without a reason. Everyone in the car had their heads turned to my parents' house.

Logan hopped from the car, opening the door for the kids before Dash could complain that he didn't need a child's lock. I took Lachlan from the other side and brought him to them.

Placing him on the ground, I looked at Logan as she chewed on her lip with that worried frown over her eyebrows.

"Stop, Jefa," I whispered. Grabbing her, I kissed her head. "Just relax. I won't let anything happen."

At least I could promise her that.

"Mmm." Dash started coming closer. His irritated tone I knew well. "If you don't want Tita to find out whatever that is... you better stop now."

Logan sounded startled, practically choking on air. Her head whipped to face me, her big eyes widened.

I cleared my throat. "Nothing is..."

"Yeah, yeah. I don't care. But if she catches you rubbing on each other like that? Good luck."

"Dash!" She blushed, reprimanding him.

And with that, he turned around and went with his siblings, already on the porch, knocking at the door.

I smiled at Logan. She looked absolutely freaked. "Well, you wanted him to like you. I think that bullshit was the closest a teenager gets to liking someone."

Her mouth twitched up, and her shoulders relaxed a little. "I guess I'll take all I can get."

I nodded at the door, right at the time I heard it opening.

"It's not like I want to hide..." I started in a lower voice.

She actually chuckled. "Like Caridad needs more reason to hate me? I'll be the wanton woman who seduced her príncipe?"

"I'm sixteen years older than you, Jefa. If anyone is seducing, it's me."

Logan arched her eyebrow. "Are you sure?" And she hurried her step, marching in front of me, that ass of hers in a skintight pencil skirt.

She had lots of those, I noticed. Even when she paired them with knit sweaters, she looked beyond hot.

And again, I wished I could stay.

"Feliz cumple, Papá," I said as soon as we got in.

"Gracias, gracias," he murmured while we hugged.

I put distance between us when his eyes turned to my right side. Logan stepped closer. "Happy birthday, Mr. Castillo."

Before Papá could open his mouth to thank her Lachlan barrelled into her legs, his face buried in her skirt as he cried. Her focus changed the second it happened.

Quickly, the uncertain look washed away from her features, and she went down to take him in her arms.

"Hey, hey, buddy, what's happening?"

His hands around her neck, he hid his face in her neck and whined.

"Not my fault!" Vienna started from the other room as she marched our way.

"That's not an  incriminating way to start a sentence." Dash snickered.

"Tell me," Logan requested.

"He found a toy that I forgot here. My toy, Lo. Not his."

She clearly left out the part when she did something to fix Lachlan's mistake. But Logan just smiled, hitching Lachlan up in her arms.

Dash groaned.

"You know it." Logan wiggled her eyebrows at Vienna.

I chuckled too, making my father watch us all with curiosity. I shook my head and pointed at Vienna. "Just watch," I told him.

"Until Vienna learns how to share..." Logan explained, but it was quickly stopped by Vienna's singing.

"Vienna needs to sing the most annoying song," Dash explained to Papá, talking over the noise.

It was one from a silly cartoon Lachlan liked. I had to go with Dash on that one. The tune was like chewing gum and got stuck in the brain. In the cartoon version, the voice was sickly sweet and high. Vienna's rendition was loud and impossible to miss.

"This happens too many times," Dash told Logan. "You can't punish us all."

"Complain one more time and I'll find a song for you to sing," Logan threatened.

He held back a smile, and when Vienna finished her awful song about sharing, Papá clapped, still confused about what was happening.

"You like that one, buddy?" Logan asked, tickling Lachlan's side.

But he shook his head and said "Lo" really low on her neck. Logan rubbed his back and told Vienna, "I think your brother needs an apology."

Vienna didn't miss a beat. "I'm sorry, Lach," she said. "Let's go and I'll show you how to play."

Lachlan moved, glancing at Vienna and then Logan.

"Go," Logan whispered.

He wiggled out of her hold, Vienna held a hand to him, and they left. Logan then turned to Dash. "Go see what the toy is. Vienna thinks literally anything belongs to her."

Dash waved her away. "Yeah, yeah."

"I'm finding you a song," she told his back.

Brushing her hair off her face, she fixed her green eyes on Papá. "I'm so sorry, Mr. Castillo. I'm trying to get Vienna to share but..."

"Children," he said, waving her off.

"Children," she agreed.

I was going to drag her away, offer her a drink when a throat cleared. Mamá was in the kitchen door, watching us with an expression impossible to decipher.

"Hi, Mamá."

"Café." She finally uttered a word. "Would anyone like coffee?"

My father moved, nodding, and I went after him. "Or something stronger?" I asked Logan with a smirk.

"Don't start." She shook her head.

"Or you'll give me something to sing about?"

Logan blinked, taking a second to reply, then she chuckled and followed me down to the kitchen. "We are so weird," I heard her say.

My hands closed in a fist, and I didn't reach for her. Dash was right, even if I didn't want to admit it. I needed to keep the touches to a minimum.

So, I slowly breathed the air out of my lungs, stepped into the kitchen and asked if there was anything I could do to help.

I NEVER SAW MY mother so quiet. Papá, of all people, conducted all conversations during dinner, asking the kids about school and for their news since that weekend they spent together. Vienna took over, of course, telling them everything, including that she was now too seeing Dr. Maya.

The hairs on the back of my head stood at attention with the daggers Mamá's sent at Logan.

She was from an old generation who thought therapy was something for those who had nothing else going on. Or maybe she had nothing against therapy and everything against Logan.

I had to talk to them.

The thought plagued me through dinner until dessert, as we sang feliz cumpleaños. I tapped Papá's back, and Logan gave him an outrageously expensive bottle of Cuban rum she ordered specially for the occasion.

Papá opened the black box and took out the beautiful bottle. His eyes widened when he spotted the label.

"Logan you shouldn't—"

"Happy birthday, Mr. Castillo," my little minx interrupted. "Alvaro said you'd like it."

I could hear in the pitch of her voice how nervous she was. We all felt the weight of Mamá's disapproval even though she didn't talk. I knew my mother hated that kind of extravagance in her house, but I told Logan it was ok if she wanted to spoil my dad.

I did too. I picked tumblers to go with the rum that were way more expensive than I usually would go for. I learned with Logan that you only got one shot at loving people. She loved fiercely, so why hold back?

"Geraldo," he requested, blinking from the bottle to her.

Logan smiled timid, taking that small step to the right direction. Everyone relaxed, but I knew the time had come.

It was never my intention to use my father's birthday like this, but it became apparent Logan was always going to be overlooked by my mother. And before today, I'd roll my eyes and say she was just being difficult. It didn't feel easy to ignore anymore.

The reality of what Sofia's life was like came crashing into my lap. So many truths I wasn't ready to hear. I knew my parents weren't ready for what I was about to tell them. I had to end it, though. I needed Mamá to start seeing Logan for what she really was.

Sofia's champion. The best person to take care of the kids. No one else would do.

When the kids left, I closed the kitchen door. "I need to talk to you about something."

I flashed a look at Logan, and she stiffened in the chair. Maybe she was afraid I'd spill my guts that we were sleeping together. Her eyes never left mine as I crossed the kitchen and sat on the chair beside her.

Papá was opening his brand-new rum, pouring it in the new tumblers as he whispered to himself how good it smelled.

"Maybe today is not the day," Logan whispered.

"¿Que pasa?" Mamá said, leaning on the counter, a tea towel over her shoulder and a mean look in her eyes.

I breathed in, not really interested in dragging this out, especially when Logan seemed ready to bolt at any second.

"I recently found out a few things about Sofia's relationship."

No whispering this time. Logan flashed me a warning look. "Alvaro."

"No. This is important even if it's painful."

"What are you talking about?" Papá stopped looking at his rum for the first time since he got it.

"Who told you these things?" Mamá asked, making it obvious she wanted it to be Logan so she could discredit it and call it a day.

I pinched the bridge of my nose. "Sit down, Mamá." I chose my words carefully. "The kids are saying a couple of things."

"They never said anything." She shook her head but sat back at the table.

"Caridad," Papá said softly, his hand coming to cover hers.

"Sofia and David's relationship was worse than we initially thought," I decided to say at once. "The kids are... scared of him."

"The kids—" Mamá started, but to our surprise, Logan cut her off.

"The kids know better than anyone what happened in the house, and they will be heard."

My parents' mouths closed in a snap, and I took it as an incentive.

"Things in the house weren't good. I haven't asked for details, but David was abusive." I heard a gasp, but I refused to look at my mother. "The only reason I am mentioning this is because the kids are healing. They are in therapy."

"Doctor Maya is great," Logan cut in. "Lachlan has made tremendous progress with her and now Vienna..."

"Is he talking?" Mamá asked, her eyes glued to Logan.

The woman by my side let go of an anxious breath as she simply nodded. Mamá looked at Papá like she needed his confirmation.

"It's true," Papá confirmed. "He called her Lo."

Logan smiled sadly. "He doesn't say much yet. I'm happy for him to take as long as he needs. But it isn't just Lachlan. They all have been through a lot."

"The reason I am bringing this up." I took a breath again. "We have to address Sofia's death."

"No."

It came quickly from Mamá's mouth. Like a whip, the word cracked in the still air.

"What do you mean, no?"

"I don't want to talk about Sofia anymore."

"We never started." I couldn't help but shake my head, confused.

"It is a sore spot for all of us." My Papá tried to reason with me.

"Of course it fucking is."

"Alvaro." Mamá was annoyed at my language, even as I stood there, grey hairs and all.

I stood to my full height. "Sofia killed herself." As the words came out of my mouth, everyone in the kitchen winced. "She was thirty. You understand how fucking tragic that is?"

"Basta." Mamá stood up, too.

"Not enough." I switched to Spanish as well. "The way we dealt with it makes no sense based on what happened. It doesn't fit. A tragic death happened in our family."

"And you want to keep talking about it?" she accused.

I couldn't believe I was the one telling them we had to talk about things. "We have three traumatized kids—"

"They are not traumatized!" She wouldn't budge, and now my dad stood up too, trying to calm my mother down.

"They are scared of their biological father. They are missing their dead mother!" I roared.

"Stop talking!" she shrieked.

"Basta!"

The power died in my lungs. My mother's eyes widened, and we three stared at Logan, who just stood up and was speaking in perfect Spanish. "What Alvaro is trying to say is that in order to help the children, we need to heal ourselves, too."

No one talked. We all just gaped at her. Her timbre changed in Spanish. I liked it a lot. Logan sat down after that, smoothing her clothes over her legs. She cleared her throat. "I'm raising Latino kids and I grew up with Sofia. Yeah, I speak Spanish."

Papá smiled at her and sat down. I remained standing watching my mother, waiting for her to turn this into a problem as well, until I felt soft fingers closing over my wrists.

The feel of her skin on mine was enough to calm my muscles from twitching. Papá's eyes followed her hand, but I didn't care enough to move away from her touch. Logan's thumb made delicate circles around my pulse, and I let out a breath and sat down again.

Mamá was the last one to sit down but she did, and I started over, not gentle anymore. "You treated Logan like she was a villain." I turned to my mother accusingly, even if my tone was low. "You acted like she was ruining our family when she was the only one who tried to save us. She was the only one who protected Sofia, and you tried to push her away."

I knew my words hit the target when my mother's eyes filled with tears. Papá, with a rage I didn't expect from him, slapped a hand on the table.

"Enough, Alvaro."

"We all sat as she suffered, and Logan was the only person who—" I knew I was ready to pop a vein, my eyes turning red with rage, but then Logan's hand was over my leg, stopping me.

"It doesn't matter anymore."

"It doesn't?" I asked, turning my gaze to her. "You come here with fear of being rejected when we should thank you? You tried to take care of Sofia, and now you're raising her kids. You did what we couldn't do, Logan."

She looked me right in the eyes, frowning as she sent me a sad smile. "I did it because I loved Sofia. And I love the kids. It doesn't matter anymore."

"It matters to me," I told her and then moved my eyes to my parents. "Logan should be treated better."

"Logan," Papá started. "We do appreciate what you do for the kids. They look great. Healthy."

Mamá said nothing. Her eyes shattered in pain. I wanted to feel sorry for hurting my mother, but my pain didn't let me.

"What were you trying to find in those old pictures?" she finally asked.

"Old pictures?" Logan furrowed her eyebrows.

I rubbed my palm over my face. "Something. A sign. I don't understand how we missed it. How bad things were that she—"

"She was here." Papá sagged to the chair, all the fight leaving his body. "She wasn't with him anymore. She was here."

Here. I understood the hurt in his voice. Because it was them who found Sofia. The kids were away at different sleepovers, they came back from church and Sofia...

I shook the image away. It was horrible. I couldn't begin to understand the pain of them finding Sofia dead, knowing nothing was ever going to be the same.

I wanted to be kind to them. I wanted to understand their misery, but my heart bled when I thought of what she went through. I couldn't comprehend how she felt, how she wanted to leave us even after years away from David.

"Because the kids were safe."

We all stopped and looked at Mamá. Her voice was raw, ripping from her throat, silent tears down her lashes. She looked at Logan and with a nod that seemed more for herself than to any of us, she turned and opened the cupboard above the stove.

Inside the cookie jar that never held a cookie in one day of its life, she took out a letter.

The letter.

I knew Sofia left a letter, but Mamá said it wasn't for me and I accepted that since I couldn't find in my heart to read it, anyway.

It was for Logan. For months I kept the secret, thinking maybe she wasn't ready to let go of the last thing from Sofia.

Gulping, she passed the envelope to Logan.

"She left you a letter."

Logan didn't ask why it took so long to find its way to her. She just pressed her fingers on top and slipped it toward her, a breath catching as she saw Sofia's handwriting on the front.

"Let's go," I said.

Logan nodded, bringing the envelope closer to her and nodding to Papá.

"I'm sorry about... your party."

Papá could barely reply. He just shook his head and looked away. No one could talk after that, and I knew it was my fault. I just couldn't do it anymore. I couldn't ignore Sofia's story one second longer.

She loved those kids. She was a great mother. I couldn't breathe thinking about how broken she must have felt to leave them behind.

The kids said nothing when we told them we were going. They just followed us to the car and put their seat belts on.

My hands on the wheel, I looked ahead, lost in my thoughts as Logan faced the window doing the same. Our ride back to the city was silent, sad. Lachlan fell asleep. Vienna hummed under her breath. Dash had his earphones on.

My phone pinged with a message. I chanced a glance, and it was all there in black and white.

Paddy: One fight and you'll never hear from me again.

I could easily say no to him, but my number was up. David wanted money to leave Logan alone. I hated he was using my will to protect her against me, but if there was ever a way to make me do something stupid, this was it.

One fight could solve it all. I could let Paddy schedule it and call his regulars. One fight to make all the money and get rid of David and Paddy in one go.

I had a reason to do it this time. I had people to look after. I had to think about the kids… and Logan. Always fucking Logan.

Like she knew of my dark thoughts, her hand came to mine on top of my thighs, squeezing it. I brought it to my mouth, planting a kiss on her palm. And then lowering it back and holding her there.

"Is tío your boyfriend now?" Vienna asked.

No, I was her ruin.

# 26

# Logan

*Lo,*

*Remember in seventh grade when you weren't invited to Marcy's bar mitzvah because you didn't let her copy that math homework even after you explained you weren't being a bitch, you were just real scared of getting caught?*

*I decided not to go, too, and we stayed at my house, watching a bunch of movies and eating gummy bears until my mother started shouting at us.*

*You said I was always protecting you. Like choosing not to go to the party of the most annoying girl in our class made me a hero.*

*I wasn't staying behind because I was kind to you. I stayed behind because I was likeyou. I didn't fit in either, but when you came to school for the first time, I didn't mind not fitting in.*

*Being alone together was way more fun. You were bright, funny, and my best friend. You were my hero, and I thought you were the coolest girl at school.*

*When I met David, I should've listened to you. But I was in love and too young.*

*I was dumb. I should have stayed behind with you that night, too. It hurts me to say that because the night I'm talking about is when I got pregnant with Dash.*

*I love my kid, Lo. You know that. But that night, I wasn't ready. I was just a kid, but David said we had been together long enough. We liked each other enough. He listed a bunch of reasons and I felt cornered. I thought he was right, so I went with him when I should have asked you to watch a movie and eat gummy bears instead.*

*So many other times I should have grabbed the phone and called you, but instead I stayed. I let him say things to me. I raised Dash in fear. I had more children because he said it was time.*

*I never reached out because he told me you were at Harvard and I was a joke to you. He isolated me and made me feel worthless, and eventually his words were the only truth I knew.*

*A teen mom. A loser. Why would Logan want to be friends with you?*

*I know that's not you. You never cared about anything but me, but sometimes his voice was so loud, Lo.*

*Still is.*

*It's always there, always telling me what to do. Always reminding me I'm not enough.*

*And then, I close my eyes and I rewind back to the night I should have stayed with you. I think about what we could've watched and how much junk food we could've eaten until Mamá confiscated it all.*

*I'm not proud of that. That's slipping, that's me trying to rewrite history and that's not fair with the kids.*

*I love them and I want them safe.*

*He can never get to them, Lo. He doesn't have parental rights, but he's smart. I spend nights thinking of all the ways he can get to me. It's not like we are hiding.*

*I'm living in my parents' house. The kids go to the same school we went to. It's him who isn't interested in us anymore, thank god.*

*But if that ever changes?*

*I'm tired.*

*I just want to find a way to make sure they are safe. That they always stay behind in a room with you, having gummy bears like I should have.*

*I'm sorry.*

*I wish I could stay.*

*Sofia.*

I HAD A SHOWER after we were back from the Castillo's home. The kids were in bed already and Alvaro went straight to the gym. I knew he needed to think. I only convinced myself to have a shower to stall. To buy myself time before reading the letter. My hair was still wet, only a sweatshirt over my body, and I couldn't hold back anymore.

I took the letter and opened it, sitting at the edge of the bed to read.

I must have read it ten, twenty, fifty times. I couldn't feel the tears streaming down my face, but I cursed when one fell on the paper.

Putting it aside before I destroyed it, I looked down at my toes. Was that enough reason to give me her kids? A night in seventh grade when she felt protected?

But even as I scoffed at her reasoning, I knew it was more than that. I knew David. She knew I'd never let the kids be with him, not when I already failed her.

The parenting books that I compulsively piled on my bedside table weren't enough guidance. I had no idea what I was doing. Every day, I learned something new. And not just because they were kids, but because they were *them*. They had their own personalities, their own quirks. I learned them all, and I loved doing it.

Sure, I probably wasn't the best person for the job but Sofia was right. I'd do anything to protect those kids. Whatever the cost.

Agony ripped my chest apart, my lips quivered, and I cried for my best friend. Cried for her fears. Cried for her life.

My head cast down. I didn't notice he came in until he tilted my chin up. He was still wet, only a towel around his waist. He frowned while his hand took the curve of my cheek.

Whiskey eyes darted to the letter, understanding coming to his features. I closed my fingers around the paper, raising it between us.

"You can read it if you like."

I could almost hear his indecision. Finally, he took it from me, but placed it on the bedside table along with my parenting books.

"Another time."

Strong arms circled my body, my legs going around his waist instinctively, my head buried in the crook of his neck like it was a practiced move.

He let me hold on to him tight, my tears falling on his damp skin. He sat us on the bed, his back to the headboard with me straddling his waist.

“I need you to stop crying, nena,” his voice rasped in my ear. “You’re ending me.”

I chuckled at the idea that I was ending the man whose nickname was El Toro.

“Tell me how to make you feel better.”

I moved to peer at his face. “Is that you coming on to me?”

He chuckled, his grip on my ass tightening. “I know you have no underwear on under that fancy sweatshirt of yours. Don’t tempt me, woman.”

Only Alvaro could make me blush like this in the middle of my tears. My hands went to each side of his face, taking him in.

“I’m sad cause she’s not here. But I’m so grateful you and the kids are.” I took in a deep breath. “She loved the kids and regretted ever meeting David at the same time. Do you think that’s life, Alvaro? There’s always a little sadness right in the middle of the happiness?”

“If it is, I will do all I can to change it for you. I’ll fuck up the world so you can only get the good parts.”

Alvaro Castillo wasn’t a prince. He was rough and moody. He was also loyal and the calm in a storm. He broke my heart and put it back together one look at the time.

“You and the kids are the good parts,” I whispered an inch from his mouth. “That’s all I need.”

We broke the space between us at the same time. His hand buried in my wet hair. My scalp tingled when he pulled on my wet strands to make my mouth take him the way he wanted. I held on to his shoulders, and then up, lacing them around his neck as he untied the knot of his towel. When nothing separated us, I felt the cold metal of the piercing against my stomach making me suck in a breath while we kissed.

"You love that piercing, don't you?"

I couldn't talk, so I just nodded, and he growled. "I'll get more for you. A full fucking ladder."

I moaned. I wasn't sure if he was just saying it, but the idea he would pierce it just for me had my hands shaking and my knees melting.

He kissed me slowly, taking symphonies of whimpers from my lips. Reaching to the bedside drawer, he took a condom, making quick work of it between us.

The question if I was riding him again almost left my lips, but before I had the chance, he dropped me in the bed, his big body covering mine.

He said nothing, only stared right into my eyes and bottomed out at once.

My mouth fell open. He set a pace and brought his hand under my sweatshirt, squeezing my nipple between his fingers.

And then he kissed me again. Slowly, taking what belonged to him. Because that was what was happening. I belonged to him, wholehearted, I did.

My heart was his to take, my body his to destroy. The love I felt for Alvaro Castillo couldn't exist in a vacuum anymore.

I couldn't contain it, sneaking kisses after dark, quickies at midnight. My love for him grew stronger, impossible, and took over my life. I couldn't be without him. I couldn't pretend he was just Sofia's older brother anymore.

I wanted to be with him and be it for him. I wanted to touch him all the time. I wanted to kiss him whenever I wanted.

I dreamed of someone looking at me just the way he did. Somewhere so deep inside, I wasn't sure when he ended and I began.

I wanted impossible love.

And I got it. *I had it.*

My body shook, the fear of losing something I wanted so badly taking over. I could hear my heart beating fast, numbness spreading over my toes.

"Alvaro..." I whispered, tears running from the corners of my eyes.

"Tell me what is wrong, Jefa."

He was still inside me, thrusting shallow until he took a good look at me and stopped all together.

Lips parted but no sound came out. How could I explain that to someone? I had everything I've ever wanted and I was still scared? Scared of being alone. Of failure. But I was scared of happiness, too. Of all my dreams coming true just to wake up the next day with nothing.

Before I could think of words in the English language that made sense to that feeling, he was nodding like I said it all with a look.

I gulped for air. He moved and I panicked thinking he was going to give me space. I didn't need space. Instead, he pushed harder, his hand closed on throat, tilting my head up and feeling my pulse at the same time.

"I've got you," he promised.

"Alvaro..." I tried to shake my head.

"Can you see me?" he asked, his eyes watching mine like nothing else was around.

I jerkily nodded.

"Use your words, Jefa."

"I can see you," I whispered.

He hummed, satisfied. And then he came down, kissing me softly. "Can you taste me?"

Tears I couldn't control spilled from my eyes, but I answered him anyway. "I can."

"Now, can you feel me?"

My hands reached for his shoulders, down his arms, feeling the hot, smooth skin under my fingertips. My shoulders relaxed, my legs opened even more, and I concentrated on the feeling of having him inside me. Like he could read my mind, Alvaro thrusted. I felt his piercing, his cock stretching me, hitting me right in the right place.

"I can feel you," I told him, the roughness in my voice undeniable.

His thumb circled my pulse, so tender, so careful. "So be here with me. Don't be anywhere else. Whatever your demons, I'm slaying them for you. I'll never let you cry. Never let you fall."

My hands dug to his skin, looking at him and only him. The lines besides his eyes, his full lips. The tension of his arms when pumped into me. The feeling of his weight over my body.

"You don't owe anyone perfection," he said. "You don't need to be anyone but you."

All the feeling came rushing back to my body, my heart chasing something good. He thrusted faster, my back arching off the bed.

"You don't belong to anxiety, Jefa," he rasped to my ear. "You belong to me."

I came with his name on my lips. He let my throat go and kissed me when he came with a growl right between my lips.

The next day, I gave him a kiss before he went to work, rolling my eyes when Vienna giggled. I ignored Dash's eyes on me and just finished giving Lachlan his breakfast.

Because he got me.

He said it.

But that was all before I went downstairs and found a letter without postage waiting for me.

It read an address, a time, and that was it.

I knew who sent it, the fear running down my spine with the thought of him in my building again.

My eyes focused on the address and when Michael, the doorman, asked, "Everything ok, Ms. Hart?"

I lied.

"Yes."

# 27

# Alvaro

"It's good. You see that?"

Paddy's grin was sickening, his eyes scanning the crowd. By the time I arrived, I couldn't even find a place to park my car. I should have known. I usually gave him twenty minutes heads up, and he found people to gamble. With a twenty-four-hour warning?

The motherfucker packed the house.

The kid I fought last year was waiting for me and all I wanted was to end this fast.

"I want my money as soon as this ends, Paddy," I said from my place, my elbows over my knees. I preferred to look at the sticky floor than him.

"These things take time, Toro..."

I flashed him a dangerous look. "Don't make me end you, Paddy. This is the last time."

He shifted uncomfortably on his feet. "Yeah, ok. Let's go out with a bang, huh?"

My chest constricted, but I wrapped my hands anyway. I'd lie to her again. She'd take in my knuckles, probably my face and body, and I'd have to explain myself. I knew the excuses. I rehearsed them, but I hated having to lie to her.

I shook off the guilt, the mission clear in front of me. Dirt with dirt. I'd pay David out of our lives with the very thing that threatened it.

I was done messing with Paddy and the shitty people he kept around. He was greedy with no scruples. I couldn't be involved with this shit anymore.

Finally, I had something to fight for and it was far away from the ring.

Standing to my full height, I pinned Paddy with a look. "Let's get it over with."

He didn't ask me to wait until he warmed up the crowd. At this point, I gave him too much already. He left quickly, and I cracked my neck as I heard his voice calling everyone's attention.

The fucker was loud. He had cops in his back pocket and never worried about being discovered. It was stupid. So many nights I was here, working out my frustrations and ignoring the people I got myself tangled with. Now, the reward seemed small for the risk.

The El Toro chant broke out, and I moved from the locker room. My eyes fixed on one trajectory—the ring. Paddy was still talking on the microphone, telling tales of my victories like the stupidest troubadour.

Nothing mattered in a fight. Not if you were coming from a losing streak or a winning one. Nothing defined a match except minutes you spent in the ring.

He could count all my winnings and still, only what I did today was going to mean anything.

The sound lowered down in my mind. I looked at the boy who I beat last year and found nothing memorable about him.

I couldn't place his face, his name, or anything about him. He was just another person I beat when I was frustrated with my own life. He was a pawn in my own narrative, and I felt that so deeply I almost told him that.

*Don't define yourself by me. I don't even remember you.*

It would be tragic if it wasn't the way of life. I closed my mouth and said nothing. With a quick move, he started.

One punch that was easy to avoid. His feet were quick, but he gave too much away.

I knew now why he had lost before. It wasn't because I was bigger. It was because he told me all I needed to know about him at once.

He punched me first, making the crowd wince collectively. Blood streamed from my gums, but I smiled. I knew all his moves now.

My bloody smile must be terrifying because that was the moment he first flinched.

After that, my hooks connected easily. I trapped him to the side he didn't know how to defend well, and blow after blow connected. My knuckles split again with old wounds. It was his blood, and the blood of others who were in the same place he stood now.

He moved with more agility than I liked. I ignored the blood streaming from my face and went for it.

The fight was me against me. My demons and now the demons of my sister.

The boy dropped on the canvas and I stood there victorious without the rush.

The crowd cheered El Toro.

*The last time*, I said.

The last time.

I moved to the ropes before Paddy attempted to hold my fist high, but when I turned emerald green eyes were all I saw.

# 28
# Logan

It was a gym.

The address David left was a gym, and something was clearly happening judging by the number of people arriving.

I shouldn't be here. I was out of place and that was clear, but the questions burned in my mind. I needed to set him straight. I wanted him out of our lives and if he wanted money…

Willa told me to file for a restraining order, but Sofia's letter had me wondering. Suddenly, I didn't want to anger him. I wanted him to back off, to be uninterested. Angry people found ways to hurt us. Maybe if I gave him what he wanted, he would leave us alone.

That theory was ridiculous and proved itself wrong the second I arrived at the gym. The address could be anything. He could kill me, and Alvaro wouldn't know any better.

I scoffed at my lunacy, ready to leave, when I spotted something across the street.

The Castillo Construction logo

Alvaro's truck.

I swung the door opened, my eyes on the old gym that looked more like an abandoned warehouse. When I stepped in I made a face, overwhelmed by the smell and the noise. The machines were moved to the side, and there were people everywhere.

Right in the middle, a boxing ring.

I could barely walk, avoiding people but they practically dragged me. Not sure where I was going, I had to stop in my tracks when the crowd started to chant.

His nickname was a rehearsed song. Turning my stomach, I held onto it in shock.

*El Toro*, they called for him.

Far away, someone started announcements. The cheers went up a notch, energy sizzling. My heart was hammering in my chest. I knew it was coming, but still felt faint when I saw movement to my right side. My eyes darted to the door just in time to see him parting the crowd.

His serious manner was simply deadly. He was all muscle, dressed in nothing but black silk shorts. Long gone was the man I kissed this morning. This one carried death in his eyes.

He parted the ropes and entered the ring as the man announced his opponent.

I watched it all with my ears ringing. Eyes following every move, each punch.

"I bet fifty on the Toro," the voice to my side said.

Dread spread over my chest, and I turned only to see for myself what I already knew.

David seemed relaxed in the middle of it all, smiling at my horror as he watched the fight with me.

"You brought me here." It was all I said without taking my eyes off Alvaro.

"And you came. Always the good girl, Lo."

I wanted to ask him not to call me that, but I didn't care anymore. I wanted him not to call me at all. When I didn't reply, he pushed.

"Told your man I won't tell anyone. But I have a price, Lo. I'm not a charity, ya know?"

"Tell what?" I faced him.

That was enough to make him open a smile. Cursing myself, I turned back to watch Alvaro again.

"This is illegal. This circus. Paddy shouldn't be illegally gambling here, but Paddy isn't good at following the rules."

I couldn't give a damn who Paddy was, but his words hit nevertheless.

"You asked for money already."

"And you ignored me. Rude. So I asked big brother. I think he was easier to persuade than you. Surprising right? I'd say he has more to lose."

"You're blackmailing him."

"Oh, no," he scoffed. "That's the funny part. I'm blackmailing *you*. He just sees himself as a superhero. I'd say he can't protect anyone, but whatever makes the money move, huh?"

Alvaro was winning one punch after another. He was ending the man against him.

"And you'll go forever?" I managed to croak. "I want you out of the country. I want you gone."

"No high school reunion?" He smiled.

"Gone, David. It's that or nothing."

He nodded right in time as Alvaro ended his adversary. I didn't wait to chat with David. Those few words we exchanged made me want to shower half a dozen times.

I moved the crowd, not being polite this time until I ended close to the ropes, just at the corner I knew he was going to exit. And right when he turned, his eyes found mine.

My lip quivered in reflex, and I stepped away as he came down from the raised platform.

Sweat, blood, and my tears.

My head was spinning. I opened my mouth, but he shook his head. "Come here."

I followed him without a word until we ended in a locker room. It stunk of sweat, like it was never washed before. The floors were sticky, making noise as I walked to the middle of the room, bracing myself. Alvaro locked the door. I never asked why he had a key.

"What are you doing here?"

"Illegal gambling?" I asked instead.

"Where are the kids?"

"Dash is home." I couldn't stop myself from replying, but I bit my own tongue. "What's happening, Alvaro?"

He rubbed his eyes, making me wince from the blood smearing his face.

"I come here to..."

"To fight."

"To deal with shit."

"Go to fucking therapy." I chuckled sarcastically. "You know who gave me this address?"

His face was confused, but just for a second, until it opened in clarity. He cursed under his breath.

"He says he'll tell the cops you're involved in illegal fighting if we don't pay him off."

"He told me that, too."

"Shit, Alvaro. When? When did you know that?"

"Right after we saw him. He asked for money and..."

"And why have you never told me?"

"Because I never wanted you to know," he roared in a tone I'd never heard him take with me before.

"Well, now I do."

"It's a fucking mess."

"The kids. I could lose the kids..." I shook my head.

That was all I could think about. I could lose the kids and Alvaro was here, dealing with whatever he wanted to deal with.

"I know."

His confession made me snap out of my head. "You knew?"

"This fight was for money to give to David. To send him away."

"With more ammunition against you? You have to be smarter than this."

"Shit, Logan, you're the legal guardian. Who cares what I do?"

And it finally came to me. I stumbled back. "You were never staying with me. You were paying David and moving on."

"Moving on is not the word I'd use."

"Leave me. Leave the kids. Go on with your life. That's better?"

"That's not fair, and you know it."

"No, it's fucking not!" It was my turn to roar. "You've been asking me to trust you, Alvaro. You told me you got me."

The vein in his neck popped. "And this is me protecting you."

"This is you hiding shit from me. I have money. I have ways to deal with this..."

"I didn't want—"

"What? To tell me you fucked up? I needed to know. For us, for the kids. So sure, make the money and disappear on me. What about them? You're their uncle."

"They never needed me before. They would be fine."

"We all need you." My voice sounded broken even to my ears. "But sure, do that. Have your sacrificing moment. I'll pay David. But you can go ahead and put me in the past."

"Logan, I was..."

"Whatever you were doing. I needed you to tell me."

His jaw was set, bloody hands shaking. I pieced together all the times I saw those bloody knuckles. All the times he lied to me. Even when I met him at Sofia's funeral, he had a split lip.

I wasn't sure what hurt me the most. Was it the lies? Was it the way he dealt with it? Or was it how he was planning on leaving rather than telling me what David had on him?

I was just hurt, broken, and tired.

I moved to my car in a haze, ignoring everything and everyone in my way. I wanted to get home, cuddle with the kids and forget that once I thought everything was going to be fine.

# 29
# Logan

My eyes ran through the last paragraph one more time with a sigh before I lowered the papers onto the table.

Dashiell watched me in silence, his left leg hopping up and down while he waited for me to finish reading his essay.

"You're a good writer," I simply said.

And that was enough to make him groan, putting his head on his hands. I had to laugh.

"What?"

"You're looking at me like I have a future or something."

I snorted. "Oh well, I know that goes against your overall aesthetic, but you're smart and talented."

He lifted his gaze to mine, a flicker of pride passing through his honey-colored eyes. "And you really think it's good? Not just because you want me to..." he trailed off.

"To go to college?" I arched an eyebrow, and he moved his gaze from me, making me chuckle. "Oh, yeah, I'm a horrible person because I want you to go to college. What else is out there?"

"I'm not Ivy League material, Lo."

I had to ignore my melting heart every time they called me Lo like Sofia used to do. It was a huge step forward, and if that same heart wasn't breaking because of the other Castillo, I'd say life was full. Perfect even.

But his absence was felt by all of us. I felt every single one of the seven days and thirteen hours we had been apart.

Refusing to let my mind go through that path again, I took a fortifying breath and made myself concentrate on Dash.

"I like how you just assume you'll get in." I crossed my arms in front of my chest, mocking him. "But I don't care where you go, Dash. I just want you to... want something for yourself. Whatever it is."

"Even if I want to skip it and work for tío?" he challenged.

I gulped, ignoring the way my heart skipped with the word tío.

"If that's what you want." I shrugged. What I wanted was for Dash to *want* something. Literally anything that wasn't running away and raising his siblings. He needed to think about the future without triggering his fight or flight instincts.

He shook his head, reclining on the chair. The office was his new place to study, away from the kids. He first said it wasn't necessary, but I could tell he liked the privilege.

Vienna and Lachlan were with Dr. Maya. I was supposed to use the time off to catch up on a couple of things, but I couldn't say no when he asked me to read his essay for English class.

"Tío wakes up way too early."

"College is a great time for you to figure things out."

"That's what rich kids do. The rest of us are thinking it will help with our life's prospect, but we end up swimming in debt for years to come."

"Look how smart you are," I offered. "You just forgot one detail."

"What?"

"You're the rich kid now."

My words had the desired effect. He groaned, making the most disgusted expression I'd ever seen on his face. I had to laugh and poke him further. "Living in a penthouse, studying at Lone Pine. That's you Dashiell Geraldo Murphy."

"Thanks," he said. "Now I hate myself."

I leaned over the table, catching his eyes. "You're smart. Go wherever you want to go."

"Why is  this is such a big deal to you?" He rolled his shoulders back. "I have time to think it over."

"Well, depending on where you want to go, you need to start choosing the right extra-curricular activities ..." I caught my tongue because he looked petrified at the idea of preparing a curriculum. "I want you to want something for you, Dash, just you and not the kids. I want you to act your age." I skipped the part where  when he antagonized Vienna, looked exactly his age. "If I need to drag you to college parties, so be it."

"You're great at parenting." He grinned. "College parties, huh?"

"I'll be there to watch. Don't be too excited."

"Never."

We fell into a comfortable silence, and he looked down at the essay in front of me. "Good?"

"Excellent," I said.

And I wasn't just trying to motivate him. He was a good writer, a natural even if he hadn't noticed yet. I glanced down at my watch and stood up. "I'm getting the kids. Come with me and we can get dinner, too."

He jumped into action. Nothing made a teenager boy move quicker than a promise of takeaway.

We got into the elevator and went straight to the garage, ignoring my second parking spot that Alvaro never used.

That was the sign I missed. Things moved between us, but his truck remained parked across the street. Day in and day out, he never really lived here. Not when he made sure only to pack a duffel at the time.

He was a guest, always a guest, and it was on me to think he'd ever be anything but.

"Can we get food from Antonio's?"

My hand gripped tighter on the wheel. Dash didn't miss it.

"What did he do?"

I cleared my throat. "What?"

"How did tío fuck this up?"

"Language."

He huffed and looked away. Even though picking up food from Antonio's was the last thing I wanted to do, I drove to that side of town.

Eyes on the road, I ignored my stupid heart every time I saw a white truck just to hurt all over again when I couldn't spot the Castillo Construction logo.

The pain was especially excruciating when I drove to Alvaro's favorite restaurant. My mind wouldn't rest, thinking I'd see him at every corner, on every street.

"I wasn't trying to be..." Dash started. "I'm sorry. We can go someplace else. Get the kids and whatever they want is good for me."

I shook my head. “No. It’s fine.” I parked the car and turned to him.

Dash’s lip twitched in a smile. “If you say so.”

I hopped from the car, not bothering to ask what he wanted. I knew the routine—we needed enough pasta, garlic bread, and chicken parmigiana to feed an army.

The street was busy as I crossed. When my hand closed over the knob, I couldn’t stop the wave of regret clogging my throat.

It was just a restaurant, but it was a memory of Alvaro, too.

There was nothing I wanted more than to forgive him. Every time I grabbed the phone to call him, I changed my mind at the last minute, reminding myself I was too angry to talk.

I looked at the menu over the counter, just in case something new caught my attention. I was so engrossed scanning the three-fold plastic menu, I almost missed someone calling my name.

My eyes flew upwards, finding Dustin watching me carefully, hands closed in a fist. Even if it was stupid, I couldn’t stop myself from looking behind him. It was ridiculous, impossible. It wasn’t like he could hide a mountain of a man from the view.

He reached over in comfort. I hated the pity on his face. Averting my gaze, I looked at his hand wrapped over my arm and said nothing, making him clear his throat and step back. “Hey there, Logan. This is my girlfriend, Mirella. Her parents own the restaurant.”

In my search for the big man with tattoos down his knuckles, I didn’t notice the happy redhead beside Dustin.

I licked my lips, begging my heart to settle, and extended my hand. "Hi, I'm Logan."

Dustin said something to her. Explaining who I was. I blinked and held my breath, afraid the tears would stream down my cheeks even as I stood there smiling tightly.

So, I wasn't as okay as I thought.

I missed him so much. I wondered if I did the right thing. Why was I angry again?

Oh yeah, the hiding, sneaking, and the overall stupidity of that plan.

It hurt. I wanted to be his partner so bad. When I found out he kept secrets, I got hurt enough to push him away. And now I was practically having a meltdown in the middle of the restaurant. My heart shattered, making me wonder if it was all worth it.

Being right never was.

"Logan?"

Next I blinked, Dustin had sent his girlfriend away, his expression worried. I stiffened when he came closer once again, lowering his voice. "I know that it's not on you. But you're the only one who can change his mind."

On high alert right then, I pressed. "What are you talking about?"

Dustin looked around again, like he was afraid someone would jump out from behind the menus.

"I tried talking him out of it. It's dangerous. It's stupid. He won't play fair. It's a suicide mission."

My blood curdled inside my veins. "Tell me."

"Alvaro," he said, his eyes dropping. "He's fighting David."

"He what?" I reeled back because those words surely made no sense. "David Murphy?"

Dustin made a face like all he wanted was not to say the name. "He's fighting him in three days."

"That's insane," I scoffed. "David is half of Alvaro's size. He's not a fighter. He's..."

"Logan," he called me from my thoughts. "There's only one reason for David to accept fighting Alvaro."

"He's going to cheat." Of course he was. David did nothing without cheating. Being honorable wasn't something he liked to do or knew how to do. "Why is he doing this?"

Dustin sent me a sad smile. "Sofia? You? The kids? Take a pick. That guy will never leave you alone. Alvaro knows it. I get it but..."

"He's going to kill Alvaro," I whispered.

The words rang between us, an impossible sentence I never thought I'd say. Fear hammered in my chest, and without another word, I said goodbye to Dustin and left the restaurant.

Alvaro was planning on killing David. Or at least harming him enough, but it was he who would end up dead. There was no way in hell David would get inside a ring with a beast that was El Toro without a Plan B.

He wasn't banking on his fists for this.

I got in the car, slamming the door shut and racing from the restaurant. I needed to call Alvaro, but I had to get the kids first and make sure they were home and—

"Logan? Where's the food?"

# 30.

# Alvaro

She called me for the first time at six thirty a week after I left her house.

Her name flashed on my screen and something inside me twisted like it got stabbed with a knife. Just the five letters of her name was enough to do that to me. I tried to taste her on my tongue, smell her in my space. It was all in vain.

My walls were without Lachlan's most recent art. My house lacked flowers.

*Magnolias.* Where were the magnolias?

The empty walls and practical furniture never bothered me until that day when I missed her home.

I had a comfortable couch and a big TV. My bed was good. I thought I liked it all until all I had were my bare walls to watch.

My life reset to the day before Sofia died. I came back to an empty apartment. I worked until I couldn't stand, and I pushed further by going to the gym. My frustrations hung on me, refusing to let me go as I tried to work them out in the ring.

I was in my forties, and no one depended on me. A ghost of a man. There but not. Life meant nothing if it wasn't for the people you loved.

Sofia's death weighed heavier than ever on my shoulders. Intrusive thoughts played in my mind all day. A constant reminder of how useless I'd been my whole life.

I couldn't go on like this anymore. I felt the fire under my skin demanding action. Then Paddy called and told me an unusual request came to the gym. I accepted.

David wanted to fight me?

He was small, with no training. I wasn't stupid. I knew something didn't feel right, but I was past caring. I wanted a chance to confront him, and he just gave me the perfect opportunity.

When the phone rang again with her name flashing, I felt the pang of hurt. I knew I should answer because her voice was all I wanted to hear.

But I couldn't.

I let it ring. And she called again and again, but I never picked up.

My sins were accumulating, crawling from under the bed and dark corners. I refused to dwell on the pain, and I moved to the punching bag hanging from my ceiling.

A silly thing I installed when I bought my apartment, when my life started and ended with MMA.

In a way, Mamá was right to hate it. This was all I knew. The walls shouldn't be so empty. My dating life should be more than a couple of disastrous dates throughout the year.

I was forty-six.

Shit. Forty-six and in love for the first time.

The bag swayed with the aggressive punch, and still I wouldn't stop tearing my own soul apart, never answering her.

Then she came around. That BMW didn't belong in my neighborhood. I could smell her perfume from across the door. She screamed my name, her fist banging on the wood, but I kept punching the bag until her voice was hoarse.

"Don't do it," she asked quietly.

I stopped right away, breath stuck in my lungs. I held the bag, frozen in place with her raw tone.

"Alvaro," she called, causing goosebumps all over my skin.

It killed me not to open the door, but I couldn't give her the opportunity to change my mind. And she could. She would. Because I would do anything for that woman.

But David killed my sister.

Sofia was the one who locked the garage doors and turned on the engine that afternoon, but it was his words that played in her mind while she did it. He abused her since she was a teenager. He crushed her self-esteem and everything that made her the ray of sunshine she was.

Sofia was softness, she was giggles and warmth. She was... like Vienna. The person who always tried to make the best of things, who laughed the loudest.

She was good. Too good. My fate didn't matter anymore, but if I was going to be dragged to hell for my sins, I was going to bring David with me.

"Alvaro, don't do it," Logan begged again.

My feet moved before I knew what they were doing. I crossed the living room, my heart lunging at the sound of her broken voice. I stepped closer to the front door, the only barrier between us.

My hand covered the door, still quiet, jaw set, trying my hardest to resist the temptation.

I could take her and pretend I didn't carry guilt over my shoulders. I could let her pay him or pay him myself like I planned before.

Many options were better than the one I was going for. I knew that was true.

But I chose my path. I'd end David like he ended my sister. I needed it. Sofia needed it. The kids and even Logan needed it.

"Go home, Logan," I called roughly, trying to scare her off.

I turned around, ignoring her voice, and my fist connected with the punching bag once more.

"ENOUGH PEOPLE OUT THERE." Paddy's eyes, full of greed, scanned the crowd.

"Do you have to do this every time?" I snapped.

Saying I was done with him clearly meant nothing, because I found myself back at his dirty gym. Paddy rubbed his hands with eagerness, pissing me off even more.

The money was never a factor, and my rage was never resolved. My empty life mocked me and this—whatever pawn I let myself be in Paddy's games—wasn't worth it anymore.

The mission played in my mind. Remove David from the kids' lives and go home.

The crowd thickened outside, making Paddy jump on his feet and turn a cruel smile my way. "Whenever you're ready, Toro."

Paddy was a wolf in sheep's clothing. He knew whose palms to grease, who to befriend. He always played the sheep card in front of me, but something changed today. I could see beyond his posture and his lies.

"El Toro," I corrected his shit pronunciation. With a last look, I went through the door. My eyes scanned every face, memorizing the moment I wanted to forget.

Parting the ropes at the corner, I stepped onto the soft padding, standing up to my full height and facing my opponent.

He didn't crack five foot ten. His arms were skinnier than the fifteen-year-old's he left behind without paying child support.

David's mouth curved in a sinister smile like we shared a horrible secret. And we did.

He was poison, and I was ready to purge him from this earth.

"Alvaro!"

Her call ripped through the air, muffling everyone else. I turned from David, my eyes darting across the room, trying to find her.

When I did, I let out a relieved breath. There was no reason for me to ever think she'd be here, but she came forward like a dream coming true.

She flung herself trying to reach me, not giving a damn if she stepped on some shoes. Once people saw who she was trying to reach, they stepped aside.

Her hair was secured in a firm ponytail. Brown boots, a soft mid-length dress that looked like it cost more than my truck. She rose on the platform, her hands closing on the ropes.

"He's going to do something. There's no way in hell he'd be in this ring with you if he wasn't ready to cheat his way out of this fight."

Her eyes locked on somewhere over my shoulder. I bet anything it was on David. Not wanting her to look his way, I pinched her chin between my fingers and turned her head.

"I know."

Her green eyes seemed shattered. "And you'll still fight him?"

"This is a score I need—"

"It's not a score." She spoke so low, I had to read it on her lips. "You're wrong. Me and the kids? We need you. We aren't doing well without you. You're my family, all of you are it for me and this..." she looked at David and winced, "this is how I lose you and I can't lose you, too."

My warmth sought her softness. I came closer to the ropes. My hands spanned over her cheeks, her eyes moving between mine, trying to read something. I was ready to spell it out to her.

"You can't get rid of me, Jefa."

"You never opened the door. And before, you said—"

"I said you don't need me." I nodded. "You don't. You don't need anyone. It doesn't mean I don't need you."

She frowned. I brought my nose close to hers and spoke to her mouth, "I never opened the door because this was something I had to do alone."

"You're so dumb," she retorted, making me reel back from the aggressive tone.

Her hand gripped the back of my head, not letting me go any further.

"There's nothing you'll ever do alone. It's me and you, alright?"

"Logan..." I shook my head. This wasn't something I wanted her to be involved in. To see, to know.

"You're going to kill him, El Toro?" she asked.

She didn't let me move, our noses touching, her hands gripping me, my knuckles turning white holding on to the ropes separating us.

Before I could say anything, she took a breath. "Finish this for me and Sofia."

And only when she was certain I heard her loud and clear, she let me go, her hands closing on the rope again. She moved down from the platform, and my eyes followed. She didn't go far. No one dared to crowd her after what we shared.

I licked my lips, dry and cracked. She gave me a single nod.

One nod to let me go. To release my fury.

I turned to face David, slowly, with my new resolve shining behind my eyes. David's knees buckled. I saw the moment he realized it was a mistake to share the same ring with me.

My fist flexed at the sound of Paddy calling my name. Logan's flowery scent was so present, I felt her right there with me. I breathed her in and looked at the man who lived with my sister for thirteen years.

The nightmare of her children.

I advanced on him in a flash, my skin burning for that first contact. I punched his stomach, watching him fold in two, curses flying off him.

A smile tugged the side of my mouth. I bent over, saying it to his right ear. "This is where you die."

David tried to straighten his spine, stepping backwards, he panicked. His eyes searched the crowd, stopping on Paddy.

I didn't give them time to communicate. I could tell there was more here, they were in on this together, yet I knew better. Paddy wasn't ever on anyone's side but his own.

I stepped closer, my hook this time finding his chin, solid enough to turn his face, blood splashing to the side.

David took a breath, his eyes trying to access the situation, as he called to the crowd, "You told me he played fair."

My eyes never left David, not interested in following their deal. Whatever Paddy said to make David agree to a fight didn't matter anymore.

Paddy profited from pain, and it was David's fault not to realize that.

Not holding back, I laughed, and I reached for David. Crowding him.

"Is that what he said? You came here thinking I was one of the good guys?"

His smile distorted his features. Lifeless pale green eyes stared back at me. We were face to face when I felt the cold sharp blade on my stomach.

"I came here to take it all."

The slash came certain, the precision of someone who wasn't a stranger to a blade. I felt the pain, the sting, and the blood oozing out.

But I also felt the rage, knowing all he wanted was the money. Nothing meant anything to him. I would have preferred if that stab was made of hate.

I stumbled back, holding my stomach with a hand, covering the slash. I glanced at Paddy, knowing he had a hand in that. He wasn't stopping the fight for a knife. He probably guaranteed David that much.

Blood trickled down between my fingers, soaking my shorts. The crowd noticed what happened, their yells taking over the gym in a rage, tension crackling in the air. My eyes found Paddy, his leveled face watching me. Everyone else was enraged.

I finally understood their deal. He convinced David to fight by promising him a dirty fight. And then he placed a bet on David, leaving everyone else to bet on me. The giant who won multiple times.

An enraged crowd asked to end the fight and begged for rules in a place that couldn't house fairness.

Raising the bloody hand, I pointed to Paddy with a promise.

And then, in the middle of chaos, her voice called to me.

# 31
# Logan

RAW PAIN RIPPED ME apart. My throat hoarse from calling his name.

His bloody hand pointed to the man at the microphone, a silent promise that brought goosebumps to the back of my neck.

*His blood.*

David was always going to cheat, the blade a small symbol of how he walked through life. He was a liar, a bully, and a con artist.

The crowd moved closer, bringing me with them. The tension was visible in every face, as was their thirst for blood. They yearned for a good show, and my man's blood was there to provide.

Before my next hiccup broke free, he changed the way he moved, his eyes on the blade between David's fingers.

I flung myself at the ropes, sneering at my old classmate. "You're a coward, David Murphy."

His eye twitched at me calling his last name in a place like this. I didn't care anymore. He stabbed Alvaro. *Stabbed.*

"Control your bitch."

"Never." Alvaro smirked before going for David.

My heart thundering hard in my chest, my eyes stung from tears, but I refused to look away from Alvaro.

He avoided the knife, planting a punch on David, making the man stumble back.

They moved around one another, Alvaro smart, quick on his feet, knowing exactly how to move. And even when he got nipped, making me wince and release a whimper, he managed to hurt David, too.

The crowd called for El Toro, and that smug expression on David's face was quickly washed off. My hands gripped the ropes, a scream lodged in my throat.

They danced for a while, David swinging the knife at Alvaro, taunting with empty words. I knew what he was doing. I watched him win that game before.

"That's all he has," I said over the noise. "End him."

I couldn't let myself step away. I kept drowning David's words with mine. Not ready to watch a Castillo lose from cruelty.

Done with waiting at the sidelines, I called Alvaro's name until my throat got raw, until he started to move faster, his punches stronger.

David kept his distance, sure the blade was enough to win a fight.

Blood meant nothing anymore. My heart hurt watching the droplets of Alvaro's blood drip onto the padded floors, but I knew in my soul he needed to do this.

After agonizing moments, David showed the first signs of exhaustion. And in that moment of weakness, he lurched, but found no purchase. Alvaro dodged the end of the blade and quickly, his hand closed around David's wrist.

I pushed on my tiptoes and watched with a sick smile on my lips as Alvaro smashed his wrist, making David drop the knife.

A wave of protests took over. Alvaro kicked the knife away and in one move, he clocked the side of David's face.

And once more.

And again.

David held his arm up, cradling his own head and trying to move to the side but Alvaro was a machine at work.

He cornered David, his punches landing one after the other without waiting, without the *need* to wait.

I refused to breathe. Then David's knee gave out. Soon he was just in a heap on the floor.

Alvaro was saying something to him. I wasn't sure of his words, but they looked as fierce as his fist.

Blood everywhere. From David, from Alvaro.

I looked around, watching as it unfolded, time suspended until David's face wasn't recognizable anymore.

That was when Alvaro stepped back.

Silence finally took over the gym. We all held our breath while we watched the man who used to be Sofia's abuser. He was nothing, bleeding for what was due.

Alvaro stood there like a vengeful god, lacking all the mercy of a mere mortal.

Voices in the crowd called his name again, low, timid, until someone came to take David out of the way.

He might have been alive. If my mind wasn't playing tricks, I could have sworn I saw his fingers move.

Alvaro turned from the scene, his eyes on fire landing on me. He ate the space between us. I stepped away so he could part the ropes and let himself out. Before I could say a word, his hands were on me, his right arm coming down to my ass as he took me in his arm and positioned me on one side, my legs straddling his waist.

Holding onto him, one arm around his back and the other resting on his chest, he moved us to the locker room, the crowd parting as we passed.

No one stopped us, no one asked anything of him.

We moved in eerie silence until he locked us in and lowered me gently to my feet.

Out of breath, I paced, thinking about cleaning him up, but I halted to a stop when he said, "Logan."

"You're hurt." I swallowed.

"I'll survive." He dismissed his own limitations.

He was stabbed today. And yet he didn't even spare the dripping blood a glance. Maybe he was running on adrenaline. Maybe he was running on revenge. Either way, he was stalking toward me, his eyes full of hunger, and he didn't stop until he had me against the lockers.

"Tell me you want me," he commanded.

It was laughable. Wanting him was all I did, even when I shouldn't. When made no—

He captured my chin before I kept shaking my head.

"You want this because you're just as broken as me, Logan. You saw it. You try so hard to be perfect because you know if they get to see the real you, they will see the broken little girl. But I get you. I can take care of you. I don't mind the parts that are cracked because they match mine."

His mouth hovered over mine, his hand slowly making its way from my chin to my neck. His fingers closed loosely around it, enough for me to take a big breath and shatter when he asked again, his voice raw, low.

"So, tell me, Jefa. Tell me you want me as bad as I need you."

I nodded first, my hands holding to his forearms. "I want you."

His mouth descended on mine before the growl even left his lips. I dug my nails into his arms, pulling him to me, needing him closer, as close as I could get him.

I spent my whole life trying to be something I was not. Wrong, broken, needy, and full of anxiety, that was all I could give. But he saw it, and he thought it was enough.

My scars and his. My sadness and his guilt. We intertwined, growing impossibly close together as he kissed me hungry and fast, nipping my bottom lip, all-consuming.

His hand fell to my waist, and with one fluid move, he brought me up and locked me between the lockers and his body.

"I'm going to fuck you here, fast and hard. We can finish slow at home, ok?"

*Home.*

"So, you're parking inside?"

He chuckled, his forehead resting on mine. "Yeah, I'll park inside."

We watched one another, a small smile playing on our lips. And then he kissed me like I belonged to him and only him. His rough hands snaked under my dress and up to knead my breast, playing with a nipple. I cried out in his mouth. I took his bottom lip in a bite when he played for too long, driving me wild.

His dark chuckle made my toes curl.

Alvaro didn't even bother to remove my panties. Under my dress, his fingers went up and down my slit, taking a whimper out of me before he moved my underwear to the side, his forehead dropping to the locker behind me. He took a sniff from my neck and followed with a bite.

"You always taste like mine, nena," he whispered in Spanish.

My fingers flexed, carving on his skin. He covered his mouth over mine the same moment he thrusted, groaning when he made himself at home. He held us together, my knees turning to liquid, my voice going hoarse again as he buried himself to the hilt and took me.

Tonight was his night. He took, and I gave. He was right. I was his from the second we met.

I threw my head back. Alvaro's hands controlled our movements like I weighed nothing. His chest on mine, his mouth on my ear. "You feel so good, Logan. I'll be fucking you just like this for the rest of your life."

My palm reached for his cheek. "Yeah?" I asked.

"This is it." He promised. "It's us now. I've got you."

Legs shaking from the position, I felt him deep inside me. His piercings hitting me in the right place, teasing my clit. I was addicted to him. I wanted more. I wanted forever.

And when my mouth opened in a silent scream, he pushed further, his pace increasing until he took my orgasm for himself. It belonged to him anyway.

His nose buried in my neck. My pussy strangled him when I came, my eyes closed, avoiding the cheap fluorescent lights.

Not long after that, he followed me, a groan so sinful I kissed him, taking a dirty swear off his mouth. Alvaro chuckled and took my earlobe in his mouth. "I love you."

I always wanted to be loved. I imagined ways I could be loved. I always thought I was unlikable, unlovable, and yet, *Alvaro Castillo.*

"I love you, too."

His thrusts were shallow, but he refused to let me go. Alvaro kissed my collarbone, my neck, and my cheeks. I breathed him in the same way he breathed me in.

And then we moved apart. He took his bag and a shirt covering his chest and extended a hand to me. I took it and let him unlock the locker room and move us to the main floor.

Still full, but no David or the man from the microphone anywhere to be found.

"I'll take care of Paddy," Alvaro said, my eyebrows furrowed with confusion. He added. "The owner."

"He let David go in with a knife," I said, gripping his hand for attention.

Alvaro nodded, keeping his voice low not to attract people. "He wanted the money. Whatever pays for the show."

We kept going until finally reaching the door, the wind quickly washing all the muggy sensation, my ponytail askew whipped with force.

"I'm done, Jefa. Nothing here matters anymore." And when I didn't reply right away, he brought me to his arms. "Let's go home."

Nothing in life was truly ever done, because it became part of us. Whatever happened that night, it was still going to follow us for a while.

We moved to separate cars, my eyes on his, until we both got in and drove quickly home, reluctant to be apart for even a second.

The city was empty. Fast, we found our way. My car first and then his truck. We parked side by side in the building's parking lot.

I jumped out, and we met in the space between our cars. He took my hand and kissed it before guiding me to the elevators. I swiped the penthouse keycard, and he tucked me under his arms, fitting so perfectly just there.

The doors opened to the sound of children's laughter, bringing a smile instantly to my lips.

I guided him to the kitchen first, unable to stay a second longer without having a look at his cuts. He let me fuss around, discarding his T-shirt to the side. I cleaned him up while the kids were distracted and got him fresh clothes, but before we followed the noise, I grabbed something from my secret candy stash.

We moved together, like I was glued to his side, until we found them in the media room. Lachlan and Vienna smiling and our reluctant babysitter on his phone.

I kissed Dash's hair, hopping through his long legs, and sat between Vienna and Lachlan. "What are we watching?" I asked, bringing Lachlan to my lap.

"What do you think?" Dash huffed, eyeing his uncle, but never asking why he was back.

He belonged here with us.

"Gummy bears?" I offered Dash.

"I do!" Vi yelled and took a couple, same did Lachlan. Dash watched me with narrowed eyes, but eventually, he accepted.

Alvaro moved to my other side, his arm over the couch at my back, and I turned so I was resting on his chest. I looked at the TV and giggled when I saw the characters singing about Bruno. So, the kids were obsessed about a movie. At least it was a good one.

I breathed in, smelled Lachlan's hair and settled on Alvaro's chest.

Nothing was ever going to be the same. Sofia still wasn't here. The kids would struggle with that for the rest of their lives. Alvaro would still carry scars that wouldn't heal.

But I never wished for a perfect family. I just wished for *a* family. My family.

I turned with a smile when the big man kissed me on the shoulder.

"What's up with you two?" Dash asked, shoving three gummy bears into his mouth.

"Nothing." I shrugged.

"Tío looks like shit."

My mouth gaped open. "That's it. Vienna go to YouTube and find a song about keeping the language clean so Dash can sing."

Not many things would interrupt a viewing of *Encanto* in this house. Making Dashiell embarrassed was one of the few.

"Come on..." he scoffed.

Vienna paused the movie at once and started her search.

And for the rest of the night, we tried to find something for Dash to sing. Vienna chose the worst songs, Lachlan giggled, and Dash scowled exactly like his uncle.

Alvaro helped me pick one, laughed, and even tried his own rendition of a few tunes. Vienna wondered if we should write one.

And right then, in that moment, we weren't so broken anymore.

# Epilogue

I looked down at my planner, releasing a slow breath through my nose. The relationship I had with it was a complicated one. I loved being organized, but my lists once drove me to a panic attack after the other.

*Plans are to help, not to pressure.*

Those were Alvaro's words. Well, Alvaro's rules. He knew I couldn't change that much, but I was supposed to step away if it brought me too much stress.

Everything brought me anxiety before. If it wasn't the kids, it was my fear of failing Sofia. That ball of pain pulsed against my ribs for many years, telling me I wasn't enough even as I checked off every box.

Like the kids, I went to therapy. Well, I came back to it after a lifetime of coming and going, so I decided to try one last time. But really put effort into it.

I wanted to be well for the kids, for Alvaro.

Oh, and he had his own therapist, as well as Dash. We all needed it. That was something I realized after it all went down with David and our lives were calm once again.

Healing never stopped. It wasn't linear, it needed to be an ongoing wish. In honor of Sofia's memory, we had to do it.

Things got better after that, and worse sometimes. But we knew one bad day didn't mean a bad life. And we were determined to have a good life.

It took me five years to look at my planners and understand I owned them and not the other way around. Accepting I was a person, and I was better to my family if I was kind to myself.

"You're staring at the planner again, Jefa. Should I be worried?"

I glanced up to find my husband with his arms crossed over his chest, a smirk on his lips while he watched me from the office's door.

"I'm just breathing." I smiled.

He nodded slowly. I knew he trusted me. It was a process and sometimes I liked to take a moment to appreciate how far I'd come. We all did.

"Everyone is ready," he let me know.

I rose from the chair, smoothing my clothes as I went. "Does that mean the kids are locked in the car downstairs?" I joked.

"I wish." He chuckled when I came closer, on my tiptoes to give him a soft kiss on the lips, which he turned into something dirty quickly.

"They're going to your parents' tonight." I said between his lips. "We can play."

"Don't call it play, Jefa. I'll make you work for it."

Taking a step forward, breathing in my favorite smell in the world- Alvaro- I almost tried to convince myself it was ok to leave people waiting.

I tapped on his chest, passing him on my way to the main room where Vi was on her phone and Lachlan watching TV. I kissed my boy's hair before asking, "Everyone's ready?"

Vi shot me a glance over her phone and nodded once. Lachlan jumped to his feet and took his little backpack over his shoulder.

Before anyone could race to the door, I raised my palms, making them both stop before running outside.

"Toothbrushes?" I called.

"Yes." Vienna replied, bored.

"YES!" Lachlan jumped.

"Pjs and a change of clothes?"

"We have all that at Tita's."

I went over to my new moody teenager, pocketing her phone and making her squeak. Then I took her face between my palms, squashing it. "You're going to miss me. Stop pretending you won't."

She shook her head, but a little smile came through. Vienna was more like Sofia now that she was older. Sometimes so much I could see the pain in Alvaro's eyes. That was the thing when you lost someone. They never went away, they lived with you every day. In your heart, or in the people they left behind.

The kids were all Sofia. Their laugh, their daring, their tone of voice. We loved to see it. It was like having a piece of her still here, even if it hurt like hell.

I never stopped telling them stories about their mother, and I had plenty. They were never tired, not even Dash, who was turning twenty-one today. Still, when he was home, he would sit with the others and beg me to hash out ancient teenage secrets we'd kept. He asked questions he already knew the answers to. Listened to the same stories again and again.

People have a lot of layers. Together we almost could make her as a whole. The sister, the friend, the mother.

Sofia was the glue that held us together, the reason we fought to be better and live a good life.

We filled up the elevator, the kids promising they had everything with them. I took the cake from the fridge, chocolate, Dash's favorite.

Alvaro drove us to the restaurant, where Dash promised to meet us. He was out with friends from the body shop he worked at, but he'd never miss dinner at Antonio's.

He never went to college, and I had to learn that college wasn't for everyone and Dash was doing well at his job. In the end, as long as he was happy, I could breathe in peace.

I handed the cake to a server when we got to Antonio's, while another girl showed us our way to the secluded table I had booked. I held a laugh back when I saw Caridad already there with Geraldo, on top of Dash, brushing his hair out of the way.

"You need a haircut, mi príncipe."

It was always like that. He needed a haircut, new clothes, to eat better. I wouldn't say Caridad healed. How could one ever heal from the loss of a child? But day by day her grief became less loud, and she slowly came back to herself again. Which meant she was criticizing everybody, not just me.

"I thought I was your príncipe, Mamá?" Alvaro asked, distracting his mother.

She told them they were all hers, and all equally important, while I found my way to the birthday boy. He rose on his feet when he saw me coming, that smirk on his mouth.

"Happy birthday!"

Dash had to curve to give me a hug. He was even taller now. “When do you ever stop growing?”

“Never, Lo. Have you looked at tío?”

Dash kissed my hair, making me think of those times when he first came to live with me.

I was just as lost as them. We were all hurting in a way that felt final, just flawed humans coping the best way we could.

We took our places, and Alvaro sat beside me, his hand on my leg. I moved closer to him, letting my head drop to his shoulder while I watched our family laugh and order an outrageous amount of food.

We had the best night, the meal was incredible and when we were finished- the last table to do so- I hugged Alvaro’s parents, thanking them for my kid free weekend.

“Of course.” Geraldo said.

Then Caridad hugged me. When we moved apart, she touched my hair, frowning.

“I think you need a haircut, too.”

I held back a reply, only nodding. Then the weight of Alvaro’s arm pressed over my shoulders, while he said, “Stop criticizing my wife.”

Caridad huffed at her son. Shaking her head, she kissed me on the cheek, “She’s a Castillo. She has thick skin.”

That she was right.

My parents never changed. They met the kids, but I kept them at arm’s length. Knowing my mother, they would have treated them like inconvenient visitors. I couldn’t trust them to not hurt them like they had hurt me, so I made the decision to push them away. Most of the things she said to me growing up were the pillars of my anxiety as an adult. I never wanted her to have a chance to do the same damage to them.

I dreamed about having different parents, about getting married and filling the house with babies. In that way, my dreams never came true.

What I learned was that familia is who you choose. The ones who you trust with your life. Even when years pass by, you know they are there for you.

Familia was that warmth of knowing you weren't alone in the world. The happiness over their success, because they were ours, too.

I met mine when I was just seven years old, alone in a new school. I met mine again in the shape of an overprotective man with scars over his knuckles and three lost children who ended up helping me find myself instead.

Familia was knowing we were just as broken as before, just flawed as we once were *and still,* accept that there was no one better in the world to share your life with.

# Author's note

I'll try to keep this short and sweet.

Since my debut, people who know me see me in my female leads. I think we always write a little bit of ourselves, but before today I couldn't imagine being so raw in front of so many people.

Since Forget me, Aisha Harris, I decided to write what was in my heart. Even if painful.

So here she is.

Logan Hart is so similar to me, sometimes it was hard to write her. All her insecurities, her desire to be perfect, and all the anxiety that comes with that. I had to step away from writing a couple of times, especially when I was describing her panic attacks.

I know this story is not for everyone. More than a romance, Keepsake is a story of how a family healed after something so traumatic.

I hope if you reached the end, you can understand where I am coming from and why writing flawed characters is so important to me. In this story more than ever.

I hope if you live with anxiety and depression, you can relate to Logan and understand where she's coming from.

Thank you, Santana Knox, for literally dragging me on her back while I was writing this. She kept me going when all I wanted was to run.

Thank you, Emily Mayer, for listening to my plot ideas, my freak outs and helping me when I needed.

Thank you, everyone who helped me in the past months. Sharing about my work, reading and commenting. Some days were tough, and you made it better.

Thank you, Chris, for all the times you held me when I cried, brought me tea after a panic attack and told me I was enough.

All my male leads are based on you.

-Amy

Printed in Great Britain
by Amazon

19165633R00189